A Question of Holmes

A Charlotte Holmes novel

A Question of Holmes

A Charlotte Holmes novel

BRITTANY CAVALLARO

Katherine Tegen Books is an imprint of HarperCollins Publishers.

A Question of Holmes
 For information address HarperCollins Children's Books, a division of HarperCollins Publishers, 195 Broadway, New York, NY 10007.
www.epicreads.com

Library of Congress Control Number: 2018962295
ISBN 978-0-06-284022-6

---

19 20 21 22 23 PC/LSCH 10 9 8 7 6 5 4 3 2 1

First Edition

For Chase, my partner in crime

HOLMES

(for Jamie, because he insisted)

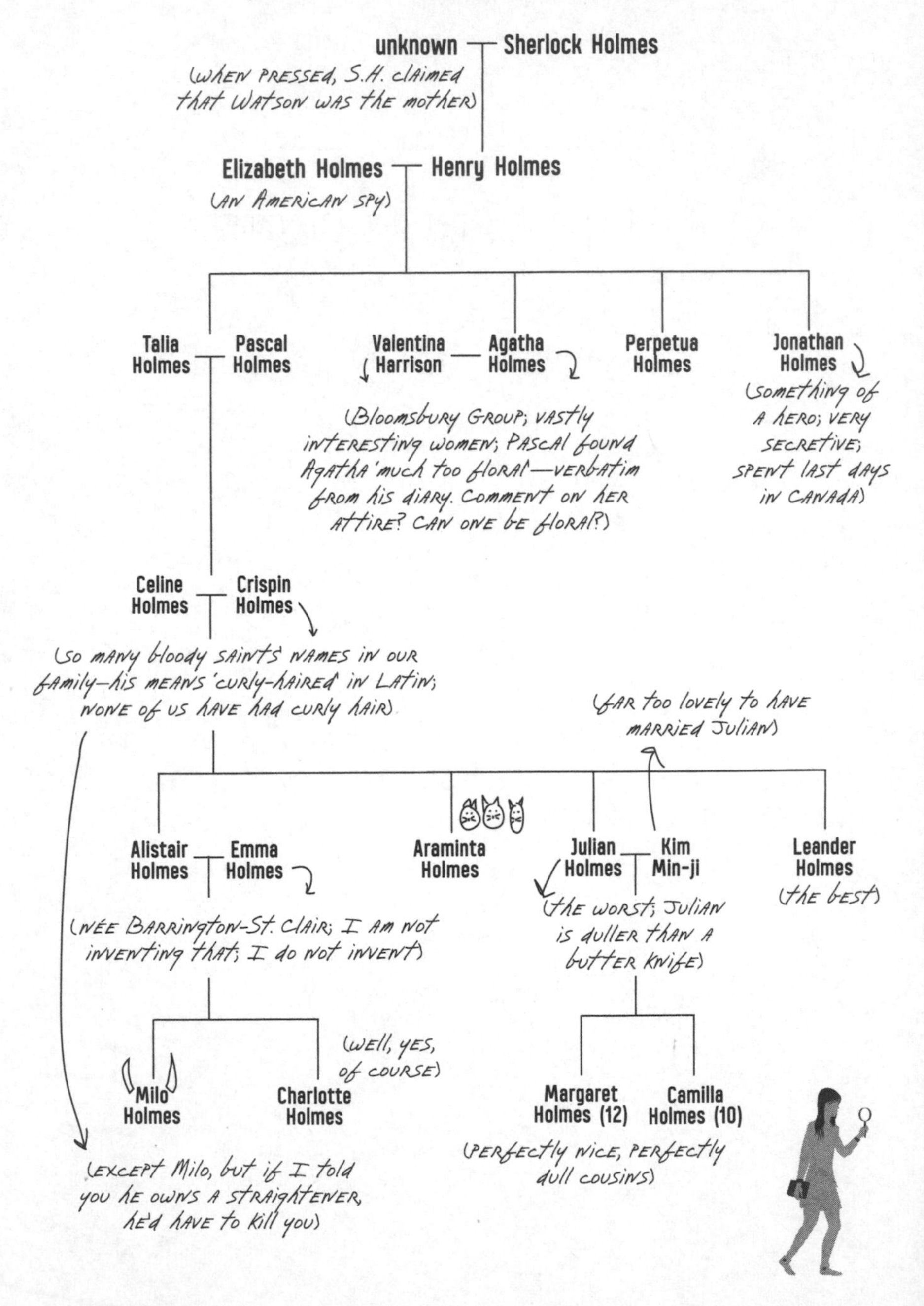

MORIARTY

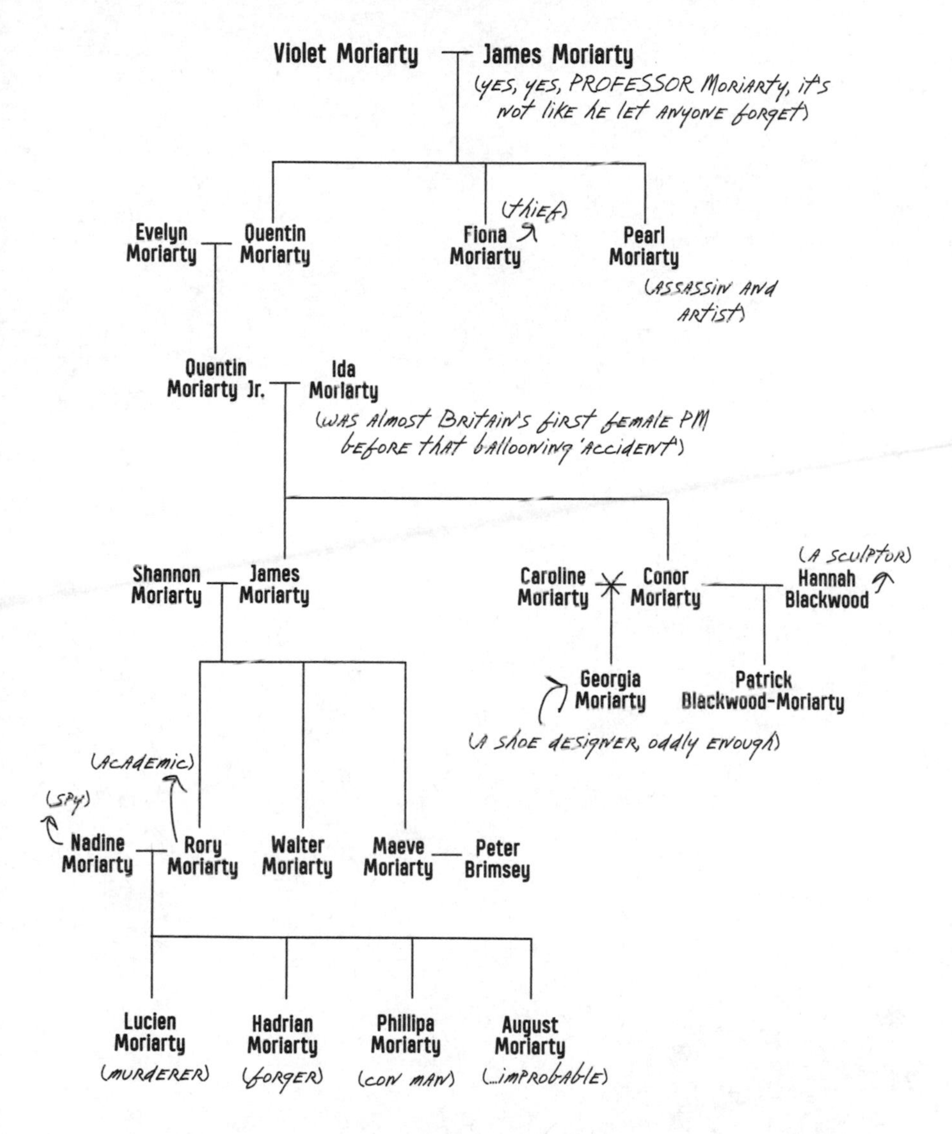

There you have them. Please tell me you don't have any plans to frame these.
-C.H.

Thus I must act as my own chronicler.

Sir Arthur Conan Doyle, "The Lion's Mane"

one

THAT MAY, IN THE WEEKS BEFORE THE BUSINESS WITH DR. Larkin and the Dramatics Society, the messages in the floodlights and the stripped-down production of *Hamlet* and the orchids, the orchids everywhere—before Jamie Watson came to stay and my life, as it often did, grew infinitely stranger—my uncle Leander took to throwing parties again.

At first I wasn't sure of the reason for it. May in Oxford is a milky, diluted affair, with little natural cause for celebration. Not to mention that my uncle was serving in loco parentis to me, a girl who had long passed the age when parenting was necessary; I must have been a burden to him. I was seventeen, after all, and I had ruined several lives, not the least of which was mine, and I had had my own bank account for ages. Surely that disqualified me from needing a father.

And still I found myself reveling in it: the hiss and splutter of the electric kettle first thing, and the double-knock on my bedroom door that meant eggs and turkey bacon on the stove; the issues of *New Scientist* in the post, a magazine my uncle didn't read, but I did; how sometimes I'd return home from the library to find my shirts and socks spinning in the little washing machine in the kitchen when I hadn't put them in myself.

How we had a childhood friend of Leander's to dinner, and he walked in with a bottle of white wine and a carrier over his shoulder, and inside, making a small ruckus, was my cat Mouse. At my uncle's request, she had been liberated from my father's "care." I was excused from dinner to take my cat to my room for immediate cuddling, and there, on the blue-and-white rug I had chosen because its pattern looked like fractals, as I buried my nose in Mouse's soft white belly and she batted my face with her paws, I realized that I had been dismissed from the adults' party like a child, and that, surprisingly, I didn't mind in the least.

These were not weighty things, taken separately, but together they covered me like a blanket, and just as I began to grow used to my mail sorted out on the counter and Leander, on the sofa in suit and American collar, watching *Murder, She Wrote* while eating handfuls of caramel corn, our days shifted once again.

I was due to begin my summer courses in a few days' time at the precollege program in St. Genesius College in Oxford University before enrolling there in the fall, and I suppose the first party that Leander threw was intended to prepare me. That is to say, he thought that inviting over a number of Oxford tutors to drink cocktails and eat miniature puff pastry in our kitchen would be comforting, and productive, and that I wouldn't immediately blurt out that one of them was having an affair with their dog groomer or blow something up on the stove—that I would, in short, have some civilized fun.

When I wrote to tell Watson of my uncle's plan, he responded What on earth is he thinking? You hate parties. Has Leander gone entirely off his tit and, if so, do you have an escape plan? Maybe through the sewers?

It was reassuring, remembering I wasn't broken for not wanting to eat fun-sized sausages with strangers. *I can tell him I'm just ducking out for the night,* I decided, and that thought took me as far as the kitchen, where people had already gathered. I hadn't even heard the front door opening and closing.

I was that far away from my former self, the girl who noticed everything.

And there, in the thick of all those tweedy people, was my uncle Leander, half-illuminated by the track lights, telling some improbable story about his time at the Sorbonne to two men in blazers and penny loafers. Standing in the doorway, I realized it'd been some time since I'd seen him with that look. That *performing* look, that is, something of a raised eyebrow and a half smile, something of an off-balance lean that meant my uncle had an adoring audience. I sighed, put a pile of sausages on a plate, and went to introduce myself to a woman—drama lecturer, divorced, two dogs—who was staring forlornly at the empty gin bottles on the counter. It seemed as though we might have something in common, though it had been some time since I'd indulged in my old vices.

The night passed slowly. I was quite happy to go to bed.

I willed myself to believe that that was the last of the parties, despite the mounting evidence to the contrary. (Obvious evidence. As in, a carrier bag full of cheeses on the counter, and my uncle, the Bach aficionado, humming a Justin Bieber song. Still, a girl could dream, etc.) Should I have been surprised when, that Friday evening, Leander interrupted my violin practice and asked if I perhaps wanted to do something with my hair, as we had company on the way?

I did nothing with my hair. I put away my sheet music (the *Hoffman* barcarolle, exquisite) and skulked out to the living room in leggings and my slippers.

"Charlotte," Leander said, laughing, as he positioned a pair of speakers on the mantelpiece. "Really. You know, it's good to be acquainted with one's professors. Think of it as an opportunity to gather material, if you have to."

"Blackmail?" I thought briefly of Mr. Wheatley, Watson's high school writing teacher, who had bugged his dorm room to "gather material." "Noted."

"Chin up. That Dr. Whatsit woman you were speaking to the other night will be back. She was quite taken with you."

A small part of my brain was always at war: *Of course she adores me,* I thought, simultaneously thinking, *that poor dumb woman.* My therapist had been working with me on this duality with limited success.

I truly hated parties.

Still, I helped Leander light the clusters of candles in the windows, breathed in their scent when he asked me to, said, *Yes, that amber one is lovely* (not because it was, but because I loved my uncle); I arranged the miniature cheeses on a platter (*Everything in miniature at parties,* I thought, *people should make themselves bigger)*; I changed into my boots but kept the leggings, and then took up a position in the armchair by the door.

The same people again. Some dons in shirtsleeves, a pair of philosophy graduate students studying the bookshelves. My uncle listening intently to—yes, there it was, to an ebulliently handsome man in the kitchen, one who had been here the time before. Now he was touching Leander's shoulder with a slim hand, as though for emphasis. It wasn't for emphasis. *Well done, Leander,* I thought, and closed the case, as it were, on the mystery of the many parties.

Pity, though. To my surprise, I found that I had been hoping for something a bit more sinister.

I was studying my uncle's suitor from a distance (blue-eyed, single, last boyfriend had given him terrible feedback on his hair) when the drama lecturer plopped down on the ottoman beside me.

"Charlotte," she said. Her name was Dr. Larkin. "Your uncle was just telling me about your interest in Shakespeare."

"My interest in Shakespeare." I wasn't *uninterested* in Shakespeare, I supposed. I liked the language. I liked the pageantry. I liked above all the disobedient girls that populated his plays, and I told Dr. Larkin that.

She tucked her hair behind her ears. "We're doing *Hamlet*, you know, at the precollege Dramatics Society this summer. We do quite a bit of Shakespeare. It goes off just fine, usually, though the precollege program is always under-enrolled and in turmoil and, well, a bit on fire—"

"You're not selling it all that well," I said, not unkindly.

Dr. Larkin laughed. "I'm not actually asking you to audition," she said. "Though I suppose, in a way, I am. We had a series of . . . incidents last summer, and so much of the program is returning—faculty and students and crew—and, in the end, we never quite figured it out."

"What, exactly?"

But she was looking just past me, her eyes gone suddenly hard. "I'm invested in it not happening again," she was saying in a hollow voice. "The business with the orchids, that is."

The party had grown louder; someone had put on the Rolling Stones, and a few people were dancing. A girl in the corner was reading my uncle's copy of *Middlemarch*. Across the room, Leander and his suitor were peering out the windows at the night, their shoulders barely touching.

None of it mattered. Something was stirring in my blood. "Begin at the beginning," I told Dr. Larkin. "And tell me, please, that you don't want me to play Ophelia."

two

"They want you to play Ophelia?" Watson asked, hoisting his duffel bag over his shoulder. His suitcase was already on the curb. "Isn't that a little, like, on the nose?"

I thumped the roof of the cab, and it trundled back out into the road. Six on a Sunday, and the city was quiet, the sun still not entirely up. Flights from America always came in with the dawn. For once, Watson didn't look the worse for wear. He never fared well on planes across the Atlantic, sleeping fitfully or not at all, but this morning his hair was so extravagantly tousled, I knew he'd spent the whole flight unconscious. Though the red lines near his temples (striated; elastic?) flummoxed me until—

"You had on a sleeping mask," I said, delighted beyond all

sense. "Tell me, was it one of those with the eyelashes printed on it? Was it silk? Was it your mother's, or—"

He pulled it from his pocket and tossed it to me; I caught it one-handed. Black silk, sans eyelashes. "You're a jerk," he said, laughing. "I bought it in the terminal."

"Why would I be a jerk? I'm only asking about your beauty sleep."

"Did it work? Am I more beautiful now?"

His white shirt was rumpled—why on earth had he worn an oxford on an international flight?—and he still had his medicinal-blue flight pillow around his neck, and everything he was thinking, every last thing, played out on his face: anticipation, happiness, a little fear. Knowing what he did about the way I worked, what I observed, he still wore it there for me to see.

Of course he was beautiful.

"Of course you aren't," I told him, but I was smiling. "It'd take a longer nap than that, surely."

Upstairs, we settled in on the sofa, his feet propped up on his duffel. The soles of his trainers would leave a mark there, but at least they weren't on the couch. Leander would have had kittens. "So. Ophelia," Watson said. "Isn't there another part for you to play?"

"Not for my purposes."

"I guess it isn't much of a stretch for you." He knew he was annoying me, and he was enjoying it. I could tell from his left eyebrow.

"I'm not sure if you're aware of this," I said, "but I have no plans to drown myself because of you. I don't see how my playing Ophelia is 'on the nose.'"

He tipped his head against the cushion. "You *are* the smallest bit tortured, you know."

I grimaced. "Less so, now. Therapy. Lots of therapy. And I'm eating breakfast. I'm a healthy, sound person."

"I'm sure that Ophelia ate breakfast."

"Pedant," I said, and pulled my legs up to my chest. "I'm just not particularly interested in playing a character whose most striking characteristic is her virginity."

Watson reddened, which was fascinating, and so I studied him until he began to squirm. Finally he said, "But you'd be doing it so you can solve a mystery, and also you've always wanted to be an actress. I mean, like, you *are* an actress. A good one. You have a literal wig box under your bed."

It was now in pride of place on my dresser, but that was beside the point. "It will be an interesting exercise," I allowed. "And anyway, I'm not playing Ophelia straight out, I'm understudying. Less time onstage, more time backstage. I need that freedom of movement."

"At least it isn't *Macbeth*," Watson said, hugging a pillow to his chest.

"I thought we did *Macbeth* last year, you and I."

"What, starring Lucien Moriarty? In the Scottish access tunnels? Sherringscotland? What does that make you . . . MacHolmes?"

"And you Lady MacHolmes?" I snorted. "I think those are the technical terms, yes."

"So what about me?" Watson asked. He was struggling to stay awake; his eyes were half-closed. "How do I help with all of this?"

"Well, I'll be quite busy. I'll need someone to do my poetry homework," I said, and he roused himself enough to poke me with his shoe. "No, there are a few different options to get you in. You could assist with the production. Set painting, lighting, et cetera. You could write a piece on the precollege Dramatics Society. Make up some American college newspaper to do it for. Or you could audition, but I doubt you'd want to, or—"

"I could be a good Hamlet," Watson murmured, and with that he fell asleep altogether.

I watched him for ten minutes or so before I went to go organize my lockpicks.

Later, closer to noon, Leander knocked on my door. He went for a luxurious lie-in some weekend mornings, and today wasn't an exception. "Breakfast?" he asked, popping his head in.

"Breakfast," I confirmed.

There were hash browns and sausages on the stove, and I perched in my usual seat at the counter, twisting back and forth on my stool. It was childish to do it, but we had nothing this whimsical in my house growing up. A seat with a mechanism!

In an attempt to stop "paying my whole bank balance to Starbucks," as he put it, Leander had invested in an espresso maker, and this morning, he was making the two of us cappuccinos. Despite its racket and the smell of the fry-up on the stove, Watson stayed asleep on the sofa, his arms around one of the paisley cushions.

"It's going to be a bit different for you two," Leander said, following my line of sight.

"Different how, exactly?" I stopped turning about on my stool. I wasn't willing to have a conversation about my love life with Watson sleeping five feet away.

No matter how much breakfast I was bribed with.

He tipped the tomato he'd sliced into the skillet. "Oh, come," he said. "You're both of age. You're both finished with school. You're free to run around setting things on fire as much as you'd like."

"We were more or less doing that before." I padded over to pick up my cappuccino.

"And now, my little arsonist, you have three months to figure out your next move," Leander said, stirring the baked beans. With his other hand he peeled bacon out of the package. I made to help him, but he brandished his spoon.

"I'm defending this little fiefdom," he said. "Sit. Have your cappuccino."

"University," I said, obediently taking a sip. "Oxford. That's what's next. That's been settled. I sat A levels. I *forged papers* so I could sit A levels without having taken the classes. I did an interview with a tutor and solved maths problems on a whiteboard for an audience."

"I encouraged it," he reminded me. "I still think it's an excellent plan. But I want you to understand the possibility here. Sometimes I worry that . . ."

I waited for him to finish, but he was looking up into the hood above the stove as though the rest of his sentence was kept there.

"This," Leander said finally, "is where your map runs out, Charlotte. We've reached the edge of the page. Nothing about you has ever been traditional, and so a traditional education might be precisely what's on order, starting with this summer program. But allow room for possibility. I know you don't need me to tell you this, but Lucien—"

My hateful, treacherous heart began to hammer just at the sound of his name.

"—is locked away. You don't need to make your decisions on the run. No one's hunting you."

"He's not the only Moriarty," I reminded him. "Remember?"

"Yes," Leander said, "but Philippa's hardly going to round up the producers of her antiquing show and set them on you with machetes."

"You never know," I said darkly.

He took down plates from the cupboard. "And Hadrian isn't after you. He sent you a bloody graduation card, God knows why."

"He might be trying to get back in your good graces," I said. "Didn't you snog him in—"

"Finish that sentence," Leander said, "and I'm feeding your breakfast to Mouse." He arranged a plate for me and pushed it across the island. "All I'm saying is that you're on the other side now. It's summer. Jamie's here. Go have some fun. Do easy things, things that make you happy."

I looked at him over a forkful of hash browns. "I picked up a case," I said.

"Yes." Leander braced his hands on the counter. "But is that what makes you happy? Do you know what does?"

I CONSIDERED WHAT MY UNCLE HAD SAID AS I WASHED UP the breakfast dishes. I'd left Jamie's on the coffee table, within wafting distance, and he was beginning to make grumbling sounds in his sleep. Leander had run out "on a work errand," though I knew that, since January, he'd dropped absolutely everything to watch over me. His income from his rental properties had been buoying us along, though we were both aware it couldn't forever. Leander was a world-renowned investigator, fast on his feet, charming, vaguely debonair. Last week, I'd overheard him turning down a case in New South Wales (something delicious-sounding—I'd heard "circus," and "throwing knives"), and he'd gone out straight after to his club, a racquet clutched in his hand like a bludgeon.

I'd felt bad for the racquetballs.

But there was no reason, now, that he couldn't be back to his usual business. I was well again. Well *enough*, I should say. I would always be an addict, but right now, I was one in recovery. I had a plan. A good one.

It occurred to me that I should inform Watson of his role in said plan.

"Good morning," I said to him, perched on the arm of the couch.

He blinked his eyes open. "Good morning," he said, stifling a yawn. "Is that bacon?"

We moved to the leather armchairs by the window, and I curled up there, studying him, as he sorted through his plate with his fork. "What are you thinking?" I asked him.

He looked surprised. "That's usually my line," he said.

"All the same."

With a forkful of tomato, he regarded me steadily. "I missed you," he said. "I'm thinking about that, and how nice it was to wake up just now to you saying good morning."

"And to breakfast," I said.

"And that," he laughed. "I'm thinking I'd like to hear you play your violin later, and that we could take a walk by the river. And I'm not sure exactly what I am to you, right now, but . . ." He shrugged. "I think we have lots of time to sort that out, if we want to."

Once, this sort of emotional honesty would have sent me running to my chemistry table, needing a good loud explosion to clear my head. Today, I only curled my toes and then uncurled them, basking a little in the sun.

Watson wolfed down his breakfast and set the plate aside. "What are you thinking?" he asked. "Turnabout, fair play, et cetera."

"Oh," I said, stretching until my fingers brushed the curtains. "I was just refining a few points."

"Points?"

"Of the terms and conditions of our relationship."

"The what?" Watson coughed. "Sorry?"

"Do you need a glass of water?" I asked, concerned.

"No," he said, "but a clarification would be nice."

"That's the goal." I sat up, steepling my hands under my chin. "I spent the last few weeks drawing it up on a legal pad. It's only about twenty-three pages long—"

"Only."

"And I tried to keep the addendums to a minimum." I was also attempting to keep a straight face, but I didn't want Watson to know that. I had given this matter significant thought. I certainly hadn't written us up contracts.

Lawyers were far too expensive.

He raked a hand through his hair. "Okay. Hit me."

"Sorry?"

"It's an expression," Watson said, and poked me with his foot. He'd done that earlier. Was that something we did now? "What are these terms and conditions? What exactly am I agreeing to?"

I took a deep breath. I knew, empirically, that it was best to begin with something small. To pop the frog into the pot of water *before* one set it to boil. "Your nails," I said.

Watson glanced down at his hands. "What about them?" he said, flexing his fingers.

"Quite often you have dirt under your nails," I said. "When I first met you, I thought you might be a gardener."

"I was living in a dorm," he said patiently. "Where would I have been gardening? The roof? Mars? Wait, actually—don't answer that."

I frowned; I'd already come up with one or two sensible

locations. “I’ve left a nail brush for your use in the en suite bathroom. Yours is green. Mine is black. Please don’t use mine.”

Watson bit his lip. “So this is one of your stipulations, then. Clean nails.”

I squirmed a little in my chair, then forced myself to settle. “You’ll . . . if we are dating, you’ll sometimes touch me, and it’s good for me to not have anything to focus on that I can be repulsed by.”

To Watson’s everlasting credit, he didn’t recoil at the horrible thing I had said. I hadn’t meant to use the word “repulsed”; I had meant to say “made skittish” or some phrase that reflected the fault of it back on myself. But the truth of it was that, after my assault, I struggled to stay in whatever romantic moment I was in, no matter how I was enjoying it. There was always the undertow pulling at my feet, pulling me away, away.

It was best to chip away at those things we could control, now, than to run screaming from him after he touched me.

“Jamie, I’m sorry,” I said instantly. “I am. You know this has everything to do with me.”

“With the both of us,” he said, and reached out to touch my knee. “I’m fine with it. The green nail brush, huh? My favorite color’s blue.”

It was a very sad attempt at banter, but I beamed at him as though he were both Abbott and Costello. He wasn’t hurt. I was getting better at not hurting him. “That’s point one,” I said, affecting unaffectedness. “Points two through ten have to do with that ridiculous list your father made you as to how to deal with . . . me.”

Watson had the grace to wince. His father had given him a strange little journal into which he had compiled a list of suggestions for how to handle one's Holmes (as though I were a small-breed dog or similar), drawing not only from Dr. Watson's own accounts but also from his own efforts with my uncle Leander back when they'd been flatmates. This was absurd on many levels. Leander was very easy to live with. He hardly ever stalked around anymore with a pistol in his bathrobe pocket.

I knew about this journal because my Watson had written about it, and we shared our accounts with each other, warts and all.

This wart was particularly large.

"For instance," I said, running the curtain through my fingers, "I seem to remember an item along the lines of 'Do not allow Holmes to cook your dinner unless you have a taste for cold, unseasoned broth.'"

Watson coughed delicately. "Holmes. Have you ever made . . . anything?"

"I have made you *at least* four cups of tea."

"In the last two years."

"I dislike cold, unseasoned broth, and my uncle Leander is quite a . . . foodie"—I despised that word—"and your father has quite the talent for hyperbole. I can't believe that Leander once made him *clear, tasteless soup.* I will make you no broth. *Verbum sap.*"

"Noted," Watson said. "I'm not proud of that journal, you know. I'm not proud of a lot of things my father has done."

James Watson had a habit of boosting his son from class to

go listen to his police scanner in the Walmart parking lot. He was a bit of a rogue, a bit of a bad influence, a bit of a silly suburban dad. The last I'd heard, he'd been fighting with Jamie's stepmom, Abigail, over his friendship with Leander. They'd been gallivanting about together like schoolboys, leaving Abigail to take care of her and James's kids and the minutiae of their lives.

"You're still not answering his calls," I ventured.

Watson sighed. "They've split up. For good this time, I think. He keeps leaving me messages . . . I think he's been spending time with my mom and Shelby in London."

"Interesting," I said. It made a certain kind of sense. Jamie's parents had a reasonably good relationship for a divorced couple, and Grace Watson had just gone through the harrowing, absurd experience of being duped into marriage by a Moriarty. I imagined they were both feeling somewhat fragile right now.

"Ten-year-old me would have died and gone to heaven at, like, the *suggestion* that my parents might get back together. But now . . ." He shrugged a bit too forcefully. "I don't care."

I touched his knee, and he put his hand over mine, and said, "You know, these aren't . . . unreasonable things to ask for. The things you're asking for."

"Compared to your parents?" I asked.

"Compared to anyone."

Generally speaking, I had no real basis by which to judge relationships as reasonable or unreasonable. My family was composed of a number of odd, sad adding machines who lived in a lonely house on the sea. They weren't precisely role models.

And as for Watson—we'd smashed our friendship into bits and rebuilt it from the ground up. It resembled nothing, now, other than itself.

"Good," I said, for lack of a better response. "Well, then, I also take issue with the idea that I don't give you compliments. Your father claimed that I would give them to you every 'two to three years.'"

Watson bit his lip again. He was going to do himself an injury.

I ticked them off on my fingers. "For someone who does not style it, you have very good hair. You are better at French than you think, though your written syntax is appalling. And you have developed an excellent right hook."

"Thank you," Watson said gravely.

"You're welcome," I said. "That should tide us over for at least the next six months."

He leaned back in his chair with a rueful expression. "Is there anything else? I know you said that you'd put together, like, twenty-three pages of this stuff, but I was sort of hoping we could walk around the college—"

"I want to date you," I said in a rush. "I want to, and I have no idea how to do it, even if I am behaving as myself. Whoever *that* is. And now I've picked up this case, and so often in the past we've played at being together to extract information that I'm not sure where that fake relationship begins and our real one ends. Or vice versa." I fidgeted, then forced my hands to relax. "What's worse is that pretending . . . it makes it easier. It lets me try out things that I might want to do for real, and there aren't the same sort of stakes. Because the stakes are very high. It's you."

"I'm not going anywhere," Watson said in a low voice. "They'd have to drag me away from you. They'd have to put a gun to my head, and even then . . ." He made a helpless sort of shrug. "I mean, Holmes, the worst has already happened, and look. We're here. We're together."

I reached out to take his hands, warm and calloused and gentle. "I don't want to pretend about anything important. But is it okay, if sometimes . . . I pretend to be a girl who would want to go dancing at a disco?"

"Is that pretend, though?" Watson asked. "Because I remember a homecoming dance when—"

"Or," I hurried on, "if I pretended I wanted to hold hands while walking to, say, play mini golf."

"Mini golf," he said, like it was a delicious, awful thing that he would lord over me for months. "*Mini golf.*"

"That is not the point."

"You with a little putter, whacking away to get the ball through the tilting windmill—"

"Watson. Focus. *Holding hands.*"

"Like we are now?"

"Yes," I said, and he brought them up between us.

"You can pretend whenever you like. But how do I know when you're pretending, and when it's real?"

"We'll need some sort of code word," I said. "Something we wouldn't ever say otherwise. Like 'kumquat.' Or 'asymptote.'"

"I can do that." He regarded me over our clasped hands. "Can I add one term myself?"

"Of course," I said, though I could feel myself tense.

"Once a week, we have to do something that cannot possibly kill us." Then he smiled, a bit wickedly. "And once a week, we have to do something that probably will."

In that moment, I loved him more than anything else.

"And that's all right?" I asked. "All this is all right?"

Watson considered it. "I . . . I don't have any agenda this summer. I feel like the last year has wiped me completely clean. I'm so tired of just surviving," he said. "And in three months everything is going to start, the whole train ride straight into adulthood, and I just . . . I want to lay around on the couch in your flat, and watch dumb television, and write stories, and I want to solve this mystery you've got. Whatever it is, it doesn't have a bloody Moriarty at the other end. So it's a chance to try out solving a crime without our necks on the line. We can try our hands at being detectives for real."

"For real," I echoed. There was something to that idea: the last few years had felt like fiction. "I agree to your terms. I'd like to give these terms seven to ten days, then renegotiate if needed."

"Or call the whole thing off?" He said it lightly, a cord of uneasiness just below.

I tried my best not to hurt Watson. I also tried my best not to hurt myself. "Yes," I said. "Should we shake on it?"

Below us, a pair of taxis went by like racehorses loosed from their gates. A tangle of pedestrians were peering into the windows of the souvenir shop, their umbrellas up against the light rain. I knew they were tourists for that; the rest of the city threw up their hoods, or a newspaper, or simply squinted their eyes and pushed on forward as the clouds gathered and the wind picked up. And above it all were the towers and turrets of the university, rain-washed, sharp-edged against the sky, some commingled promise of what was past and what was to come.

It would start, it would start soon, and if Watson was hurt, he was also happy, and that was the way it always went, with us. "Shake on it?" he asked, disentangling our hands. "I sort of think we already have."

three

Precollege Program Orientation was scheduled for two days after Watson arrived, and I discovered a few things in the meantime.

1. My uncle Leander has a memory like a steel trap. He took Watson and I to the all-you-can-eat Indian buffet around the corner from our flat, to the antiquarian bookshop to look at first editions of Faulkner, to the teahouse painted to look like a starry night, all of which Watson had mentioned in passing that he loved, and whose repetition now left Watson in a state of expansive joy.
2. I should have found this delightful. I did not. As, throughout all of this, Leander referred to Watson as my boyfriend.
   2b. Loudly.

2c. He did this as often as he could.

2d. To wit: "A latte for my niece and her young man"; "Charlotte, wasn't that your Jamie's favorite, *A Light in August*? Faulkner's later work—"; "Child, go and get your boyfriend another napkin, we aren't *barbarians*." And then that smile Leander had, something like a wolf after eating a fat peasant child.

By the time orientation rolled around, I was, in fact, feeling quite barbaric. Watson, true to form, was too delighted by the stack of paperbacks he'd bought and the pigeons on the corner and the raspberry cake he'd had with his tea to register any of the above as obnoxious.

It wasn't that I was upset by the thought of Watson being my boyfriend. It was something else that bothered me. Whatever Watson and I were to each other was our business, no matter how the world leaned in and breathed against the glass, and Leander, my excellent all-knowing uncle-slash-guardian, should have known that. And not found it half as funny as he apparently did.

Even if his intentions were good (Watson was, emphatically, not "easy"; he was, however, someone who "made me happy"), I was still mad. This was a complex idea, but I was fairly certain I could convey it to Leander through a very extravagant sulk, and so I did my best.

I didn't, of course, count on the collateral damage.

"You're unhappy," Watson said in the kitchen, that second evening after supper. He was pouring steaming water into a mug, avoiding my eyes. "Have I violated the terms? Or . . . if you haven't had enough time to yourself, or something, just tell me. I'm not supposed to move into the dorms until tomorrow, but they might be able to let me in tonight—"

"Why would you do that? Don't do that," I said. In the other room, Leander rustled meaningfully. I cocked my head toward my bedroom, and Watson picked up his mug and followed.

After I arranged myself in my chair, legs over the armrest, he surprised me by dropping down to sit at my feet.

"What's on your mind?" he asked, shoulders tensed.

It took quite a bit to make me speak plainly about how I felt, but Watson in distress tended to provide that bit. "I'm nervous," I admitted.

"Nervous?"

"Nervous. We're starting up at a new place, and together," I said. "We've never done that before."

He sighed, considering. "Maybe I'm slow or something," he said, "but why does that make you nervous? We have each other. We'll be fine."

"We'll be fine, but we'll be on display, a bit. We'll be expected to do the whole Holmes-and-Watson dance, which neither of us likes doing. And on top of that, we'll need to make new friends."

"We will?"

"Yes," I told him. "My therapist said so. So that we don't go do our 'folie à deux thing,' as she calls it."

"Folie à deux thing? As in . . . the shared private madness

thing? You have a hyperbolic therapist."

It had seemed fairly on the nose to me. "Still."

"Holmes," he said, tipping his head back to look at me. "I don't mind it. There are worse things in the world than making new friends. Murder. Kidnapping. Scorpions."

"I'd take scorpions over socializing any day."

"You could take your mind off it by telling me about . . . I don't know, this Dramatics Society situation. You still haven't given me the details."

"All in good time," I said, because I was rather comfortable here, him looking up at me with his soft eyes, and the last thing I wanted to do was to bring a case into the room with us.

It was sudden, the sound of breaking glass, and before I heard the low roll of laughter that followed, I was already on my feet, Watson in a low crouch. It took a beat before we registered that the sound had come from the television in the next room.

I could hear the muffled sound of Leander cursing, the volume going down. Watson and I rearranged ourselves wordlessly, and after a moment, he laughed, dabbing at his front where he had spilled his tea. "I guess it's either we rehash this mystery, or we go watch *Friends* with your uncle."

"*Friends*, then," I said, to Watson's evident surprise. I rather liked the Joey character. "I think there's ice cream in the freezer."

Orientation was a bit more formal than I'd anticipated, this being a precollege program. We were ushered into the sort of long, paneled, beautiful room that one would expect from a cocktail party in the eighteenth century, or as the setting of a trial.

Spaces like this reminded me of home. That wasn't a good thing. I paused at the door.

"God, this is gorgeous." Watson unwound his scarf from around his neck. "Like Hogwarts," he said, and pulled me inside.

We'd moved him into his rooms that morning, just the two of us. He'd only had the two suitcases. He was sharing a stairwell with some other precollege students, but the only one there when we arrived was a cheerful brunet boy in a cardigan who shook both of our hands and asked straight off what we were studying and if we wanted to get a pint later, there was a pub nearby he loved, well, not a pub, a bit *swankier*, but we should go, it would be *wicked*—

Watson had cleared his throat. "I'm sorry, I didn't catch your name," he said cautiously, as though the boy was about to whip off his mask, announce he was Tom Bradford's twin brother, and then mug us for our wallets.

"Rupert Davies," the other boy had said, and then, apropos of nothing at all, said, "Excellent! We'll all meet later, then!"

Now, at orientation, Rupert was waving us over to a block of seats he'd reserved with an umbrella, a coat, and what appeared to be one of his shoes.

"Dear God," I said.

"I know. I keep flashing back to Sherringford. I am having," Watson said, "murderous déjà vu."

"We should go, or he might strip us for parts." I eyed the shoe Rupert had left on the seat beside him. "Imagine how many seats he could reserve with your trousers."

"Mr. Watson!" Rupert cried as we approached. "And I didn't catch your name—what was it?"

"Charlotte." I didn't offer my surname. "Are you waiting for others to join you?" I badly hoped that he was, and that those others weren't us. It wasn't that I didn't like Rupert—I didn't know him at all; how could I form an opinion?—but that there were a few hundred people in this room, and I was getting bits of their stories by looking at them (wasn't sleeping; came from California; would drop out in two to three days' time), and I was processing so much data that I was having difficulty being polite.

I wanted to improve on that—politeness—as I disliked being bad at things. So I stuck a smile on my face and hoped it would soften into a real one.

Rupert, bless him, was still talking. "Yes, well, this is my second year here! And my first year I met this boy Theo on the train and he wound up in my stairwell. And Anwen—oh, you'll love Anwen. Ended up with her by mistake. Someone thought she was a boy by her name, stuck her with us, but no matter. We stayed up all night talking about music and Wales—we were all thick as thieves, the three of us, before you could snap your fingers." For effect, he snapped his.

This was too much information. I had to stall while I sorted it out.

"I love a fast friendship," I said, pulling Rupert's umbrella off the chair so I could sit. "Tell me more about Theo. Is he originally from Wales as well?"

What are you doing? Watson mouthed to me. *Stop what you're doing.*

"America," Rupert said happily. I imagined he would still be thrilled if Theo came straight from the bowels of hell. "Boston, maybe? Providence?"

"I love Boston," I said. "And Providence."

Watson eyed me, then the seat with the shoe on it. "Is it okay if—"

"Oh, yes, of course," Rupert said, and set it on the floor beside his socked foot. "You know, Anwen and Theo—"

And at that point, the program director mercifully took the stage.

As for Anwen and Theo, they didn't arrive until orientation was under way. In fact, quite a few people slipped in late, and from the confident way they found their seats, I decided they were largely returners. None of this information would be new to them; might as well linger outside.

On our end, there was quite a bit to learn. Watson paged through his folder as the program director ran through the regulations. All meals off-campus or in one's kitchen; a long, disturbingly specific list of things not allowed in the dorms or flats—fireworks, cigarettes, goats, houseplants. ("We had an incident with a Venus flytrap last year," the director said darkly.) There was a brief session about the Oxford tutorial system, as well. In addition to twice-weekly lectures we'd attend as a class, we'd meet in small groups with our tutor to discuss the material in depth.

"You can't fake your way through a tutorial," the director said. "Don't even try."

So much for the two of us lying around, watching television. Watson looked a bit pale. He was here to study fiction writing, but I think he had imagined this would be the same sort of classroom-workshop setting as at Sherringford. It was something altogether different to sit in a small room while a decorated writer paged through your story mere inches from your face.

Then again, perhaps it wouldn't be anything like that. Perhaps, after everything, we'd finally found ourselves in a healthy learning environment.

"They're going to eat us all alive," Theo said, flinging himself down next to me. At least I assumed this blond, broad-shouldered boy was Theo. The flap of his messenger bag was open—three brand-new Pilot V4 Very Fine pens, a dog-eared copy of *Hamlet,* an apple in a plastic bag.

"Oh. Sure. Well, that's fine." Watson went pale. "Totally fine."

At that, Theo smiled. "I'm making it sound pretty bad, aren't I? Sorry. We like to bait the new blood."

They appeared to want to continue talking, so I kicked Watson in the shins. Just in time—the director had turned a gimlet eye on us. After a moment, he continued monologuing (proper comportment amongst older students, program reputation, etc.), and Theo relaxed his shoulders, and a redheaded girl slipped into the seat between him and Rupert. She didn't have an orientation folder, or even a bag. She had, in fact, nothing with her, and she sat there in her dark dress and boots as though that was all she needed to bring to the first meeting of a prestigious credit-bearing university program.

I had always admired that sort of insouciance in a girl, as I am nothing if not prepared. If I don't have my orientation folder (or similar) it is because I have a primary goal (sleuthing) that negates my secondary one (everything else).

For a slightly delusional half second, I checked Anwen over for any signs that she was a detective. Nothing from her fingers, smoothing her dress; nothing from her unfocused eyes, her relaxed mouth—

Watson poked me. "Stop staring," he whispered.

"I'm not staring."

"You're staring at her like you're carving her up."

Really, he was so unbearably dramatic. "I have no plans to quarter her."

"Like you're thinking about making pork chops, or something—"

The director clapped his hands twice. "All that said, welcome to the Oxford Precollege Program! We'll see you all at the welcome dinner tonight."

"I hardly ever eat pork chops," I told him, putting my folder into my rucksack. "I don't eat *human* pork chops at all."

Next to me, Theo laughed, a sound that tunneled into a snort, and Anwen shook her head, and Rupert said, "You two are bizarre. Where should we go to eat?"

Watson looked down at his schedule. "The JCR, it says?

The Junior Common Room, in an hour?"

"That's where *they're* eating," Anwen said. "We'll go for a pint later, but for dinner, we can do better. Where are we going, Rup? D'you want to book us in at that Italian place over by Trinity College? Next to the used bookshop, the good one. The food was terrific last year."

"I'll ring over," Rupert said, digging out his phone, and Theo stuck out a hand and said, "You must be the two that Rupert was telling us about," and as the two of them shook, I watched Watson's shoulders drop down from where they'd been, somewhere around his ears.

"New friends, then," I said to him, as we were hustled out the door.

"*I'm* going to end up making friends with them," he said. "You, on the other hand, are going to pump them for information about William bloody Shakespeare and then leave them for dead on the side of the road."

I hooked my hand through his arm. "I think you have some strange ideas about my bloodthirstiness," I said, and he shrugged, trying not to smile, and we wandered along that way, our shoulders bumping along together into the night.

"You have a plan."

"I do not."

"You lucked out into meeting three of the actors straightaway," he said. "Or . . . one actor and two hangers-on. I'm not sure yet."

"The Dramatics Soc is the most popular summer club," I reminded him. "It's hardly luck."

He looked down at me. "Still, you see an opportunity. To learn more about last year. Which you still haven't told me about."

"I might," I allowed. "I might also just want pasta."

I liked this part of Oxford. I hadn't spent all that much time around the university, considering. By now, I would usually have known my city down to the ground: the sewer systems, the bus lines, which alleys were shortcuts and which ended blind. That would be what I was looking for now. Thoroughfares. Quick exits.

Instead I was studying the way that the road ahead of us curved up and slightly to the left, how the sun still hung high enough in the sky to be seen over the Georgian buildings at the top of the hill. We had another three hours of sunlight; we were approaching the longest day of the year, here at the top of the world. It was close enough to the end of term that undergraduates were still wandering the streets, dazed from the completion of their exams or the graduation of their girlfriends or, in one case, the grandeur of their plans for when the sun finally set. *Punting,* I thought, as we passed a pair of girls planning where on the river to meet up later. *Didn't James Watson used to go out punting with my uncle? Didn't—*

Dear God. I found myself slowing until I came to a stop, as ahead of us, Theo and Anwen and Rupert walked on in close concert, whispering about something that I was sure was of some tangential importance to my case and which I had missed altogether. Even now, Theo's mouth was pinched, Anwen was tossing her hair over her shoulder.

I looked hopelessly up at Watson. "Well," he said, scrolling through his phone, "at least we know now that your hunch was right. They're talking about *Hamlet*; they're some of the right people to follow. I wonder who they'll end up playing. Theo's sort of princely, right? Maybe him for the lead?"

Pretending to scroll through his phone. Watson had been paying better attention than I had, and it wasn't him helping that was such a surprise as much as my needing help at all.

Dear God. Was I any good at what I did anymore? Did I even want to be?

"Well done," I said to Watson as serenely as I could, as Theo strolled up to the restaurant's front door. "Do you think they do a good chicken picatta?"

four

By the time we had been sat at a table in the corner, I had managed to recalibrate. I would not be admiring the tablecloth, the minimalist décor, the waiters' black bow ties. I would not be watching Watson's eyes go dark and soft in the candlelight. I would instead do what I did best: empty myself of all wants except the one at hand.

I would extract basic information about the Dramatics Society from these three sitting ducks, and then, and only then, would allow myself to return to my daydream about going punting with Watson tomorrow.

"It's been a whole year. Can you believe they still remember us?" Theo asked, as the waiter brought a round of cocktails that no one had ordered.

"We certainly spent enough money here last summer," Anwen said.

Watson looked down at his drink. "For a minute there, I forgot I was back in England. I haven't had a legal drink in ages."

"America sucks, mate," Theo said, with a thick fake accent, and Rupert chucked a roll at him that Theo caught neat-handed. Anwen rolled her eyes.

I sipped my water. "Did you all keep in touch between summers?"

"Of course," Rupert said, and Anwen looked down and said, "Not really," and Theo leaned back to signal the waiter, and didn't answer at all.

Not a good question. I watched Watson clock it the same moment I did. "You're from Wales, Anwen?" he asked, and you could almost hear the sound of things realigning.

"I am," she said, "from all over," and the waiter brought another basket of rolls and a plate of beef carpaccio that made Rupert look ill and Theo ecstatic, and I watched her, Anwen, as she immediately changed the subject to the houseplants she'd brought with her, if they were getting enough sun in her summer digs.

As the night went on, I realized I kept doing that: watching them, not individually, but as some kind of three-headed person, a benign hydra. Benign? Perhaps. There was some tension here, something I wanted to tease out.

This was a problem, yes, but it had training wheels on. Precisely what I needed. *We* needed.

Though Watson didn't seem very sleuth-like at the moment, at least not from where I was sitting. He'd rolled up his sleeves and was relaxing back into his chair—his blood orange cocktail had smoothed out his edges. As for me, I drank my water and ate my chicken and felt myself return. I kept asking questions, flattering ones, ones they wanted to answer—the best nights most people seem to have are those where they're allowed to shamelessly talk themselves up—and though I kept edging them back around to the theater, the theater and the accidents last year, I kept stumbling over a smaller, more intricate mystery in the way.

Why had these three friends, despite their seeming closeness, despite this being their first night together in a year, chosen to invite out two strangers to their favorite restaurant to break bread with them? Had they wanted to avoid each other, they would. Had they wanted to be together, they wouldn't have invited us.

I cracked my knuckles, so to speak, and dug in.

Rupert was a youngest child from Norfolk. "The youngest of six," he said, and I looked at his ruddy cheeks and his hands, calloused not from holding a pen or playing an instrument but from lifting and carrying, and asked where his family farm was. He liked that, the "trick" I'd just done, deducing he was a farmer—it told me almost as much about someone if they found my read of them fascinating or invasive—and said yes, part of the reason his parents had had so many children was so they had help with their sheep and their cows. He didn't appear bothered by that; he didn't feel used. He loved the farm, he said, feeding the baby lambs with a bottle. But his accent was more city than country, and his boots were expensive—hand-tooled Italian leather—and he wasn't planning on being an actor, he was here to study economics. "It's my current project," he said, "when I'm not farming." The rich did this sometimes, I'd learned, chose words that were technically true but that obscured whole worlds of meaning. I asked if he spent all year on the farm, and he blushed—Rupert blushed quite a lot, it was charming and seemingly genuine—and he said no, in fact, he went to Eton during the school year, it was silly to attend a school so posh and expensive but his father had gone, his uncles too, and anyway his parents were away most of the year doing business in London, and that's when Anwen leaned over and stage-whispered to me, "Rupert Davies. As in, Davies Fine Leathers. They do the saddles for the queen? His family has Rup and his brothers come home to work the barns in the summer, they think it keeps them from becoming spoiled tosspots."

Rupert did not, in fact, appear to be a tosspot, though I reserved the right to change my opinion given further evidence. At any rate, I didn't resent him for coming from money, or for wanting to hide that fact. It was, in fact, such a logical decision on his part that I lost interest in Rupert temporarily. What I did find interesting: Anwen's satisfied smile at outing Rupert, Theo rolling his eyes.

Unlike Rupert, Anwen didn't talk much. Only in asides, redirections, the odd sarcastic comment. When I asked her a question about herself, something as straightforward as how she found out about the Oxford program, she would say, "Well, Theo learned about it from his dad . . ." and he would smoothly pick up where she had trailed off. Everything an evasive maneuver. Still, there was no nervousness in her gestures, no tells that she was lying, no self-consciousness at all that I could see—and I almost always found self-consciousness, particularly in other teenagers. Her dark dress was simple but well cut. It had a high collar but fit close to her body. Her hair was a dramatic curly tumble down her back—she clearly hadn't brushed it; the not-brushing was deliberate, and it gave her a wild, fairy-tale look. Her nails were filed and painted translucent, so they had a subtle gleam, and she wore no jewelry except a signet ring (bought new, made to look vintage) on her smallest finger. It was, as my mother would say, a *look*, a push-pull between shined-up and attractively undone.

What I managed to glean about her was all in those details and in the things she let slip: she was here to study Russian history; she designed clothes and painted as a hobby and would be helping out with sets for *Hamlet*, even if she auditioned and won a part, "but only because Theo dragged me into it, naughty boy"; she had been accepted to Cambridge for the fall and professed to not care if her credits from this summer would transfer, which was the one moment I could tell she was lying, though I couldn't tell if it was about Cambridge or about the not-caring. All I knew for certain was that she had both a polish and a bratty insouciance that drew her friends' eyes to her over and over again.

Soon enough, Watson was looking at her too. Looking

to evaluate, I thought, not with any real interest; and still I wished I hadn't noticed, because my fondness for him tripped me up. Made me invested. It kept me from running my game as I liked to.

Still, it was a compromise I was willing to make.

Theo and Watson got on like a house on fire. They read the same books; they listened to the same grunge rock from the nineties; they both wanted the carbonara for dinner and the tiramisu for dessert. Theo had on a cheap military jacket cut to look stylish and shoes that he'd bought secondhand. He was attractively rumpled, a boy with strong shoulders and a slim waist, like a diver. Unlike Rupert, Theo didn't have much to say about his life back home, only that he'd always wanted to do theater in Britain, ever since a Shakespeare troupe had come to do a workshop at his school in Boston and told him he was talented. It was true, he had a certain clarity of expression, a certain resonance to his speaking voice. He would do well playing a shipwrecked prince or a well-intentioned pirate; for now, he told us he'd set his sights on playing Hamlet. "The audition's the day after tomorrow, and I shouldn't be drinking at all—my voice, you know—but I'm a little nervous," he said. He didn't seem nervous. He had a boyfriend back home in Boston, and when Anwen poked him for texting under the table, she said to us, fondly, "Theo's like this whenever he dates anyone. Smitten. You should have seen him with his girlfriend last year." It was important to her for us, for whatever reason, to know about the girlfriend, to know he was bisexual, or pansexual, that he wasn't only attracted to boys.

But he didn't give her any response, so there was nothing more for me to go on. I watched Rupert twirl his spaghetti. Watched Anwen flag down the waiter to order another glass of wine. Watched Theo pick a white thread out of her hair, shaking his head, saying, "I always find string there. Where on earth does it come from?" As Anwen laughed, Rupert darted his eyes over to Theo, then to me, then back to his plate, so fast I wouldn't have seen it if I wasn't looking.

"I'm auditioning as well," I told them. "For Ophelia."

Watson ran a finger down his water glass. "She's a terrific actress. Totally transforms herself into someone else. It's like she disappears."

Theo said lightly, "It's a relief, sometimes, isn't it?"

"To disappear, or be the one watching?"

"Both," Rupert said, to my surprise. As far as I knew, he wasn't someone who had issues with being seen. "But—" He glanced at Anwen, then back at me. "Have you heard at all about what happened last summer, in the theater department?"

Aha.

"They're just stories," Theo said.

Rupert fidgeted. "The orchids—"

"Were someone's idea of a sick joke. An expensive sick joke. Do you know how much those things cost?" Theo rolled his eyes. "Someone just wanted to scare us, that's all."

"What was it?" Watson said, as if on cue. I admired him, then: he'd established himself earlier as the sort of boy to ask the brash question, and then did so. "Everyone keeps talking about *something* that happened last year—what was it?"

"Just . . . just some accidents." Anwen grimaced. "They weren't . . . they weren't terrible, you know? But they weren't nothing, either."

Rupert's eyes widened. "Matilda *isn't here.* All right? Matilda didn't come back, she's *gone—*"

"She's not dead," Anwen said. "She's just not, you know, *here—*"

"Theo, you of all people should be upset—"

"I am upset. And now we're done talking about it," Theo said. He stood. "I haven't seen the waiter in, like, a year. I'm going to go get the bill."

Anwen tossed a handful of cash on the table, and followed him.

Rupert watched her go. "I'm sorry about that," he said. "But it's important that you know, if you're thinking of doing this year's play. They never found out who was behind it."

Watson nodded. "Thanks for the warning. We'll think about it."

"'We'll'?" Rupert asked, with some interest. "Are you auditioning too?"

The light outside was fading, and as Watson sat, deliberating his answer, the young hostess walked around, touching the tea lights on each table with a match. A stroke, a light, the brief smell of sulfur. And then all the candles lit, like small stars in a dark night.

"I might be," he said finally, as Theo and Anwen returned. Together, I noticed. He had waited for her at the restroom. To have a tête-à-tête away from prying eyes?

It came to me then. One of those moments I spent months chasing, through calculus or pills or a list of deductions so swift I arrived at the answer before I'd begun to articulate the question.

We're going deep here, I texted Watson under the table. Do you trust me?

He met my eyes. Mouthed *yes*.

"Well," I said to them, "thanks for inviting us out. Honestly, we were both a bit nervous coming along."

"Oh, don't be," Anwen said, and she reached out to touch Theo's arm. Any excuse to do so, it seemed. "The academics aren't that hard, right, Teddy? I mean, they *are* hard, but—"

There really was little I hated more than someone condescending to me for show. Still, I fixed a smile on my face, one that showcased my incisors. "Oh, not *that*. That'll be fine. No—just socially, I mean. Jamie and I have been dating now for a few years, and I think we both get a bit nervous that we won't meet anyone because of it. We can be a little bit reclusive."

A glance between Anwen and Theo, whisper-quick, and that was it, the nudge I needed to cast my wager.

I dropped Rupert's eyes. Then I slowly, deliberately ran my foot up his leg under the table.

He didn't blush, or look down; he didn't even look surprised. He had exactly the reaction I knew he would.

He smiled.

five

"I KNEW WE WERE DATING. BUT I DIDN'T KNOW THAT YOU were cheating on me."

Watson had worked himself into a state, standing in his sock feet in the middle of my bedroom. He was furious at me, and also he was trying very hard not to laugh, and it was something of a personal failure on my part that this was how I found Watson most appealing.

"That does seem to be accurate," I admitted.

He ran a hand over his face. "Holmes—"

"Yes?"

"We're dating and you're cheating on me," he said, his voice going higher in pitch. "You're the kind of cheater who plays footsie with country squires while I sit there eating *lady-fingers* across the *table*."

I frowned. "It's the twenty-first century. They aren't country squires anymore. Rupert is a gentleman sheep-farmer-in-training."

"I was drinking a *decaf cappuccino* while my girlfriend had her foot up a gentleman sheep farmer's pant leg—"

"Yes," I said, and really, I was moments from laughing in his face, "you are a cliché, I've made you some kind of awful cliché. I apologize. I grovel. I throw myself upon your mercy."

Watson rolled his eyes up to the ceiling and finally, after a long moment, he sat down on the bed. "You're lucky I adore you," he said. At last he was smiling, and I resisted the urge to go to him, to put my hands in his hair.

I considered him, then, sitting comfortably on the white cloud of my bed. I'd decorated this room sparely, the better to fill in details when I knew them. I had a rail for my clothes, a desk in the window, a table for my experiments that right now stood bare. At Sherringford, back in my supply closet, Watson had fit in amongst the teeth and the vultures and the marked-up books like he, too, had been something I'd collected. The thought had given me pleasure. I remembered studying him through the bow of my violin, thinking, *Why are you here, why are you here—why do you sit so still like that, watching me?*

But he didn't look like a curio to me anymore, not in this bedroom that I'd left quiet and open. He looked like a boy.

One who, by his presence, was beginning to fill in the blank space around him.

I wasn't sure I was comfortable with that either, and I snatched up the dressing gown off the back of my door and put it on like a suit of armor.

"I also ran my foot up Rupert's leg in a way that made him think it was Anwen's," I told him, belting my robe. "Unless my aim is incredibly poor."

"Jesus, Holmes. You could have led with that, you know—"

I raised an eyebrow at him.

"But you didn't. Okay. At what point do you fill me in on what's happening here, exactly?" He twisted his hands. "If this isn't anything more than a puzzle, why have you kept me in the dark?"

"Because I needed your interest tonight to be genuine," I said. He was on my bed. Why was he still on my bed?

Frowning, I pulled a cigarette from the packet in my robe and began casting around for a match.

"Will you please just tell me?" he asked, and it was either I did so, or I sat on his lap and put his arms around my waist, and I wasn't ready for that, not yet. Terms or no terms, I wasn't particularly good with romance unless one or the other of us was about to die.

Fortunately (unfortunately?), that wasn't on the table. I briefly considered poisoning us both so I could take him to bed, then discarded the idea.

I needed a distraction.

"Fine," I said, and stuffed the unlit cigarette back into my pocket. "It began last summer."

"Not just the facts, Holmes. Tell it like a story."

"Like a story," I said. "Fine. Fine." After all, Dr. Larkin had provided me with a number of dramatic flourishes when she had told it to me.

It had been a hot June, a damp one. The air had lain thicker than usual over the dreaming spires of Oxford, and underneath that suffocating blanket, as the Dramatics Society painted their sets and learned their lines for a production of *A Midsummer Night's Dream*, the company had fallen, too, under a spell from which they couldn't easily wake.

The Dramatics Soc hadn't always done Shakespeare, but they'd gotten into a pattern: comedy and tragedy in alternate summers. *Midsummer* had been Larkin's idea, a way to showcase their finest actress, the reason they'd been doing all the Bard's plays in the first place. Matilda Wilkes—tall, with burning eyes and with an understanding of the language that far outstripped her years—had come from London the previous year and laid everyone flat with her talent. She was only a rising junior when Dr. Larkin decided on *Midsummer*: Matilda, with her air of natural authority, would play the fairy queen, Titania, and the roles of the four lovers—the ostensible leads—could go to seniors, who hopefully wouldn't realize they were being upstaged.

After the auditions, Dr. Larkin had posted the casting list and taken her customary place in her office across the hall, in hopes that she'd catch any malcontents early to comfort them. This was, after all, a precollege program; the goal was education more so than performance. Still, the posting of the cast list still brought students to tears.

("It's an *extracurricular*," Watson interjected. "We all have to take other classes. It's just acting."

"You'd feel differently if someone yanked you from your fiction workshop because 'it's just stories, he can take something else.'"

"Yes, okay, point.")

The students came and went, in their clogs and ripped jeans and crop tops, with their neon-colored hair; there had been good-natured ribbing ("Of course you're playing *Bottom*") and some dickering over details ("Uh, I don't think I'm 'delicate' enough to be Hermia, but whatever?") but largely they all had been pleased. The only surprise had been Matilda Wilkes, lingering near the back of the crowd, her face dark and drawn. She'd fled as soon as Dr. Larkin caught her eyes.

Why? The reason soon became clear. Matilda Wilkes had stage parents. More accurately, stage *parent*—her father had called Dr. Larkin not ten minutes later, upset that his daughter had passed over acting programs at Royal Scottish and Juilliard to be cast in such a humiliatingly small role.

("Brat," Watson said. "Not her, her father. 'Oh no, can't believe I had to send my daughter to *Oxford*.'")

Mr. Wilkes had threatened to pull his daughter from the program, a move Dr. Larkin thought was a bluff until she received a call from her director. An extracurricular should not be causing this much turmoil, Larkin was told. If this girl was really the best, she should have the best role, regardless of seniority.

"Fix it," the director said. "Fix it, or else."

("Entertaining enough?" I asked him. "I'm attempting to channel you."

Watson was shaking his head. "This is what I sound like when I talk?"

"You're much more . . . emphatic.")

Dr. Larkin capitulated, but on her terms. She called a meeting, told her students that *Midsummer* was off the table ("I made some excuses about not getting the rights," Larkin told me, "which was ridiculous, but no one noticed"), and introduced a new play: *The Importance of Being Earnest* by Oscar Wilde. Auditions were held. The cast list was posted. Matilda was given the lead.

The next week, the accidents started.

Small things, at first. Scripts went missing. A light fell from the grid above the stage in the night; the company arrived in the morning to find it there ("like a robot's broken heart"). After the first round of costume fittings, the dresses meant for the girl playing Miss Prism had all of their seams let out. When she tried them on again, she was drowning in a sea of lace and ribbons.

All of this was exactly innocuous enough that it could have been ignored. Passed off as a prank, or a mistake. But the day after Harriet Feldstein, the girl playing Lady Bracknell, twisted her ankle dashing out of the dressing room—there had been a tangle of wires just outside that no one could remember leaving there—she came back to find an orchid (an *odontoglossums*; lovely) waiting for her at the makeup mirrors. Its tag was addressed to her. It said, *Watch your step.*

Naturally, no one stepped forward to say they'd sent it. Harriet Feldstein wanted to drop out, but Dr. Larkin convinced her to stay by installing a nanny cam in the dressing room for another level of security. The professor told no one except Harriet and the program director that she had done so.

It worked, to a certain extent, in that no further incidents happened there. They happened everywhere else instead.

The backdrops were painted and hoisted up into the fly space above the stage with ropes, and stayed there—until one of those ropes was cut during Algernon's monologue. He jumped backward just in time to avoid being clobbered by a hand-painted garden. That had been Theo Harding.

During tech rehearsals, the tea the characters "drank" onstage was replaced with motor oil; Matilda Wilkes spit hers out in a long black arc across the stage. The lighting cues were reset, every night, and had to be fixed by hand. The black-painted stairs behind the stage that led down to the dressing rooms—their edges had been marked with glow-in-the-dark tape, since the actors had to thunder up and down them in the dark. During dress rehearsals (tech week, as those in the theater called it), that tape was removed, and Harriet went flying down the steps. She twisted her *other* ankle and bruised her face.

Harriet was sent a moth orchid the next day. The tag

had her name, typed, and below it the words *watch your step.* Thankfully, it was in character for her to perform her role with a cane.

The orchids, it seemed, were only delivered on occasions that the victim had been successfully injured. No one saw the flowers arrive. No florist in town would claim responsibility.

Fear grew. Students stayed in pairs at all times, cried quietly in corners, dropped out of the smaller parts in droves. (Anwen Ellis, who had been cast as the "manservant" Lane, was the first to go.) All unused rooms were locked and could only be opened by a key that Dr. Larkin held on her person at all times. Parents called vociferously for the play to be canceled, and Dr. Larkin had an all-day meeting with university administrators the day before *The Importance of Being Earnest* was set to open. She had made up her mind, she told me, to call the show off in her concern for her students' safety.

That night, Matilda Wilkes had been walking home from a night out with friends. They were cast members from *Earnest*; they had all gone one way, and Matilda had gone the other. One could follow her path from one CCTV camera to the next—that's what the police did the next day, poring through the grainy, washed-out footage, trying to put together a timeline. A narrative.

When they found her, though, there was no story. Her bag over her shoulder, her head down, her pace steady, quick, that of a girl eager to collapse into her bed. But not because she was being followed. Not because she was afraid.

And then, at the end of a long block, she had glanced up as

though to check the name of the street she was turning onto, and for just a moment she looked directly into the camera's dark lens. The streetlights had washed her face into a blank. A suggestion of dark eyes, a haughty chin. She had nodded to herself and rounded the corner, out of sight.

That was, of course, the last that anyone had seen of her.

As though she had cut a hole into the night and climbed through it. As though she had erased herself from the bottom up.

(I was familiar with that feeling.)

Her father, who had come down from the city to see her perform the next night, stalked around the police station, shouting at the detectives; her mother had haunted the theater, begging information from students, from teachers. She had known nothing of the orchid attacks. She had called her lawyer. Matilda's boyfriend, Theo Harding, refused to perform. And without Cecily and Algernon and with the lawsuit the Wilkes family served the precollege program, the play was definitively canceled.

"Dr. Larkin stepped away from the precollege program at the end of the summer," I told Watson. "Of her own volition, supposedly, but the way she talked about it made it sound as though she'd been forced out. And took a pay cut, based on her new shoes—cheap—and her jacket, handbag, and scarf, which were very much not. I think she wants her job back."

"This is all, like . . . really awful," Watson said. "I can't believe they're letting the program continue."

"It's quite an old program, and a popular one, and really,

I think people are just indescribably stupid sometimes about their own safety." I retrieved the cigarette from my pocket and lit it. Watson winced, but said nothing. It was my last remaining vice, and not one I intended to keep for much longer, and still his disapproval stung a bit.

"Was she sent an orchid, too? Matilda?" Watson asked, his eyes on the thing between my lips. I frowned, then stubbed it out on my armchair, and Watson winced at that too.

Mouse emerged from under the bed and wound her way over to me, and with a sigh, I gathered her up in my arms. "She was. Not that she was there to collect it. It didn't go to the theater—at this point, the culprit must've known they would be closely watched—but to her rooms. The suite she shared with Theo and Rupert."

"And?"

"Not to be melodramatic," I said, "and do know that I'm just quoting Dr. Larkin here—"

"Oh, come on, just tell me—"

I cleared my throat. "The orchid was a bright, bloody red."

SIX

"RED? LIKE, THEY DYED IT?"

I shrugged. "I didn't see it. And unfortunately, orchids don't fall into my areas of expertise. Though from what I can tell, it *is* a fascinatingly complex field—"

With that, Watson flopped backward onto the bed as though he'd been shot.

"I refuse to apologize for having an interest in botany," I said, trying not to laugh. I was always trying very hard not to laugh.

It's possible he could tell. I never knew with him. Either way, he sat up on his elbows, smiling at me a bit lopsidedly. "Red orchids, white orchids—I'm sure you'll dig in soon enough. Either way, they're creepy. We're headed back into creepy territory, here. And this is a cold case, a year old. Matilda could be anywhere."

"The last case we had was hot enough for a lifetime," I said. "And I don't think we're looking for Matilda. Not exactly. What Larkin wants is preventative work. Protecting the students who come this year. I'd prefer to do that than to clean up a Moriarty's mess."

He grew serious at that. "Do you have a plan?"

"I do," I allowed. "But it's getting quite late. Unless—unless you wanted to stay. It would be fine. With me, I mean, if you stayed."

Caution was my watchword. Watson and I were rebuilding something, and I wasn't quite sure what it would end up being, and in the meantime I didn't want to push things unnecessarily, and also he still made me incredibly nervous.

Watson was watching me. "I want to know what you've deduced that made you take this insane leap," he said finally. "But—won't it foil whatever dastardly plan you have, if I'm not in the room with Rupert tonight to hear his reaction?"

"A bit," I said.

Watson shrugged. "Then I'll see what I can do."

"Tell me what he says in the morning. And I'll tell you what I've surmised."

"An intelligence swap, Detective?"

I felt my lips twitch. "Indeed, Doctor."

"Tomorrow, then," he said. "Breakfast before your first lecture?"

"Come by at eight. We'll have scones. I'll walk you to class."

He smiled to himself, his eyes gone soft. Off somewhere in a memory, or another life. Back at Sherringford, perhaps. "'Night," he said, and before he left he pulled me in and kissed me on the forehead, and this once, my body let me accept it without flinching away.

It was becoming abundantly clear that, contrary to appearances and negotiated terms, I had no idea at all what I was doing.

I WAS AWAKE AT SIX THIRTY, AS I HAD BEEN SINCE I'D BEEN back on a proper sleep schedule. (It had been some time since I'd been up smoking til dawn in a nest of my own research.) Leander was still in bed when I got up—he'd come in quite late the night before, past midnight—and so I made myself a quiet cup of tea, poured it into a takeaway mug, and set out for a wander so that my footsteps wouldn't wake him. It was a pacing sort of morning.

There had been some truth to what I'd said last night at dinner, that I was anxious at the thought of entering a new social sphere with Watson at my side. It wasn't that I didn't want him there. I wanted him there desperately. But I was worried about the weight of expectation—well. I was worried about my expectations for myself. I had been presented with a pretty little puzzle box of a mystery, here, and already I was showboating for his benefit rather than considering the case.

As in: Did I really *need* to run my foot up Rupert's pant leg? There were many paths up the mountain, after all. And yet here we were.

Here, right now, was the little café down the street from our flat. It was called Blackmarket, though there was no whiff of any illegal activity on the premises. They sold coffee, and muffins, and a "cheeky snowman" latte that I only ordered when alone, so that as few people as possible would hear me say the words.

It was what I was doing just then, placing my order (and asking them to skip the snowman face they drew with strawberry syrup onto the whipped cream, I did have some last reserves of dignity) when Anwen walked up beside me. It wasn't yet seven o'clock, but the café table behind her was heaped with books. I could just see the title of the one on top: *Speech and Motivation in Shakespeare's Tragedies.*

"I'd thought you looked familiar last night," she said, by way of greeting. "I must have seen you here before. I'm here most mornings in the summer."

"Oh," I said, because I hadn't had my latte yet, and that was about all I could muster.

She'd been up for some time, clearly: her hair in a fishtail braid, her nails freshly painted. I could still smell the polish.

She seemed to want me to continue, so I said, "So you come here often?"

"I mean, yeah?" she said, as though I was daft. "Uh, yeah, this is one of our regular spots. Convenient to St. Genesius—the theater's right over there, do you see it? Through the window. Which doesn't matter much to Rup, he'll follow me and Theo pretty much anywhere."

I nodded. The barista handed me my drink.

Anwen looked at me again, as though she was waiting for me to give her something in return. Talkative people didn't often do this, pause for the other person to speak; usually, when presented with a willing listener, they'd prattle on until stopped. But Anwen seemed to want something specific from me.

"I live down the street," I offered.

"Oh," she said. "It's quite a nice address, isn't it?"

"Yes," I said, and waited.

"Jamie's very nice."

"I've often thought so." Despite my request, the barista had gone and drawn the snowman face onto my drink anyway. When I took a drink, I made its eyes bleed across the whipped cream. Anwen watched, fascinated. Her eyes flickered back up to meet mine.

I don't often feel the need to apologize for myself or my actions in a social setting (really, I've come to like myself quite well in the day-to-day) but there was something about this girl that made me feel deeply ridiculous. My snowman wasn't helping.

I thought for a moment. "I don't have a lot to say before my coffee." It was the sort of thing, after all, that people said.

"Rupert suggested that I ask you to run lines with me," she said. It was a particularly ham-fisted sort of insult. Framed this way, *Anwen* herself would never want to run lines with me; she was only suggesting it out of obligation. "I'm doing costumes, but I'm auditioning for Ophelia, too. Rupert says I play her a bit unusually. It would be interesting to have your take."

I had told her the night before I was auditioning for the part. This was either a bald-faced power play, or she was so assured in her own talent that she thought I ought to bask in it as well.

Or she wanted to be my friend. That was, perhaps, the scariest of all.

She didn't know I'd already been called in to understudy the role, so the pressure was entirely off. And the possibilities ripe. "Do you want to meet at the theater?" I asked, putting just the tiniest bit of quaver in my voice. There it was, the whir of my brain; the coffee must have kicked in.

"Perfect," she said, reaching out to lightly touch my arm. "I'll meet you at the doors at noon."

After an encounter like that, I wasn't going to stick around.

Instead I had my usual constitutional. I chose a building on the St. Genesius grounds I hadn't yet explored (the boathouse) and mapped it top to bottom. I loitered by the door, looking intently at my phone, until the clerk at the desk disappeared into the back, and then made a quick inventory. The number of punts; the number of poles, aluminum and wooden; the entrances and exits, the photographs on the walls.

I charted it all down in my head. The next day, I'd explore the meadow across the river. It would be good to know how long it would take to cross it if one were running flat out (being pursued by wild dogs or similar). I was still setting up a hypothesis in my head when I rounded the corner to my flat and found Watson at my front door, a paper bag in hand.

"He thinks it was Anwen's foot," he said.

I snorted. "Good morning to you too."

Yawning, he held out the bag between us. Inside was an untouched blueberry scone and the crumbs of a second. "Rupert kept me up until dawn. 'What was Anwen thinking,' and 'Anwen said *this* last year to me in the pub but maybe I misheard her what do you think did she really say "I want to kiss your neck" or maybe my neck had mist on it?' and 'God, Jamie, Anwen's foot felt just like heaven—'"

"He did not," I said, laughing, and he took my arm as we set off back toward school.

"He came pretty close. Is that what you wanted? For him to need to spill, and for me to be there?"

I nodded. "He couldn't tell Theo. You're new, so you have no alliances, and you have a girlfriend, so there's less chance you want Anwen for yourself. You're perfect."

We passed the St. Genesius library, its weathered brick (excellent for climbing) and high stained-glass windows (somewhat less ideal). "Theo made it sound like we're going to live in there, with all the work we'll be doing," Watson said, craning his neck.

"You're only taking the one course," I told him. "I'm taking four."

"Four? I thought you were taking seven."

"I took on a case," I said. "That's three courses in itself. And also the administrators were a bit concerned about when I would sleep. I told them it wouldn't be an issue, that I had my methods, and then Leander gave me that look as though he was going to send me back to rehab without even tossing my room first, and it seemed far simpler to just keep the chemistry courses, and my poetry tutorial, and be rid of all the rest."

"Poetry," Watson said, casting a look at me. "*Poetry.*"

"There is something wrong with you, if that's the most concerning part of what I said."

"You're not using again," he said, a statement.

"I'm not."

We were passing the theater then. Cream brick, several stories, built in the fifteenth century. Watson could tell you more about its eaves and towers, I'm sure. I was counting its windows and wondering how much trouble I'd be in if I had to break one.

"Then my biggest concern," he was saying, "are the nightmares I'm going to have about all the morgue poems you're going to write. The murder poems. The *I made this poison for you, poor swain* poems—"

"I have layers," I reminded him. "What if all my poems were about my grandmother?"

"You have a grandmother?"

"I didn't spring whole from the head of Zeus."

"Scary. Pass."

"Kittens, then," I said. We had made it to the steps of my lecture hall. "I could write about kittens. Tulips. My future wedding—"

"Completely terrifying."

I squeezed his elbow. I adored him. "My lecture is about to start. Can you please sum up, without rhetorical or dramatic flourishes, what you learned from Rupert?"

Out of respect for my methods, he laid it out in a numbered list.

Rupert was attracted to Anwen and had been since he'd taken her suitcases up three stories to her room early last summer.

He had believed, based on fairly conclusive evidence, that she might feel the same way. (Staying up all night talking about television they'd loved as a child; her repeatedly touching his shoulder, his hair, etc.)

Rupert had then introduced Anwen to Theo, and immediately her attentions, and perhaps her affection, shifted targets. Theo did not reciprocate: he was interested in Matilda Wilkes. This didn't seem to matter to Anwen.

Rupert did not resent Anwen or Theo for this turn of events. Instead, he made himself indispensable to them.

"It doesn't feel like he's just been creepily hanging out, waiting for Anwen to love him," Watson said, "or, like, waiting to push Theo off a cliff, but it also doesn't *not* feel like he's doing those things?" He glanced down at his shoes.

"For the record, I've never thought you were creepily hanging out, waiting for me to love you," I said, as it felt necessary.

Watson did not look back up at me. "Well, I think Rupert's sort of sad," he said, "as in pathetic-sad."

"I have two minutes," I said, as I literally did not have time for Watson's unfounded bit of self-flagellation.

He ran a hand through his hair, shifted his bag, glanced up at me.

"No one knows anything about where Anwen's from," he

said. "Her parents. Her family. Where exactly in Wales, and Rupert thinks that if she didn't have the accent he wouldn't even know that much. She avoids the subject totally. But—

"Even though Theo denies it, Rupert thinks he knows her whole story."

The students were streaming around us now, up and down the long steps to the lecture hall.

"You have biochemistry," Watson said. He could be quite obvious.

"Yes. And then I'm meeting Anwen at noon at the theater. To run lines."

"I'll catch up with you after?" He took a step toward me, then hesitated. "Do we—do I—"

"Oh," I said, realizing, and threw my arms around his neck. My schoolbag thudded satisfyingly against his jacket; I had forgotten what it was like to touch someone like this—or had I? When had I done it last? "Good-bye, poor swain."

"I hate you," he said, his nose in my hair. "Have a good lecture."

seven

One feature of my very particular upbringing is that I am able to absorb large amounts of information while my brain loiters somewhere else altogether.

An illustration: my father, at the dinner table, liked to engage my mother in lengthy conversations about horse racing or sea anemones or a vaccine she was developing at her lab, and just as my eyes would unfocus (it didn't concern me, after all), he would turn and have me recite their words back verbatim. By age seven I was able to do this easily; by age eight, I could do it while thinking about something else.

All of this is to say that I could recite the entirety of my first Oxford biochemistry lecture (thank God, as I had a tutor quizzing me on it the day after next), and still I hadn't heard a word. I had spent the hour in the small mirrored room in my head, where I examined myself and my motives, as another feature of my upbringing was that, since I was not allowed to have feelings as a child, I continued to have difficulty having feelings as an eighteen-year-old girl.

For instance: Why on earth did Watson touching me make me feel so disordered? I had applied rules to our courtship. Rules were, by definition, orderly. And still I felt too hot, that my skin was too tight. In the past when I'd felt this way I'd played something feverish on my violin and exorcized it from my body.

I didn't think that that would work now.

Part of me recoiled at feeling so out of control; another part examined closely the part that recoiled; another hugged herself tightly and tried not to look at herself in the mirror.

As usual, the muddle of myself was too much to work out, and I arrived at the theater hoping for an easier mystery to solve. The place had a certain charm, I had to admit: like the other buildings on the St. Genesius campus, the white marble was scattered about with light. The front was rounded to incorporate the rows of seats inside, and when I tipped my head back to see the roof, I spied a small white tower that looked as though it had been hot-glued on. A crow's nest, I thought. I wondered what its purpose was.

The doors were wooden, built into a larger wooden wall reinforced with crosshatched metal, and when I stepped into the vestibule, that small space was as hushed as a Catholic church I visited once in New York. (I'd needed to change my wig in the vestry.) It had a similar smell, too, like cloth and dust, though what I could see was spotless. There was a small ticket office to one side, built an obvious four centuries after the rest of the building, and a coatroom at the other, and when I walked through the second set of doors into the theater itself, I paused for a moment to get my bearings.

Rows of seats leading down to the stage, red velvet and gold leaf, everything oppressive with age and still, in its own way, beautiful. I was coming to notice this about Oxford, the heavy sense of history, how it made one feel important and insignificant in the same breath. I'd been around wealth before, or the appearance of it; my parents had done a very good job pretending they hadn't lost their fortune. But our own claim to fame could only be traced back a hundred years and change. Before that, we were humble country squires, and before *that*, I didn't know.

Subtract another five hundred years, and Oxford would still have been standing.

This was all rather abstract for me, this musing about *atmosphere*, but it wasn't as though I had immediate matters to absorb me. Coming to a mystery a year after the original incidents meant that you did a bit of useless wandering before you struck on anything gold. Still, I had some time before I was scheduled to meet Anwen, so I decided to start looking around.

It took forty-five seconds for me to trot to the bottom of the aisle, minimal effort to hoist myself up onto the stage. I stepped into the wings and traced a path past the lighting board to the set of stairs in the back, for the actors and crew to access the dressing rooms in the basement. The stairs were painted black, as Dr. Larkin had said, and the fluorescent tape at their edges looked new. Twelve steps down, a small, spare hallway at the bottom. No other obvious exits other than the one back up through the theater. Anyone who had crept in to deliver orchids to their victims had, on first blush, to have been backstage already to do so.

Still, there was something different about the quality of the air than I expected. Basements, as a rule, were cooler than the floors above, especially basements made of cinderblock, as this one was, and yet I could feel a whisper of hot air on the back of my neck.

I shut my eyes to listen.

A bicycle bell. A man laughing. Not loud, not obvious. For me to hear those sounds in a building whose walls could have happily survived a siege, there had to be another exit to the outside. Perhaps walled off, perhaps hidden, but *there.*

Later I would have time to investigate further, but for now I had to peer back into the human element of this case. When I reemerged onto the stage, it was just past noon, and I hurried back out the front doors to look for Anwen. I had no intention of upsetting her this early in our relationship.

Well. This early in the case. I wasn't here to make friends. (Which was something I couldn't say anymore, as Watson said it made me sound like a reality television star.)

But I pushed through the doors to find the street empty. A family of tourists straggled by, listening to a walking tour on headphones and pointing silently at the imposing building across the square; a girl I recognized from my biochem lecture walked by with a golden retriever on a lead. I was temporarily distracted by this—how was she allowed a dog? Where was she keeping it? It was a bit too large and happy to have been kept in a closet—and then I realized that she was on her way to the Sainsbury's on the High Street to do her grocery shop (set of canvas bags, water bowl for dog waiting on street). She lived here, as I did.

Ten minutes had passed, and no Anwen. I turned on my heel to see if I had possibly missed her inside the theater (though the aisle carpet had no prints other than mine since it had last been vacuumed). Then stopped short when I came to the second set of doors.

A note. *I'm in the sound booth upstairs. Meet me there?*

I studied it, a bit bemused. I hadn't seen it when I'd left, which didn't mean it wasn't there—but it was certainly taped up after I'd first arrived. Which left a ten-minute window. We'd just missed each other. The handwriting didn't look particularly feminine, but neither did mine, and anyway, *I* was the one who was running late.

I took the note and put it in my bag.

There was another set of stairs here in the vestibule that I had imagined went up to Dr. Larkin's office, and when I climbed them, they proved to do just that. As well as to a door that read SOUND BOOTH.

I paused, my hand on the knob, before I barged in. *You are being very stupid, Holmes,* I thought. *Behave like yourself. Pay attention.*

There wasn't any sound inside. The building was still. I looked down to examine the floor beneath my boots, and it was hardwood, old and creaky. Had there been anyone waiting beyond the door, I would have heard their shoes, or their chair. No one stayed perfectly still, waiting.

Hardly anyone, anyway.

I knocked. No answer.

Next to the door was a bulletin board, and on it, a calendar. ORCHIDS OF THE WORLD.

It looked new.

"Anwen?" I called again, and I may have been many things, but I wasn't an utter fool. Anyone trying to murder me would at least need to put in some effort. When I yanked the door open, I took a quick series of steps back and to the side.

In time to keep the blood-soaked figure from falling directly on top of me.

It was fair to say that, after the events of the past few years, my nerves were still somewhat shot. So I hoped I would be forgiven for yelling, "ABSOLUTELY NOT," before I leapt quickly backward.

After a long moment in which I was not beheaded, I straightened. The figure was still on the floor. A cursory inspection showed that it was in fact made of bedsheets knotted together into the shape of a body—head, shoulders, and so on—and fallen faceup. A photograph of a girl's face had been pinned in the appropriate place. At a glance, I thought it to be Matilda Wilkes, and a quick search on my phone (Facebook; infinitely useful) confirmed my supposition. Hardly surprising.

What was: the piece de resistance, a plastic dagger stuck into the figure's chest.

It was stuck in the *wrong* side of the figure's chest, but then, I supposed the perpetrator's heart was in the right place.

(I took note of that joke to repeat it to Watson later. I was on something of a crusade to prove to him that I had a sense of humor.)

"Amateurs," I said as I bent beside it, snapping on a pair of latex gloves; I kept them in my bag for such occasions. I ran my hands over the figure, then lifted it slightly, both to gauge its weight (less than ten pounds; easy enough to prop up inside the door, no matter the perpetrator's size) and to see if the dagger would fall out. It didn't. It had been wedged into a knot, which kept the plastic blade stable, and I wasn't about to dislodge the evidence. The knife itself was a standard costume shop prop; they could have bought it anywhere, taken it from the basement of this very theater. Still, I found its serial number, then photographed it. Then sniffed the splatter of ketchup around it, made to look like blood.

A good corn syrup mixture was much more realistic.

The knot itself was more interesting. I examined it, photographed it, and made a note to look into it later. I'd just leaned back to take some shots of the scene when I heard footsteps on the stair.

"Holmes." Watson pelting down the short hall, his trainers squeaking on the hardwood. "I heard you yell—I—" He pulled up short.

"Not a body," I said.

"No." He looked down at it. "More like a dead sheet monster."

"Anwen stood me up."

"She's actually right behind me," he said, squatting down next to the figure. "With Dr. Larkin. She'd gone to meet her to get the keys, in case the theater wasn't unlocked. But I guess she had to run around to track her down, Dr. Larkin was in a meeting in another building—"

"With the Soc's new director, actually," Dr. Larkin said, stepping into the hall, Anwen just behind her. "You'll meet him tomorrow night. Dear God, Charlotte, what happened?"

A clumsy but effective announcement that this campaign of fear hasn't ended, I thought, but what I said was, "I don't know, I'm all shaky," and threw myself into Watson's arms, my fists tucked up against his chest. Quickly, I pulled off my gloves and stuffed them between the buttons of his shirt, then down. He stifled a yelp. I suppose it would be surprising, having a ball of warm latex shoved under your clothes without warning.

"Pretend I'm upset," I whispered.

"She's had a scare," he told them as I pushed my face into his shirt. "I don't know if there's someone you need to report this to, or what, but I think I should get Charlotte out of here."

I looked up tearfully at Dr. Larkin, whose brow was

furrowed—*Who do I call,* I saw her think, *what do I say that can keep the program open*—and at Anwen, whose face was a perfect blank.

"They're going to cancel the show," she whispered finally, and there was something different about her voice, about her accent.

Dr. Larkin jumped in before I could place it. "Don't say that," she told Anwen. "I've called in help, you know."

"But you're not—"

"Even if I'm not the director, I still care," Dr. Larkin said, because of course she did. She wanted her job back. "We're working with some really excellent consultants to get to the bottom of this, and I'm sure . . . I'm sure . . ."

She trailed off, perhaps in part because the consulting detective she had hired was still sobbing prettily into her boyfriend's arms.

"I'm sorry," I said. "I'm sorry. I lost someone close to me last year, and—"

Watson stiffened. I suppose it was in poor taste to bandy around August Moriarty's death like this, but I also thought that August himself would probably not have minded. Any port in a storm.

"I can still run lines," I told Anwen. "I think. Maybe? But can we just go somewhere else?"

"I'd prefer that the both of you leave," Dr. Larkin said. Her eyes flickered down to the faux body, and she thought, *They'll cancel the program entirely, we'll lose our endowment, my car payments will keep being late, I'll lose my flat—*

How did I know? She said a version of those things to me when she asked me to take on the case. When faced with our worst nightmares, we don't tend to think new thoughts.

"Are you calling in the police?" Anwen asked the professor, and her voice was back to normal: Welsh, feminine, musical.

"No. Why would I? Harmless prank, really. No, the two of you go off and run lines—perhaps at Charlotte's flat? I visited her uncle there. He's lovely. Nice big space. Yes, excellent—" and she began casting around for the supply closet.

Anwen uncrossed her arms, adjusted her skirt. She glanced from me to Watson. "If it's not an imposition," she said. "You can come too, Jamie. If you want."

At that, I pinched his leg.

"No!" he yelped. "No, go on. I, ah. Have a lecture."

"Are you sure?" I asked him, sniffling.

"I'm sure," he said, and reached out, very gently, to brush away a tear from my face. His dark eyes softened. He really was a better actor than I gave him credit for. "I'll see you later, pumpkin."

As I led Anwen out to the street, I texted from my bag: Watson?

Yes, pumpkin?

New condition: you cease and desist all gourd-related nicknames.

Done. But pinch me again, and I'll start calling you pickle.

Do that, and I will find and then publish your diaries on a website with a vociferous comments section. Though I was not a gourd, I was most definitively not a vinegar-soaked phallic object.

Noted. Good luck with Ophelia. Dinner tonight?

Yes.

Somewhere nice? I'd like to take you somewhere nice.

"Coming?" Anwen asked.

Fine, I said to Watson, and "yes," I said to Anwen, though the shake in my voice was from a fear of something visceral, something terrifying and strange.

A date with Watson.

eight

HAD IT BEEN MY DECISION, I WOULD HAVE NEVER ASKED Anwen back to my flat.

Why on earth would I give a suspect access to my living space? At the very least, they might be able to draw conclusions about me or my habits that might blow my cover (I would, for instance, have a hard time justifying the brick-sized moisture-analyzing machine I kept on the radiator, which was still not providing accurate information on why my cat Mouse had developed an alarming little cough). At most, the suspect would be able to sabotage me where I lived. I had recently spent a year of my life ripping apart each room I lived in for recording devices, small explosives, itching powder, and similar; I was rather invested in never having to do that again.

Even then, I had learned very little about Anwen that was immediately alarming. Humans are simple creatures; the most highly accomplished of us even more so. When you pair intellect with the sort of razor-sharp focus that brings you to a school like Oxford, you're more or less slapping a pair of blinders on the human horse. Your goal is dead ahead; distraction is all around; it does not behoove you to think of anything but your heaps of homework and whatever small hobby you've adopted to keep you from losing your mind. You don't have time to consider things like the psychological profile of a girl (me, for instance) who owned both a complete professional-grade chemistry set and a pair of well-worn velvet loafers with embroidered alpacas on the toes.

Anwen, however, was different.

I'd noticed her caginess the night before, at dinner, when she'd continually drawn our attention back to Theo and Rupert. I'd noticed her slip from a perfectly unremarkable Welsh accent into something far rougher and burrier in the theater. I hadn't drawn any conclusions yet, though I'd been tempted to. If nothing else, I'd learned my lesson about theorizing in advance of having all the facts.

It was tempting, though, to wonder why Anwen looked so taken aback as she walked into my flat.

Watson, in his previous accounts of our adventures, has fussed about the strangeness of my previous living quarters. As they were my quarters that I had arranged how I pleased, I can't comment on their eccentricities. (Plenty of people collect *spoons*, of all things. Why on earth am I not allowed to collect skulls?)

Really, the space I shared with Leander was quite standard. The living room was floor-to-ceiling books, largely texts that interested my uncle (mysteries, true crime, botany, Leander's full collection of Evelyn Waugh novels), some of mine (my childhood encyclopedia set and a well-thumbed copy of *The History of Dirt*), a memento or two from our journeys (the aforementioned skulls). Sofas. Blankets. A bay window. A kitchen with nothing untoward boiling on the stove.

I *had* boiled a pair of socks that past weekend for an experiment, but she could hardly know—

"This is all yours?" she asked, casting herself down on the sofa with rather more force than necessary.

In the few steps it took to join her, I had completely rewritten my persona to suit her comment.

"It's my uncle's," I said, with a bit of an eye roll. "He's richer than God and never here, which works out just fine for me. This place is like a weird-old-man palace."

There was an expected response to that statement: *ugh,* or *did your parents make you stay with him?* or some other opening into a conversation about how, while my uncle was wealthy, I was not. (Which was, at this point in my life, true.) Anwen would be able to laugh off her discomfort at my social class, and—

"Oh," Anwen said, twisting a red curl around her finger. Her face had gone blank again. "Don't be self-conscious about it, you should see Rupert's ancestral home. It goes on forever, and even though his family's massive, you can wander it for days and see no one. No, I was wondering if you lived here with Jamie."

I raised an eyebrow. "We've been dating for a long time, but we aren't there yet."

"No? I thought you were serious." She smiled. "It sucks that you have to live with your uncle. I always thought that that was the best part of graduating, that you got to be on your own."

Since when was Anwen running this interrogation?

"It's nice not to pay rent," I said, "especially when you're taking too many courses to have a job. And as for me and Jamie . . . we're eighteen. We don't need to shack up together right away, especially when he's off to London for uni this fall, and I'm staying here. Anything else you need an answer for? I could go change my clothes, if they're not to your taste?"

Her eyes widened almost imperceptibly, and too late I realized what I'd done: fallen directly into one of my customary traps. Find someone's sore spot and press down hard enough, and they'll reveal far more than they ever intended.

I had just, more or less, told Anwen that my relationship with Watson was my own personal bruise.

"I suppose this means you're living with Theo," I went on, a bit desperately. "The two of you seemed friendly last night."

"I told you he has a boyfriend," she said, and pulled a dog-eared copy of *Hamlet* from her bag. "We all live in the same stairwell, but we aren't dating."

She was attempting, again, to rile me up. "Oh. I'd gotten the impression that something else was going on," I said.

"No, just a friend." Her voice was calm. She was, in fact, far more composed than I was, sitting on Leander's sofa (velvet, gray, vastly impractical) with her tattered paperback on her knees.

I felt silly, suddenly, for thinking even momentarily that this girl had wanted to be my friend. Anwen was playing her own game, and it wouldn't end with the two of us online shopping until four a.m. while drinking tea. (I missed Lena rather badly.)

Still, I had to reset this conversation somehow.

"Which monologue did you want to run?" I asked, standing. "I'll just put the kettle on. Jasmine? Earl Grey?" My voice was frosted over, but then that couldn't be helped.

"Do you have English breakfast? Twinings?" Anwen followed at my heels.

"We do," I said, and set out two Sherringford mugs. Leander really had to get rid of those.

Anwen wandered over to the window above the sink and looked down onto the street, like some improbably beautiful vulture. "I'm sorry if I was weird, just then," she said at length.

Had I been someone else, I would have perhaps dropped the teakettle. I hadn't been expecting such an admission from her. Something about this cool, unflappable girl was confounding me.

It was important that she keep talking, and the best

strategy for that was to let the silence hang until she felt she had to fill it.

"It's just—we haven't talked about that thing? In the theater? The . . . sheet body?"

When I saw her trying to meet my eyes, I reached into the cupboard for the creamer, the sugar caddy, two ramekins for our tea bags.

"I'm just . . . scared," she said, but she didn't sound scared in the least. Was she shamming? Was she playing me the way that I had played her? "Whatever that was, it's a threat, and I feel like I barely escaped last summer as it was. I quit the play right after the accidents began happening . . ."

"Mm," I said. What else could one take for tea? I took a lemon from the fridge, then returned it in favor of whole milk and half-and-half.

"Maybe you don't know why it's important? Or what happened at all, maybe? I know it got awkward last night, when Rupert brought it up . . . but we had such a good thing going, the three of us, until then, and everything got so messy and complicated, and Theo was spending every night at the police station and Rupert wasn't *talking* to me . . ."

Nodding, I poured the whole milk into the ceramic creamer and left the half-and-half in its disgusting little carton. That was Leander's; he called it his "nasty American habit," though he said nothing about the Oreos he had to buy from the international store for eight pounds a package and then kept under his bed. Most likely because he didn't want me to know they were there.

The best way to keep a disinterested face was to be interested in something else. I wondered what flavors Leander had squirreled away this week. Red velvet Oreos? Birthday cake? Candy cane? Perhaps that was just at Christmas.

"But I was scared," Anwen said, staring down into her empty mug (it was as though I wasn't there, exactly what I intended), "I was so scared, and after what happened to Matilda it all just went to shit, and what if it happens to me?"

I took a calculated risk. "Matilda?"

"It's *all her fault,*" Anwen said, and a moment later, began to cry.

The kettle went off then, a punctuation mark.

She startled back to herself. "Where's your toilet?" she asked, and I pointed down the hall in defeat.

Anwen returned from the bathroom with her blank expression back in place and a fresh coat of mascara. I made a mental note that she kept makeup in her bag. A girl interested in maintaining her mask.

That mask remained firmly on after that. "It's not that I hate Matilda," she said. "Hated? I don't know if she's even still alive. But she and I were never friends. She was really only into Theo. Anyway, I have trouble with that—making friends with girls. I'm not really sure why. Guys are just easier."

I raised an eyebrow. I despised this attitude, how it shoved all girls together into one category, how it carried the smug suggestion that male friendship was better.

"We should really start rehearsing—don't you have a lecture at two thirty?" Unfortunately, I did.

"Oh God," I said. "Do you mind if I watch the time on your phone? I don't know where mine is."

I took it from her and settled in at the kitchen island. "You're low battery," I said, pulling a cord from my pocket. "I'll charge it for you. Whenever you're ready—go ahead!"

Her Ophelia monologue was excellent. "'As if he had been loosed out of hell / To speak of horrors,'" she whispered, a hand up as though Hamlet's pale face were there before her. Ophelia was a vulnerable character, a girl driven to madness through her beloved's disregard, and I hadn't thought someone as self-possessed as Anwen could pry herself open that way. And yet, in my living room, her red curls crackling around her, I had the sense I had whenever I watched someone transform, onstage or elsewhere. That a quiet door had been opened somewhere, that a wind was coming through.

I performed mine for her—from after Ophelia had lost her mind, when she rants and sings in *Hamlet*'s fourth act—but I did my worst version, all rolling eyes and mock-rended clothes. I wanted to see what kind of notes Anwen would give me, if she would be honest.

She wasn't. She told me I was "great," cast another careful look around my flat, and exited, as it were, stage left.

I had approximately ten minutes to do the following things:

Ensure that the text messages between Anwen and Theo that I downloaded off her phone (when I'd taken it to charge; she really should have been more careful) had made it safely to my inbox.

Confirm the appointment I had just made for tomorrow morning.

Decide what the girlfriend version of myself would possibly wear to dinner with Watson that night.

A dinner. Somewhere nice.

What version of myself could I construct before then that could be even passably acceptable?

nine

I WAS EARLY FOR DINNER, SUPPOSING THAT WATSON would be late, as he so often was.

The restaurant he'd chosen wasn't a fancy place, though I will be the first to admit that my standards weren't exactly standard. I had spent my childhood attending stifled, terrifying dinners at any number of Michelin-starred restaurants across Europe. I had beheaded many tiny cauliflowers and broccolinis while my father stared me down across a white tablecloth. This was not that. Neither was it counter service. It was the sort of place where the waiters wore white shirts tucked into denim, and the menu featured no fewer than four tarted-up versions of macaroni and cheese. At least that was what I could tell from the website, which I'd scanned (rather nervously) in the back of the taxi.

I would arrive early. I would settle into our table. Watson would approach. I would then say, "Hello, Watson," and then I could ask him about his day.

This is how people behaved. For two hours, I could behave like a person.

Only Watson was not late. He was waiting for me on a bench in the vestibule, toeing the gray-washed hardwood floor.

"Holmes," he said, standing as I walked through the door. "I think our table's ready."

"Hello, Watson," I said. (That much I could manage.)

He had on his brown leather jacket and a white shirt, open at the collar. He looked very much like himself. Was that a good thing? Should I have imagined he looked different? I searched myself for the sort of response I was meant to have in this scenario, a first proper date with the boy that I cared for. Should he have a golden sheen around him? An inner glow? Should he be looking at me as though I were a treasure, or a princess? Biting his lip? Averting his eyes?

Should I be imagining us doing this—dining out at strangely posh comfort-food restaurants—for the rest of our lives?

I was spiraling. I took myself back to what was in front of me. Watson looked handsome, in the way he always did, which is to say clean but not manicured. The only difference was that he smelled a bit like cologne. Something, again, clean, like water if water had been supercharged into having a smell. Perhaps he'd made an effort. Was *that* exciting?

I *was* excited, I supposed, in the way in which I wanted to throw up from nerves.

I realized then that I had been standing in front of Watson for forty-five seconds without saying a single word.

"Miss?" The hostess hovered behind him. "Um. Your table's ready?"

"You look a little like you've short-circuited," he said, smiling, and took my hand gently as we followed her to the back corner of the restaurant.

Brick walls. A leather banquette. A votive candle on the table, and a sprig of lavender in a mason jar. The silverware was not silver but copper, polished to a shine. For a moment I was terrified that Watson might do something wretched like pull out my chair, but he gestured instead toward the booth side of the table. I slid in and immediately pulled up my feet. Sometimes it helped to make oneself more compact in combat situations.

Across from me, Watson fiddled with his watch, pulling it out from the cuff of his jacket and then sliding it back in. "How did it go?" he asked. "With Anwen?"

"Good," I said brightly. "Fine."

"Did you learn anything?"

"Not really." That was untrue, but I didn't want to be my clinical self just now. The rest of the world got that self. Tonight, I wanted for once to be the Charlotte beneath all the Holmes.

Whoever that was.

"Oh," he said. His disappointed eyes met mine for a second before dropping again.

If our date were a test, I was failing. I had no idea how to do it right but still knew I was doing it wrong. I had no real examples for this sort of thing. Books? I didn't read fiction. Television? The characters in *Friends* were hopelessly mean to the people they dated, and besides, I only watched that show to watch Joey, who was very attractive even while consuming entire pizzas. I thought back to the films that Leander and I had watched when I was convalescing these past months—screwball comedies from the 1940s, brightly lit mid-2000s films about "crashing" weddings to meet girls, the odd Transformers movie or two—and despaired. I should have curled my hair. I should be touching my face. I should be tastefully revealing bits of my past in anecdote form, until he found something with which he connected or which he found hopelessly charming.

Aha, I thought, and leaned forward. "Have I told you about the time that my aunt Araminta tried to teach me to handle the hives at her apiary?"

"No," Watson said. "It's a big one, right? Her apiary?"

"Hundreds of thousands of bees. She tends them herself. The honey, when she jars it, is a beautiful amber color. Some of it's flavored—she has a tarragon one that's quite sharp, and a lavender." I touched the little bloom in the jar. "She does the infusions out in her workshop. It's the original one, built about a century ago."

"Sherlock's, then." He was watching me, now. Watson always had a fascination with my family history. Was it terrible to exploit that?

The villa, as my ancestor had called it, wasn't far from the manor where I had grown up. His was a southern-facing set of buildings that overlooked the chalky cliffs that led down to the Channel. The cottage itself wasn't particularly grand; it had a garret stuffed with books, many dating back to the turn of the last century, and the kitchen was one of those prodigious old caverns with an Aga stove and a tabletop for rolling out biscuits. Araminta made wonderful biscuits, made still better by the honey that dripped down into the little crevices of dough, and as a child I had gone down the lane—when issued an invitation; I had always been required an invitation—to eat those and look out over the sea.

"Yes," I said, "though she's expanded a bit. It isn't a commercial production, her honey. She sells it in a few shops in town. A neighbor boy helps her in the summers, but I think she intended to have me come on as her partner. I hadn't known that until my parents decided to send me to America for school. She was very resistant. Didn't like the idea of my being so far away."

"I didn't know you were close."

"Physically, she was right down the road, in that cottage on the hill. Emotionally . . . I don't know how close she was to anyone, really. I certainly didn't know how to speak to her. She was quite a bit older than my father. Had a job as a codebreaker in the 1970s, until something awful happened—"

"Walter Moriarty," Watson said, surprising me. "Leander told me. She found out Moriarty was negotiating the illegal sale of a nuclear warhead. He cottoned on that she has turned him in, killed all three of her cats."

I thought of Mouse, and shuddered. "I'd heard something like that. She acted . . . not as a grandmother, exactly, but something like it. She took us on errands to London and to short weekend trips to Prague and Munich and Rome. We'd be marched through a few museums, photographed against a river or two, taken to a nice restaurant. And then at night, Milo would inevitably end up watching me in the room while she went to the theater."

Over his shoulder, I noticed the waiter hovering, but Watson was watching me again now, his eyes warming back up, and I realized that the look in them was a sort of tempered delight. "Araminta didn't take you with her?" he was asking.

I took a steadying breath and addressed the waiter. "A beer for him—something floral, I imagine you have it—and a French 75 for me." He jotted it down and said he'd return for our dinner orders, though we hadn't yet looked at the menu.

Watson lifted an eyebrow. "Something floral," he said.

"Yes."

"Floral."

"You don't drink often," I told him, "and you make a bit of a face whenever you have beer, but you insist on ordering it, now that we're back in the UK—I think it pleases you to have it. The pint glass to cup your hands around. The color of it and how you look when you're drinking it. You sip it slowly, so you can make it last the whole night, and that's cheaper for you on the whole, which should be moot anyway because my uncle will be paying for this meal, and any meal, and anything you need, really, because he loves you like a son. But. The beer. I'm not going to presume to change your order entirely, but I may as well send for something a bit easier for you to drink."

"You may as well." He used finger quotes around each word.

"Watson, I'm only helping you achieve your ultimate goal of imagining yourself drinking a beer while you're drinking it." I folded my hands on the table.

Without dropping my eyes, he reached across the table and took one of them in his, running his thumb against my knuckles. "Floral beer," he said softly. "It seems like a good solution."

"It is," I said, my voice higher than I intended. "I thought it through before I came."

"And the French 75?"

"I saw it in a film, and I liked the flute it came in, and—"

Gently, he turned my hand over, running his thumb along my palm. The skin was more delicate there, and I could feel his callouses from riding his bicycle this spring, from gripping the handlebars too tight. I could feel the soft edge of his nail.

We had been in bed together. I had pressed myself against him in the dark and said his name. And now we were out in the open, and he was touching me in a way that was almost innocent, and still I was flushed and freezing and babbling like a fool.

"—and I thought I might look nice drinking it, that you

might like the look of my holding a flute more than a wineglass, especially considering the ones for red wine, they're so large and silly, like a soup tureen on a stilt. And my ordering a strong cocktail would be ill-advised. You know I really shouldn't let myself have things like that, not with my past, my habits, but the doctor said if I'd like, I could have a single drink, and—"

"And so you ordered this one." He should have been laughing at me, but he wasn't. "It checks out."

"My deductions check out? Fancy that."

"You're very smug."

"You," I said, "are terrible at compliments."

He took a breath, running a finger down the center of my palm. "Ask me again," he said, voice low, "when we're alone."

"Ready to order?" the waiter asked, setting down our drinks. I startled. I'd forgotten we were in a restaurant, in public; I'd forgotten the fact of other people. I'd forgotten myself.

My whole self, except for the palm of my right hand, his finger tracing its lines.

There was something to being Charlotte, only Charlotte, for the night.

"Not yet," Watson told the waiter, still watching my face, and the man nodded and walked away. "Is this what you wanted?"

"What I—" I shook my head a little, but I couldn't stop smiling. "I don't know what I want. I spent the last year running through possibilities in my head, what a night out would look like, you and I as ourselves—"

With quick fingers, he'd undone the cuff of my sleeve. Slowly—achingly slowly—he ran his thumb over the line of my wrist, as though he were smoothing out a length of cloth.

"You sound like me," he said quietly. "Telling yourself stories."

"There isn't much else to do when you're on the run. Didn't you do it? When we were apart?"

"I did," he said. "I'm trying something else now. None of that worked for us before. What if I don't want some grand story?" His eyes were very dark. "What if, right now, I just want to touch your wrist?"

My voice came out faint. "Yes," I said, then: "asymptote."

"Asymptote?"

"Is this real?"

"It's always real," he said. "Holmes . . . do you still want dinner?"

His eyes were kind. His mouth had more complex ideas.

These were not the kind of games we'd played before.

"No." I stood too quickly, and I saw the panic rise in his eyes, as though he thought I'd bolt out the front door and away for good. There had always been a chance of that in the past. There would be, always, despite the time passed and the help I'd received. Watson had always let me take the lead in these things before, had always waited until I'd approached him.

I wasn't used to not being the one running the show.

These thoughts, I should mention, were ones I had later, when I was able to analyze this scene at my leisure. At that moment I wasn't thinking anything at all except how quickly I could get him out of that restaurant and into my bed.

He drained half his beer. I left my French 75 on the table. We dropped twenty quid for the waiter, more than we needed to, and he took me by the elbow and pulled me out onto the street, and we were only blocks away from my uncle's flat but I couldn't stop touching him. As we waited to cross he fitted his hands around my waist and dipped his head and kissed me. My hands went up and underneath his jacket, and I was shaking. I didn't know why I was shaking. I wasn't short, and he wasn't tall, and I'd never done this before, kiss someone like this, dash across traffic hand in hand with a boy, desperate to get someplace quiet and dark and alone. At least not when we weren't running for our lives.

Though if this wasn't dangerous, what was?

It was still light out, eight o'clock in the evening, and the streets were nearly empty. The air was close and heavy, the clouds low in the sky, and as we rounded the corner to my street it started to rain.

I stopped before my front door, looking up to our windows. "There are lights on," I said, pushing my damp hair from my eyes. "I thought Leander might be going out, but—"

Watson stepped up behind me. "We can go to mine," he said, his breath hot against my ear.

Anwen, Rupert, Theo. The case. I couldn't let anyone see me this vulnerable. I had to stay here—this night, this self, this boy. Even now he had moved his lips down to my neck, his arm keeping me fitted against him. As I fumbled my keys from my bag, I felt too hot, too tight in my body, and when I finally had the door open we spilled into the stairwell like a thunderstorm.

"Quiet," I said, and he whispered hoarsely, "There's no way we weren't heard," and still it didn't matter, how could it—I pushed him up against the wallpaper and he was laughing, bright-eyed, as I pushed his jacket down his shoulders and began undoing the buttons of his shirt. He hissed at my fingers, cold against his chest.

"Hi," he said, stilling my hands against him.

"Hi."

"Hello."

"Hi," I said again. I was a bit unsure why we were greeting each other.

"God." He ducked down to kiss me, then pressed his lips against one temple, the other, the top of my head. "I—"

"What?"

"Nothing." He laughed again, in disbelief. "We can't go in, not like this. We can't go back outside, it's pouring. And I don't want to leave you. Not yet."

I took a steadying breath. "Let's sit and wait a moment. We can . . . straighten ourselves out, and then go in and to my room and he won't suspect anything." Of course, we both knew I was lying. My uncle, the private detective, would suspect everything, but he would at least wait until morning to make fun of me.

We settled ourselves on the top carpeted stair. Watson buttoned his shirt, blushing a little, murmuring something I couldn't quite hear. I asked him to repeat himself.

"Maybe you should finish telling me your story," he said. "About your elderly aunt. And the things you did as a child."

"Do you want me to also pour a bucket of cold water over your lap?"

He grinned. "If you have one handy."

"I don't remember," I said, running a hand over my hair to smooth it. "Oh. The theater."

"The theater."

"How she used to leave me and Milo, and go alone." I took a steadying breath; I was still so distracted. "I wondered about it for years, you know. Once, late at night, she came back to our hotel room when my brother was already asleep. And she was weeping."

Watson studied me. "Do you know why?"

"I asked her what was wrong," I said, remembering that night. The heavy curtains. The polished sconces on either side of the out-of-date television. The twin beds the hotel had given us, and my aunt, who had insisted on sleeping on a rickety cot by the radiator. "She said she had been someone else for a time, and now she wasn't. I think she might have been a bit drunk."

Watson sighed, adjusting his collar. "I imagine that's metaphorical," he said.

"I put it out of mind, until that day I was telling you about. She'd asked me to see her before I left for Sherringford. More specifically, she asked me to see her 'hives.' I thought she meant that we would look at them and talk—someone might ask you down to see a café, for instance, but they mean to have a conversation. This wasn't like that. She wanted me to work."

"She put you in a suit," Watson said. I could tell he liked the idea: the heavy white garment, the netted headdress, the gloves that grew your hands into a giant's.

"She did. She led me out into the apiary. I was to help her transfer a hive. We had it stacked up, ready to be moved on a dolly . . ." I studied my boots, the toes pushing into the carpet two steps below me. "I'm usually very precise. I imagine I would be an obvious choice to help with a delicate operation.

"But it was odd. She didn't offer help, just gave instruction. *Load the hives. Move them slowly.* She watched me, and all was going well until the wheels of the dolly I was pulling hit a rock. Two of the hives fell. Burst open. The bees began rioting. I panicked and pulled off my headgear and I was stung, and I hadn't ever been stung before, and though I'm not the sort of allergic that needs to go to hospital, I'm allergic enough that I swelled.

"I wasn't weeping. I was fascinated, in the middle of all that . . . destruction. And my aunt Araminta stood and watched me. After a minute or two, she brought me inside, gave me some tea. Pulled out the stingers with tweezers, washed my face with soap and water. Wished me luck at school, and off I went. I kept feeling as though I'd failed a test.

"We haven't spoken much since then. Birthdays. Christmastime." I dropped my head against his shoulder, and his arm went around me, an instinct. "Is that enough cold water for you?"

He squeezed my arm. "Why tell that story?"

"Leander says she's planning a visit," I said, "to meet with some shops here to sell her honey. Maybe she's wanting to expand her business? I'm not sure. But she'll be in the flat for a few days, sometime soon."

"I'd like to meet her."

"You're into any Holmes you meet," I said. "You want to add us to your anthropological study."

"That's not nice."

"It's true. It doesn't need to be nice." My voice came out stiff.

He tipped his head to the side, considering. It was more than I deserved. "You don't want me to meet her."

We sat together in a silence that wasn't particularly companionable. Inside, I could hear my uncle beginning to stir—he was pulling pots and pans from the cupboard. The deep, hollow bell of the Dutch oven on the countertop. The drawn-in breath of the kettle as it settled on the stove.

My upbringing had taught me to listen and to assign meaning to what I heard. Both the formal training, and the informal—those moments when I woke in the morning, determining how safe it was for me to go downstairs.

It was the only way I knew how to be in the world.

"She's a version of myself," I said. "She hides in plain sight. She might be interesting to you, for that reason."

"Every version of you is interesting to me," he said.

"I know," I said. *I had been someone else,* I remembered her saying, *and now I'm not.*

He, who more than anyone saw every part of me, could feel the shift and stutter of my mood. It had turned, as it always did; I was like the water that way.

"Do you want to go in now?" he asked.

I listened. There was another voice in with my uncle—the handsome man from the party. I remembered his clear tenor. *She wants me to step in,* the voice was saying, and in the background, the water in the kettle began to turn over. A hiss, a splutter.

You shouldn't do anything you're not prepared for, my uncle's boyfriend told him, and I could hear the shuffle of his feet in slippers, the sharp sound of the spoon against the pan.

"I can leave," Watson was saying. "We can pick this up tomorrow. I know we haven't talked at all about the case."

"The case." I'd forgotten. The sheet monster with Matilda's face pinned to it, the gang of feuding friends around the supper table, Anwen in her floral dress. *It's all her fault.*

I reached for his hands and settled them on my hips. "Come in with me," I said. "Stay over."

Inside the flat, a pot clattered loudly against the stove, and for once, neither of us startled.

"What are you thinking?" he asked. "I can see those gears moving. What do you want?"

I wanted to know who I was, now, in what felt like the aftermath of my life. I had survived my childhood. I was an adult, standing with the boy I loved, doing meaningful work that I had trained for.

I reached up to smooth Watson's brow. The neatness of my life now was shocking to me, a girl with such ragged edges. I wasn't sure if I could fit inside its borders.

But I wanted him. I always did. "I want to tell you more stories about my aging aunt," I told him, instead, and when he realized I was teasing, he wound his fingers into my hair and kissed me, a promise in a language I couldn't yet speak.

ten

I WOKE IN THE MORNING TO THE SOFT, RHYTHMIC KNEADing of my cat's paws on my stomach. When I opened my eyes, Mouse peered at me, shook herself all over, and then leapt from the bed.

Watson didn't stir at such slight movement. It took more than that to wake him—I knew that from lingering in doorways, seeing him passed out on his back on his father's couch, his eyes bruised underneath the arm flung over them. I often felt like some kind of wretched war bride, watching him recover from whatever trouble we'd gotten ourselves into. Moments like that, brief and far between, before I pulled him off to the next adventure.

But we had nowhere to go this morning, not yet, and still

I couldn't keep myself from stirring. I slid out from under the coverlet and picked up my dressing gown from the floor. My black mood had evaporated, as it often did, with the dawn. I had at least a few hours until it returned.

I had a cigarette by the window, a cup of tea in the kitchen. On the counter was a note from my uncle, written in his leisurely cursive: *In London with Stephen through the weekend; he has tickets for* Hamilton*! You and your young man have fun. Call if you need anything xxxx.*

I read the note over again. The flat was ours, then. I'd always been allowed a measure of freedom (see: boarding school, Berlin, the boy asleep in my bedroom), but Leander had been so present these past months—making meals, arranging doctors' appointments—that I found myself reflexively looking over my shoulder, expecting to see him in the sitting room with a book braced against one knee, calling out, *Charlotte, do you want toast soldiers with your eggs?*

My stomach rumbled. I did, in fact, want toast soldiers with my eggs.

After spending some time with Anwen's text messages, I stubbed out my cigarette in a coffee mug and began pulling things from the cupboards. There was a loaf of good sourdough bread on the counter, a pot of Araminta's honey, a pair of avocados, some jam. There was a carton of brown eggs in the fridge, vegetables in the crisper. Onions in a wire basket, and potatoes. Butter and margarine.

Oil was for cooking. I knew that abstractly. I opened up the cupboard above the stove and pulled down bottles one by one. Olive oil, sunflower, sesame, coconut. I lined them all up on the counter, then redid my alignment alphabetically, then from largest bottle to smallest. I picked up the avocado and poked at it, the way I'd seen people do in markets. I lifted each egg to the light, then shook them, then placed them delicately back in the carton.

It wasn't that I couldn't prepare food. I had done so, often, for myself. Sandwiches, wraps, a salad. Things that required assembly more than art. I had grown up with a housekeeper, which was the sort of privilege that made one into an ornament, a useless decoration of a girl; I had never in my life made something for someone else that wasn't a cup of tea. True, I could download a food app on my phone or leaf through one of the cookbooks Leander kept on the counter (though I didn't want to consider why he owned a copy of *38 Meals for Your Picky Toddler*), but I was intelligent. I was capable. I could figure this out for myself.

An hour later, I nudged open the bedroom door, carrying a tray.

Watson sat up on his elbows. "What do you have there?" he asked, his voice coated in sleep.

"I made you breakfast."

"How domestic of you." He picked up his glasses from the bedside table and put them on. "That's—that's a rather large plate you've got there. Plates?"

"This is tray one of four," I said, placing it at the end of the bed.

He blinked at me. Perhaps he was still tired.

"Don't begin eating until you see all your options," I told him, and went off to fetch the next platter.

By the time I'd arranged it all on my coverlet to my satisfaction, Watson had roused himself appropriately. He'd put on one of my oversized sleep shirts—CHEMISTRY IS FOR LOVERS—and poured himself a cup of coffee. That surprised me; he usually took tea.

"I need real caffeine to deal with this." He lofted a piece of toast. "Can you explain this?"

"Salt, fat, acid, heat."

For a long moment, Watson inspected it. "Holmes," he said. "This sort of looks like cat food. So you should maybe explain."

"I read it this spring, in a magazine, in that facility in London." I sat down in my armchair, resisting the urge to light another cigarette. "I was supposed to reconfigure my relationship with food, you know, and so my therapist as an experiment gave me a stack of cookery magazines and told me to pick out what sounded 'good.' None of it did. All these garish close-ups of food arranged in pans, as though they were strange decomposing art. But one of the chefs they interviewed, some Danish man, said that the only thing you needed to know to cook was that every dish had to balance 'salt, fat, acid, and heat.'"

"And you stopped reading there."

"The brain can only hold so much information," I reminded him. "If that was all I needed to know on the subject, I could move on to studying something interesting, like blood spatter."

"And so what am I holding?" Watson asked, gesturing at me with the toast.

"That," I said, "is tinned herring, cottage cheese, lemon juice, and a green substance from a jar with a rubbed-off label that smelled like tomatillos and motor oil."

"I see," Watson said, his expression perfectly blank. "And this one?"

"That is bacon, egg, avocado, sriracha"—he was already putting it into his mouth—"and a drizzle of Diet Coke."

Watson only paused his chewing for a moment. "It's not bad," he said, mouth full, and went in for another slice.

"I added lemon. I know you like a lemon with your soda." I sat back. "The rest of those are in similar permutations; the bread was an easy vehicle for their delivery."

"Their *delivery*."

I ignored him; I was enjoying spinning out my train of thought. "I wake before you. I should make breakfast. Therefore, I thought we could determine what you like for breakfast this way, all at once, rather than my undertaking a series of trial and error over the next few weeks."

He smiled at me, all rumpled and covered in crumbs. "So you're planning for the long term, then?"

"I am," I said hesitantly.

"Well then. This one," he said, holding another toast happily aloft, "looks like anchovy, carrot, and fig. And . . . pickled pig's feet. Bombs away."

Watson ate on the bed; I ate quickly in the kitchen. He swapped his glasses for contacts, and we both put on our boots, and the two of us were out the door by ten. Oxford, outside, was in all its May glory; Watson was waxing rhapsodic as we walked up the block, winding our way away from the college.

"Does it just *smell* better here?"

A bus had just braked hard in front of us, coughing out a cloud of exhaust.

"Better than where, exactly?"

"Than Sherringford," Watson said, laughing, "or New York. For sure better than New York. Like, there aren't bags of garbage along the streets baking in the sun, here."

"How would you describe it, then?"

"Home. Or *a* home," he amended. "And you?"

To me, Oxford was a patchwork—the corner of our road smelled like the chip shop (grease and fish and the occasional hot-sugar smell of a Mars Bar in the deep fryer), and the next road down was fresh soil from someone turning over their front garden for the summer, and St. Genesius like grass and the river and dust, and the High Street, where we were headed, like commerce.

"Commerce?" Watson grinned at me. "That's pretty metaphorical, for you."

"It's a marker. Everything has one. I need to be able to differentiate where I'm going in the dark, or in case I'm blindfolded."

"Like that happens."

I gave him a look. "You should know better than to say that, pumpkin."

"You're a jerk," he said, reaching out to tousle my hair, and I ducked. "No, for real. Show me how you to do it."

"It's simple." I took his hand and shut my eyes and let him pull me along for half a block. "Stationery shop, bookstore, used bookstore, kebab shop. New paper and ink; new paper; old paper; lunch."

"Lunch?"

"I like kebabs."

He tangled his fingers with mine. "Nothing lost on you, then."

"Not a thing," I said, and he tugged me up against him for a moment, and because he was Watson, because the sky was milk-white and open and the morning smelled clear and because he trusted me (somehow, he trusted me), he didn't ask a single question about where I was leading him.

"So Leander gave us the place to ourselves," he said. "Do you want me to stay with you, then? Keep you company? Keep the wolves from the door?"

I raised an eyebrow.

"I did once knock out Lucien Moriarty in a restaurant bathroom," he reminded me.

"Point," I said. "I'd of course like you there." I glanced down at our clasped hands. "Here. Alongside me. But it might also be useful for us to spend some nights digging up dirt on Theo and Anwen and Rupert, and your staying in your rooms makes it easier."

"Are those your suspects?"

"I don't have suspects. They're our entrée into this community. Did I tell you about the text messages I lifted off of Anwen's phone?"

Watson slowed to a stop.

We were in front of a café. "Oh. Are you still hungry?" It seemed improbable, given the acres of toast he had consumed, but many things about Watson were improbable.

"I need . . . something," he said, after a moment. "And you . . . you need to sit there and not touch anything."

Five minutes later, I had settled in to watch Watson drain a cup of tea. "You lifted her texts?" he asked, finally, creasing the cup with an anxious hand.

"She made the mistake of letting me watch the time on her phone while she practiced her monologue." I shrugged. "I still have one of Milo's 'little mice' from our jaunt in Berlin; I plugged it in, stuck it under a magazine, and thirty seconds later I had her text message history."

"And she has no idea."

Anwen was fairly perceptive, but I didn't think she'd clocked me as the particular threat I was. "No. And to be clear, I didn't download all her information." I would have, had I had more time, though Watson didn't need to know that. It was always odd to me what upset him (small violations of privacy; blunt truths) and what made him proud (breaking someone's nose in a restaurant bathroom). Though as I've grown, I've found that to often be the case—most are more comfortable with explosions and bodily harm than the expression of ideas using language they don't like. "The results were scattershot. I only have *some* of her messages. Nothing between her and Rupert. Quite a few between her and her mates back in Wales, setting up study dates. But—and here's the kicker, as they say—I have nearly everything between her and Theo for the last nine months."

"Back to September, then." Watson leaned in, despite his earlier compunctions. "So?"

"Theo and Anwen were texting semi-regularly through the fall. Nothing about the attacks—"

"The Orchid Attacks?" The capital letters were implicit.

"Watson," I said. "We are not naming this case."

"The Adventure of the Bloody Orchids." He waved a hand to indicate a marquee. "The Curious Case of the Untaped Back Stairs—"

"That sounds like a euphemism—"

"The Adventure of A Midsummer's Night . . . mare?"

"—in fact," I continued, "their messages seemed to deliberately avoid the subject. How are classes; how are 'things'; a picture of a Cornetto with the caption 'thinking of you'—an inside joke, I imagine. Then, apropos of seemingly nothing, October 12, Anwen asks Theo how he's holding up after, and I quote, 'Matilda broke up with you.' Had they been in regular phone communication, she wouldn't have had to add the caveat. No matter the context, it feels a bit like salting a wound. The girl had disappeared. Who cared if she had dumped him?

"Theo responded tersely. 'Fine.' Like that, the one word. And really after that there wasn't much to their messages.

Whatever Anwen had wanted from him, she didn't get it. Then, silence, until the end of December, over the winter holiday. It makes sense. They're away from class and friends and daily distractions, and they think to catch up with those they haven't seen. December 23. Anwen wrote Theo to ask what he wanted for Christmas; Theo sent an image of a menorah, ostensibly to remind her that he was Jewish; Anwen apologized, said that 'my house is making me crazy and forgetting things now too lol.' Chitchat about gifts, food, Theo's brother watching too much hockey. Then, on Boxing Day, the tenor of the conversation changed."

When I paused, Watson knit his brow. "And?"

I would be lying if I said I didn't love these moments—him looking at me like I had in my hands a curtain pull, that I could reveal the underbelly of the world. "Theo said, and I quote: 'You need to call me as soon as you get this.' A period at the end of the sentence, which hadn't been his style before. Anwen responded instantly: 'can't get away what's going on.' then three question marks. An hour later Theo responded, 'Anwen. Call me now.'"

"And?" Watson said. "And?"

"I don't have the call logs," I reminded him. "It's also possible they used a video chat app, as Theo lives in America. Whatever it was—whatever was said—it effectively ended communication between the two of them."

He sat back, thinking. The breeze ruffled his hair.

"You need a cut," I said, sitting on my hands to keep from reaching out to push a curl off his forehead. And then I remembered that I could, and that he wouldn't mind—that he might in fact like me to—and so, slowly, I did.

"Hi," he said softly.

"Hi," I responded. I still wasn't sure of the point of this ritual, but I appreciated it for its simplicity.

"That was it for them?" he asked. "Nothing after that?"

"Not until the first week of May," I said, "when Anwen asked, 'are you coming back?' Theo responded 'yes.' With the uncharacteristic punctuation once again. And though I can't be sure, I think that was it until they sat down for orientation."

"Things to dig up."

"Indeed." I stood, and he followed. Walking a city that I was still learning was how I preferred to think—there was the surface data (the city map), which provided enough stimulation for me to make more subconscious connections below it. (I also thought quite well while brushing out and organizing my wigs.)

"We're not headed to the theater," Watson said, though he didn't sound bothered. "Weren't auditions today?"

"At two this afternoon. Callbacks are directly after, at five. The cast list will be posted immediately after dinner, and then the new director will bring in Dr. Larkin at seven tonight to lecture on *Hamlet* and the history of the Dramatics Soc."

"That's a weird choice," he said, "seeing as they fired her."

We'd reached the part of the High Street with two drugstores, a Sainsbury's, and several shops in a row that sold readily consumable fashion for girls. Here the crowd grew thicker, though it was before noon on a Thursday, and I had to pause as I cataloged the information coming at me as I walked. Two German girls who worked in a pub in this neighborhood—one still wore her work shirt, and the other her no-slip shoes, and even without those markers they were still talking about the git who stiffed one on her tab. An administrator with a briefcase full of files and a pair of expensive patterned socks that he showed off with pants tailored a quarter inch too high. Dogs on too-long leads. A small child buckled into her pram, old enough to walk but worn out from the morning's jaunt. Her mother had a bit of cereal milk on her jumper.

I filed it away, to dump out later if I needed, and pulled Watson through the throng. We had a schedule to keep. "It is a bit brutal, but Dr. Larkin did technically step down before they could sack her. Still, she's teaching the seminar on Shakespearean tragedy this summer for the precollege. It would be strange for them *not* to bring her in. Either way it works for us; I'm looking forward to seeing how the students react to her being there. Are you coming to auditions? Do you have class?"

"Not Tuesdays and Thursdays," he said, "so yeah, I'll be there. Maybe I can audition to carry a spear."

I frowned. "I don't think there are spears in *Hamlet*."

"It's an expression." I had tugged him over to the curb, and he looked down at me plaintively. "Are we going to lunch?"

We were at a bus stop, which he would know if he looked up. Bus stops did not sell lunch. "How are you possibly hungry again?"

"Holmes," he said, "people generally eat more than once a day."

"Watson. You ate an *hour* ago."

"Don't tell me you're going to march me home to eat more toasts."

"There are plenty of anchovy ones left."

"They were so good," he said solemnly, "that I wanted to make them last."

I checked the timetable again. Our bus was running two minutes late, and I found myself slightly put out. I had wanted to spirit him right onto it and on our way. "You're a terrible liar," I told him.

"We've established that. Where are we headed?"

"You want to know now?"

"I always want to know," he said, putting his hands into his pockets, "but I'd rather follow you to find out."

"Follow me, then," I told him, and there it was, the bright red bus trundling up the road as though it had been listening, as though it wasn't late at all.

eleven

WATSON INSISTED ON SITTING ON THE SECOND STORY OF the bus, I imagine for the view. None of the seats were clean—they never were—and I amused myself by imagining what exactly had been responsible for the stickiness of the vinyl we sat on. I had come up with a number of explanations and had wound around to suggesting "cat vomit" before Watson turned green. He took a stray newspaper—the arts section—off the seat beside him and sat on it, as though that would mitigate any cat-related damage.

The city ambled by us, as slow as if we were behind a horse in a hansom cab, and when we were still a stop away I hammered down the steps and jumped off, Watson at my heels, the newspaper section (sticky) in my bag.

"The police station," Watson said, sounding a bit disappointed.

"Did you want me to bring you to the circus?" I asked, holding the door. He rolled his eyes and walked in.

There was a policeman, a constable by the insignia on his arm, stealing a pen from the cup at the front desk. He was in his fluorescent high-vis vest and still looked fairly alert. His shift in traffic must've just been beginning.

"I have an appointment with DI Sadiq," I said. Watson cleared his throat. "We do, rather."

He scanned the list at the desk. "You'll want the criminal investigation department, then. Let me see . . . ah, here we go." The PC squinted at me, then grinned toothily. "Charlotte Holmes, huh? Got any ears for me, Charlie?"

"No. And you can call me *Ms.* Holmes," I said, crossing my arms.

I could always tell when someone had read that *Daily Mail* story on us that had come out the year before, after Lucien Moriarty was put away. The *Mail* provided a list of bullet points called "Key Facts" before the article, and one of them had read "Charlotte Honoria Holmes and James Watson Jr: a modern-day Bonnie and Clyde, with ANGER ISSUES? Their Sherringford classmate tells all!" Yes, we had taken down a criminal mastermind; yes, I had lost people I loved as we had done so; yes, I did in fact have that wretched middle name, but despite what Cassidy from Watson's French class told the

Mail, I had never once bitten off someone's ear because they wouldn't give me a cigarette.

If the need had been urgent enough, I would have simply *taken* one.

"Miss Holmes," the PC said, with exaggerated courtesy, opening the door to the hallway behind him. We followed him down to the CID. The desks were clustered together in fours, and most were empty, the computer monitors off, files safely tucked away. "DI Sadiq is in with a suspect, but she'll see you shortly."

"You shouldn't read the *Mail,*" I told him. "It rots your brain."

"Holmes," Watson said. "Thank you, sir."

"You're a mouthy little girl, aren't you," the PC said, and I perhaps would have said more, but Watson clamped his hand around my arm as the man left.

He sighed, plunking himself down. "Can you please not get us locked up? Especially in a place where it's so very *convenient* for them to lock us up?"

"Sorry," I said. "I remembered the taste of cartilage, and went temporarily mad."

"Are you scaring off my constables?" asked a voice behind me.

"Your constables are too easily scared," I said, and DI Sadiq laughed.

She wore the kind of viciously tailored suit that told me she'd been taken less than seriously before in her life and was done with that, thanks very much. It was several seasons old, a take on the 2015 Balmain blazer and slacks. (It behooved any good detective to follow fashion; a more readily classifiable means of self-presentation didn't exist, except perhaps one's grooming.) Her hair was in a perfect chignon; she had a pencil stuck through it for convenience's sake, or because it softened her look an infinitesimal amount. She was early forties, give or take, had two piercings in her right ear, smile lines on the left side of her face, and she was reaching out to shake my hand.

I liked her immensely.

"Your sergeant asked me about the ears," I told her. "This is Watson."

"Jamie," he said, standing. They shook. "I didn't realize that anyone remembered that story."

"The story about the teen sleuths who took down Lucien Moriarty?" DI Sadiq settled down behind her desk. "Everyone here remembers it. Especially that you're a Holmes. You know, of course, that the Metropolitan Police's crime database is named after your forebear?"

Watson didn't, I could tell by his face. I fixed a smile on mine. "Home Office Large Major Enquiry System."

"HOLMES," Watson said, delighted.

DI Sadiq shrugged. "Proof is in the pudding. Anyway, we all followed the Moriarty case. It's a good thing you're here over lunch, or you might be signing autographs. Lucien was a big fish, you know. DI Green was happy to get her hands on that one. *DCI* Green, I should say."

Detective Inspector Lea Green had, understandably, been promoted after Lucien Moriarty had been extradited home for his crimes. For now he'd been remanded, so he was languishing in prison until his trial at Old Bailey at the end of the summer.

I counted this exchange as the two minutes a day I allowed myself to think about Lucien Moriarty. I took a breath in, a breath out, and then I refocused my eyes on DI Sadiq.

She hadn't missed my reaction. I watched her note it, then move on. "Lea and I took our detective exam around the same time. Stayed in touch, after; it isn't easy being a woman on the force. She called a few months back to tell me she was passing along an informant, to give you whatever information you wanted, if you wanted it. I pulled the file you requested, but I'd like to hear why from you first."

At that, Watson clicked his pen. He'd produced a notebook from somewhere and had it open on his knee.

"Within reason," DI Sadiq said, eyeing Watson.

"I'm studying at St. Genesius this summer. As is Watson, here. There were a series of incidents at the Dramatics Society performance last summer—I'm not sure if you're aware. Purposeful accidents. That sort of thing. Culminating in a girl named Matilda Wilkes disappearing."

"I'm aware," Sadiq said, and for a minute or so she didn't say anything more. "Matilda—that was a high-profile case."

"Missing white girl," Watson said. "The media loves that."

She gave him a sharp look. "Yes. The media does. But aside

from the theoreticals, she's a person. Not an idea. And she's still missing." Slowly, her shoulders relaxed. "I was assigned to her case. Not as the lead detective—I was assisting. Oftentimes, you think you have a kidnapped girl when what you have instead is a runaway, so I was looking into her family. It wasn't any good, you know. We don't know where she is. Is that your interest, Charlotte? Tracking down Matilda?"

I shook my head. "Not primarily."

Sadiq nodded impassively, and there was something to her manner that suggested that I had failed her, so I hurried on. "The adviser for last year, Dr. Larkin, asked for our help now that all of last year's players are back for the summer. I'm hoping to prevent further incidents from happening this summer. Think of it as a way of conserving police resources."

"I see."

She and I stared at each other.

"You're just consulting for us, then." DI Sadiq had a glimmer in her eye.

"Something like that."

She unlocked her drawer and pulled out a file, then slid it across her desk. "Twenty minutes," she said, not unkindly. "I need to get back to my investigation. He can take notes, but don't photograph anything. And if you pick the locks on anyone's desks while I'm gone . . ." She glanced meaningfully up at the camera in the corner of the room. I had clocked it when I'd walked in.

"That goddamn *Daily Mail* article," I said. "Is it really my fault if people insist on buying the most basic locks—"

"Yes," DI Sadiq said, and left.

She'd disappeared on a Thursday. It was more or less as we'd been told. On the night before *Earnest*'s opening, after their final dress rehearsal, she had gone out with a group of friends—Anwen, Theo, Rupert, and a boy named Sebastian Wallis—for a drink at a pub called The Bell and Book. They'd stayed out later than they intended, and it was one in the morning by the time Matilda made her way home. She would normally have walked with the other students back to their shared housing, but her parents were in town to see her performance the next night, and so she was staying with them at their hotel just outside the city center. She hadn't taken a cab, despite the hour. She'd wanted to "walk off her two pints," and the weather was still warm late that night.

It was, ultimately, a mistake.

There hadn't been a CCTV camera on that final street she had turned down, Waterbury Lane. A brief bit of road, connecting two larger thoroughfares.

The next day, officers had canvassed the area, knocking on doors and asking if any residents had heard a commotion, a scuffle, anyone scream. Two different women, both with bedroom windows facing the street, had told police that they'd heard a heated argument. It had been brief and not particularly loud. They'd seen no reason to call the police. When played a sample of Matilda's voice (from a video she'd posted to social media, her running a David Mamet monologue), neither could positively identify Matilda's voice as one that they'd heard.

As for the street itself: there had been no blood. No sign

of a struggle. All they had found was one of Matilda's earrings, a pair of diamond solitaires her parents had given her on her sixteenth birthday. It hadn't been torn from her ear (at that note in the file, Watson had shuddered); it looked more like it had fallen naturally.

Her father, George Wilkes, had reported his daughter missing at dawn. By the morning, he was at the police station, hounding detectives for information. He was followed by Theo Harding, followed finally by Matilda's mother, at nearly noon. The latter had taken longer because she'd driven straight back to Kensington—their wealthy London suburb—and returned with a bag of Matilda's things "that might be important in the investigation." This had struck the officer as extremely odd; the bag was full of class notes and diary entries that suggested nothing more than your bog-standard teenage girl. When questioned, George said that his wife was "a very nervous woman, not quite right, but desperate to do what she can to help" and soon after provided a letter from his wife's psychologist and a pair of prescription slips substantiating his claim. CCTV footage of the street outside their hotel showed that she had left when she'd said and not before. The detective chalked up her aberrant behavior to nerves and cautioned her against driving in such a state again.

("She didn't go back only for Matilda's things," Watson asked, reading over my shoulder. "There had to have been something else. What was she picking up?"

"Or," I said, "what was she taking home to hide?")

CCTV wasn't any help in identifying who else could have

been on Waterbury Lane that night. A raucous group had left a venue a few blocks over after an "'80s vs. '90s" club night, and many of them had taken the same path as Matilda as they left only fifteen minutes later. When tracked down and questioned, none reported any sight of her.

Oxford had a higher crime rate than many other British cities, but those offenses ran more toward bicycle theft than kidnapping, and in the weeks after Matilda's disappearance students stopped going out after dark. Especially young women. The newspapers had a field day, interviewing Matilda's friends back home, her distant family (her parents refused to answer questions), splashing the same haunting photo of her across their front page. Matilda, her lips pressed together, her hand raised as if swearing an oath, her face a mask of fury: it was a stage shot, her in character, but it made her look dangerous, electric.

It made her look alive.

As time passed, the consensus changed. No ransom was asked for, no new information came to light, and ultimately, despite DI Sadiq's best efforts, the case had gone cold. It was decided officially that Matilda was either a runaway, or dead, though there was still suspicion on her tight-knit group of friends, whose stories about the night she disappeared were so uniform that they seemed rehearsed. I searched again for anything interesting in the interrogation notes, but Theo and Rupert and Anwen and Sebastian Wallis's interviews all read the same: Matilda had been fine when they left her. They'd all gone home together and found out she'd disappeared the next morning. Anwen had sobbed through her interrogation, something I couldn't quite square with the composed girl I'd seen so far. Rupert had called every day asking for updates. And Theo haunted the police station for the weeks up until his flight home, bringing coffee to the detectives, doing his schoolwork in their waiting room. Desperate, it appeared, for answers.

I read through his transcript a second time. A third. *I should have walked to the hotel,* he'd said, over and over. *What kind of boyfriend am I?*

He'd never told the police that they had broken up.

(Watson nodded when I pointed it out. "It makes sense," he said. "Messy breakup, and then your girlfriend goes missing? You'd be their prime suspect."

I raised an eyebrow at him.

"This is not me sympathizing with him," he protested. "Criminal psychology! I'm getting into his head!")

And though my father's training taught me to begin with facts and not with theory, I couldn't help imagining it. Theo, in The Bell and Book with his friends, watching his ex-girlfriend sitting next to another boy. Putting a hand on his shoulder. Stealing sips of his drink. Sebastian? Rupert? A stranger? Them leaving at last call, Matilda splitting off with a wave—and Theo staring after her. Telling the rest that he'd forgotten something at the pub. He'd see them in the morning.

Running after Matilda. Grabbing her by the elbow, wheeling her around. The two of them arguing—I knew the sorts of things this Theo would say, *you should know better,* and *making a fool out of me,* and then—

There were many ways for a girl to disappear.

And for his friends, the next day, to circle their wagons, to insist to the police that they walked Theo all the way home. The alternative was unimaginable.

Of course, I had a very precise imagination.

As I flipped through the file once more, looking for anything else I'd missed, DI Sadiq returned. "Thoughts?" she asked. "Questions?"

"Theo Harding," I said. "He'd split up with Matilda right before she'd disappeared."

Sadiq sighed. "We did learn that eventually," she said. "But only weeks later, when speaking to some of the other theater students. When we returned to Theo, he categorically refused it. This is the sort of thing I'd like for you to look into—you're in a position to earn his trust."

"Noted," I said, while Watson made an actual note. "Do you remember anything about George Wilkes? The note here said he was frantic, and despite that, still uncooperative."

Sadiq frowned. "The girl's father, yes?" When I nodded, she said, "Parents can be like that when their child is hurt or goes missing, especially ones with money. They treat us like we're their personal security force. I'd be more upset at the idea if we hadn't utterly failed him."

Watson flipped his notebook shut. "You sound pretty upset."

"I am," she said, straightening her blazer. To avoid looking at us straight, it seemed. "I don't like unsolved cases, particularly when it's a child gone missing."

I filed that information away. I wasn't sure if Sadiq had children—she was far too precisely done up for me to read any clues on her clothing, and I disliked looking for such signals on a woman's body. It wasn't immediately important. Either way, the moment of vulnerability from her was endearing, and I found myself doing something uncharacteristic: asking for permission. "I've taken down George Wilkes's phone number. I'd like to follow up," I said. "Perhaps he's remembered something since last summer. Something his daughter said. Something to help keep this from happening again. Can I use the phone here?"

But Sadiq was already waving me off. "Whatever you need," she said. "I need to wrap up, get back to my own business. It's nice to meet you—Charlotte, Jamie."

"Likewise," Watson said, shaking her hand, blushing a little the way he did whenever he met an attractive woman.

I called George Wilkes from the telephone on Sadiq's desk, but he didn't answer the number listed for his house, or his mobile. On the latter I left a message: "This is Charlotte Holmes, following up from the Thames Valley Police Department. If you could give me a call back at your earliest convenience . . ."

"This isn't really aboveboard," Watson said, after I'd hung up and left a note for Sadiq telling her to expect George Wilkes's call.

"It isn't?"

Watson scratched the back of his neck. "You're not a detective. I mean, you *are* a detective, but you're making it sound like you work for the police—"

"I said no such thing. If Wilkes infers as such, that's hardly my fault."

"Holmes."

"I just *told* DI Sadiq what I'm doing," I protested. "How could I be doing anything wrong?"

Watson was always this way, some strange jumble of accelerator and brake pedal, and I never knew what line he'd drawn for himself in the morning. This spring, when we were writing back and forth across the Atlantic, I'd pointed out that it didn't make logical sense to be fine with breaking and entering but less fine with, say, my secretly texting with his then-girlfriend to check in on his well-being; at that, he'd added "emailing Holmes" to the list of things he was decidedly *not* okay with, and went silent for a week.

Less often, now, he made excuses for me, was less interested in redrawing his moral landscape so that he could keep me slotted in some Edenic garden, someplace where I would always be the hero. Or the villain. It felt now that we had more of a sliding scale by which to measure the other, as was only fair. Some days I could keep myself together quite well. And other days I would do anything in the name of expediency.

"I need to prepare for my tutorial," he said, passing a hand over his hair. "And—don't you have your poetry tutorial at one?"

I did. And what I hadn't told him yet was that I wasn't planning to go. That I'd made the decision that morning in the kitchen, spreading butter on endless pieces of bread while he slept in the other room.

"I'll walk back with you," I told him. "The tutor said it's fine if I'm a little late."

twelve

After I deposited Watson at the library—I didn't kiss him good-bye, it was too much and too light out and I already felt ill about lying—I picked up a sausage roll from a little shop outside the gates and ate it slowly as I walked, running through my monologue in my head.

How should I your true-love know
From another one?
By his cockle bat and staff
And his sandal shoon—

It was one of a series of nursery rhymes that Ophelia sang—laughing, crying—after her father's death at her beloved

Hamlet's hand. Nursery rhymes, and a song about a girl losing her virginity, and the obsessive wishing of goodnight. *Goodnight, ladies, goodnight, sweet ladies, goodnight, goodnight . . .*

If I had disdain for her character, it was in the way Shakespeare used her: a weathervane for everyone else's wind. She is told by her father to betray Hamlet, and does, and when Hamlet shortly after loses his mind—something, I might add, which is entirely his own problem—Ophelia blames herself. Hamlet will not marry her; he will instead murder her father, and she blames herself for that too.

Later, she climbs a willow tree, falls from it, and drowns, as one apparently does.

Though I knew a bit about Shakespeare, it wasn't as though I had all that much experience with theater. When I was a child, Leander had taken me to see *My Fair Lady* in the West End, and during a warm, languid summer when my father had been inexplicably even-keeled, we'd watched the Kenneth Branagh film adaptations of *Much Ado About Nothing* and *Othello* and *As You Like It* and *Hamlet.* I was ten, and I'd been taken with Ophelia, all red curls and white dresses and then, at the end, lovely even in her straightjacket as she writhed on the black-and-white tiled floor.

My father had seen something in my expression, some flicker of fascination, and he had reached out to touch my shoulder. "She isn't a girl," he'd said gently. "She's a bad idea."

Perhaps he'd meant to say she'd been poorly drawn, or characterized. Or perhaps he'd meant exactly what it sounded like. That summer, as I'd known it, only lasted a few weeks longer. We'd make it through *Love's Labour's Lost* and half of some made-for-television *Macbeth*, and then one night my father wasn't in the living room when I went down after supper. Some small new indignity had driven the tension back into my father's body, and he sat like a tensile coil in his study through the waning days of August.

I had looked out the window, and dreamed.

A bad idea.

I arrived at the St. Genesius theater a few minutes before two, even though my audition time wasn't until much later. The heavy doors were propped open for the occasion; the sun stretched in long, slim branches of light onto the wine-colored carpet.

I crept in on cat feet. On the stage, a man was pacing to and fro, calling out directions to someone just offstage. A pair of high curtains began to rise, abruptly seized, then lowered all at once. Someone cursed loudly from the wings. Laughter kicked up from just below the stage, a chorus of it, and I refocused my eyes to look.

The Dramatics Society, all forty-odd of them, clustered together in the first few rows. They leaned on each other's shoulders, bent forward to whisper in each other's ears; their bags were flung over seatbacks and left to spill out in the aisles. They were high school–aged, all of them, bright like peacocks, and I heard Americans and Irish and a boy speaking excitedly with a Parisian spin on his words, gesturing with his hands.

His friend nodding, slicing an apple with a sharp little knife, sharing the pieces of it between them.

As I walked down the aisle, not a single one turned their head to look at me, though my boots were making more noise than I'd intended. I felt unaccountably self-conscious. Why on earth was I fussed? I didn't want them to look at me anyway.

"Charlotte!" a voice said. Theo. He was sitting front row center, beside Rupert, and when Rupert saw me he began waving as though he were drowning in a paddling pool. I picked my way over people's legs and backpacks and sat down in the seat Theo cleared for me.

I glanced at him—his broad smile, his even teeth—and, with an internal shudder, glanced away.

Thankfully, he interpreted my disgust as nerves.

"You decided to audition." At my nod, he leaned in and said, quite matter-of-factly, "Don't be nervous. Really. You have great presence. And even if you're shit . . . well, you're not as shit as what you're about to see."

"What's that?"

Before Theo could respond, the man on the stage cleared his throat. "Attention," he said, clapping his hands. "Attention!"

To my surprise, no one quieted down.

He cleared his throat again, and this time I took a better look at him, this man in suspenders and penny loafers, shifting his weight from foot to foot. He couldn't have been older than thirty, but he was sending his shirts out to be starched, and his suspenders were moth-eaten a bit at their edges. His eyes and nose were far too petite for his face, but his smile, though nervous, was kind.

He looked, in short, like an easy mark.

"Attention!" he called again.

"Shut up, Quigley," someone said from behind me, and the Dramatics Soc, as a whole, snickered.

Theo shot me a look—half amusement, half despair. "Someone's feeling brave," he said in an undertone.

"I understand that you are all unhappy," Quigley was saying. "I know that the events of last summer were difficult for you all—"

"Where's Dr. Larkin?" a girl from behind me called.

"She will be here this evening to give the lecture. As you all know." Quigley cleared his throat. "And she's also agreed to assist me in overseeing auditions."

A ragged cheer.

"But, as you are all *aware*, I will be making up the final cast list on my own." Into the heavy silence that followed, he said, "Please remember that I once sat in your same chairs. I too participated in the Dramatics Society—well, the full-fledged, academic year Dramatics Society—and I am very pleased to be back here, working with you all."

I was fascinated by how he kept reminding the students that not only was he in charge, but that they knew it. I was also fascinated by the way he had casually insulted their program as a lesser cousin of St. Genesius's undergraduate society. As I watched him fidget onstage, I thought he was on the verge of asking us not to eat him, please, if we would be so kind. He eased himself off the stage with a pasted-on confidence; his hands were clenched into little balls.

Theo turned to me. "So," he said with a lazy smile. "This should be a shitshow."

"Oh, come on. The man is trying," Rupert said as we stood, gathering our things. Theo pointed to the back corner of the auditorium, up by the sound booth, and I followed him up the aisle.

"Yeah, but you can *see* him try," Theo said. "It's sad. You never want to see someone try."

"'There is no try,'" Rupert intoned, the voice of someone quoting something I didn't know.

"Still," I said. "Is there a reason Dr. Larkin is so popular? I mean, she couldn't stop what happened last year."

Theo flung himself down into the seat closest to the wall. "Are you talking about the accidents? Nobody could stop them. They came from everywhere and—and nowhere. But they definitely didn't come from Dr. Larkin, and she was the one they hung for it."

I had more questions, not the least of which was why we had moved to sit so far away from everyone else (and also why there wasn't any such thing as "try," when the word was right there, in the English language, for us to use) but Dr. Larkin was hurrying down the aisle, a legal pad in her arms. She settled down in the front row, empty now other than Dr. Quigley, and left a few seats between them. Still, despite this gesture of distance, the two leaned in together to discuss something briefly.

Quigley shook his head, but Larkin pressed on, cupping her hand around her mouth to shield her speech.

Quigley shook his head a final time, and stood. "First up, we have Florence Keener," he said. The room quieted, and a tall, strong-shouldered girl in the row popped up and ran down to the stage. "Let's begin with some applause, please. It isn't easy to go first."

Theo clapped heartily. "Florence," he said, "Florence is *terrific*," and it was the first time I'd really seen him like that, glowing for someone else. Of course, he was objectively quite handsome, with his thick blond hair and full mouth. But when someone existed as Theo did, in opposition to everything around them, I spent so much time tracing the invisible lines of their personality *out* that I never thought to follow them *in*.

All of that is to say, I didn't usually find murderers handsome. Was I imagining it, or was his smile not quite stretching across his face?

"She's great, right?" Theo asked.

"What?"

"Florence. Try to pay attention—it'll distract you, if you're nervous about your audition."

He'd utterly misread my fidgeting. "Thanks," I said, but when I focused in, I realized that Florence was, in fact, "great." She was reading for Gertrude, the role of Hamlet's mother, and her height and the rich curvature of her voice lent themselves to queenliness, to the suggestion of danger. She would be an excellent choice.

So would the next girl, and the next.

That was the tragedy of it: so many roles in *Hamlet*, and only two written for women. If Quigley and Larkin had any sense, they'd be reimagining some of the male roles for their talented female cast—there wasn't any reason, say, that Hamlet's schoolfriends Rosencrantz and Guildenstern couldn't be played by girls. There wasn't any reason that the title role couldn't be, for that matter. But I wasn't the director.

I wasn't fantasy-casting the show, either. The notes I was taking—and I was taking copious notes—had a different aim altogether. I was here, primarily, to solve a mystery. When sleuthing, I refused on principle to theorize in advance of the facts.

But that meant, of course, that I needed . . . facts.

Florence was confident, easy in her manners: this meant nothing. It would take confidence to orchestrate a series of "accidents" under everyone's noses. The next two girls, Keiko and Beatrice, had been at Oxford the year before. (Keiko did an excellently understated Ophelia, all subtle, discordant worry.) The first boy to audition, Asher, *hadn't* been, and I noted how short he was, how he licked his lips before he began to speak. His eyes kept fluttering over to Theo and Rupert and me, up in the back corner, which meant everything and also nothing. (Theo was, again, very attractive.) A pair of twins got up and asked shaky permission to perform a scene together, rather than a monologue; I noted their nervousness and was writing *new?*, when Rupert murmured, "That's a brave move on Mateo's part."

"Braver than he and Elio were last year," Theo said; again

the note of approval. He'd been appreciatively nodding through all the monologues we'd heard, cheering loudly after they'd stepped down. "Last year," he told me, "they split the part of a manservant. Getting their feet wet. Good sense of humor on Teo, and Elio's great. Brought snacks to rehearsal all the time last year. Good guys."

Quigley and Larkin consulted; Teo and Elio were allowed to perform together. They were passable actors, but barely. I wrote *snacks* in my notebook. I noted Theo's hand on the armrest between us, his eyes drifting down to the notebook in my lap, like a lion lazily regarding his prey.

I did not like sitting next to him. I didn't like it at all.

I should mention that, as usual, I was writing in my own shorthand, one I had developed as a child; it borrowed something from calligraphy, something from number substitution. Any notes I was making would have looked like scribbled abbreviations to a pair of prying eyes. And Theo's were.

Rupert leaned over. "I like your doodles."

"Nervous hands," I said with an apologetic smile. "'Doodles' is a generous description."

Theo had been so long-limbed and casual, so utterly fixed on the stage, that I was surprised when his name was called next. He jogged down the aisle to a flurry of high fives; he was well liked here, despite his seeming tendency to isolate himself from everyone but Rupert and Anwen. Trauma could do that, I knew.

So could guilt.

And perhaps that's what he drew on for his monologue,

that snarl inside him, the wanting to shove it all into a container that could fit it. "I'm doing a monologue from the Scottish play, as the main . . . Scottish character," he said, and there was a titter through the audience.

"Macbeth," Rupert said, too loudly, and was shushed. "He's doing Macbeth," he said to me in a whisper, because perhaps I hadn't heard him when he was louder.

"It's bad luck, isn't it? To even say the name."

He looked like he wanted to clap a hand over his mouth. "He's really pushing it," he said. "So many of us are already on edge—I knew he was planning to find a monologue outside of *Hamlet*, but—"

"'Tomorrow, and tomorrow, and tomorrow,'" Theo was saying, and I waved Rupert quiet. Not that I would have needed to. The room itself went quiet, and telescoped in, and in, until all I was watching was Theo's face. The quick knit of his brow. The back of his hand, quickly, across the forehead, and then his feet, pacing—or no, beginning to pace, but not, and all the while the language spun out of him like he was making straw into gold.

"'A tale told by an idiot,'" he said, "'full of sound and fury, / signifying nothing,'" and there was humor creeping in the depths of his desperate voice, and it was that that sold it.

I realized, after he'd finished speaking, after the silence gave way to applause and Theo was trotting gaily up the stage, that my pen was still poised over my page.

"Theo," Rupert said, extending a hand to Theo as he walked down our row. They shook. Rupert reached his free hand to grasp Theo's arm. "You know you're a marvel, don't you?"

He grinned. "Never a marvel til it's proven," he said, and I liked him, then, and I wanted to be far away.

Below us, Quigley and Larkin were shuffling papers. Larkin announced a break; we'd begin again in five.

"You're very good," I told Theo, still processing.

"Ah," he said, kicking back in his seat. "There it is. Your real voice. It's hoarser than what I'd imagined."

The tension inside me kicked into high gear. Had I had a gun, it would have been out and trained on his forehead.

"Don't worry, Charlotte," he said, amused. That didn't do anything to ease my flash of anger. "Everyone has one. The *please-like-me* voice. Yours went on for so long, I almost thought it was real."

Behind me, Rupert sighed. "Ignore him. He's just testing one of his pet theories."

"Not a pet theory," Theo said. "Actual fact. You had one too, Rupert, but you lost it pretty fast with me. The shitty thing is, women end up keeping theirs for *days* after I first meet them. Self-protection, maybe?"

I folded my arms.

"Your body language, too. It's been almost too open. You keep your arms at your sides. I'm noticing it now because they're across your chest—sorry, not looking like that—but before, you've had this . . . invitation to you. Like you want—"

I had heard enough. "You don't know anything about me," I told him, and I pitched my voice still lower, the bottom of its register, scraping out each syllable from its gravel. "You know *fuck all,* Theo. Stop talking, or I will make you stop."

"—me to tell you all my secrets." He looked at me curiously. "But I think I've just learned one of yours, maybe? Um. Sorry."

I had been sitting next to him, ignoring the instincts that had told me to *run,* because I knew that instincts weren't logical. Especially mine, which ran so quickly toward self-protection.

My neutral expression is that, neutral, but listening to a stranger wax poetic about my "physical availability" in the years after my rape was nothing close to a neutral experience for me.

Theo straightened a bit. "I'm sorry," he said again. "I can be kind of an armchair psychologist. People just . . . I think a lot about how they tick. It helps my acting."

"Think about it, then." I could hear it, the disgust in my voice, the thread of fear. (Matilda on that street corner, Theo reaching for her neck.) "But keep your mouth shut."

I could hear Rupert shift in the seat behind me.

"I'm sorry," Theo said again, quietly. "I really am."

"Everything okay?" a voice said. Watson. He made his way down our row, face smiling, eyes cold. "I saw your audition, Theo. You were great."

"Thanks," he said. "I think I just scared Charlotte. Didn't mean to."

Watson looked at me for his cue. I nodded, and he relaxed, infinitesimally. We both knew I didn't need protection, but occasionally, I did need backup. "Everything's fine," I said.

Asymptote, I thought. But no—that was the word for when I wasn't acting.

"I watched Theo from the doorway," Watson said, popping down next to Rupert. "So, he's Hamlet, right?"

"He's probably Hamlet," Rupert said proudly.

"Probably." It was fair to say as such without seeing the rest of the company audition. There was little chance they were hiding another Theo in their ranks, and even if they were, I didn't think I could be there to see it.

I was only moments away from crying—a reaction, nothing more, and yet I didn't want these strangers to see me vulnerable.

Something about this case was crawling underneath my skin.

Swallowing, I pulled out my phone. I need to go home and lie down. You stay here? Take notes.

You're not okay, Watson wrote back. Let me come with. We're not going to miss anything.

I was fighting myself. I couldn't fight Watson too. "I need to go." My fake voice again, but shaking this time. "I'll see you all later," I said, and he followed me out the door and all the way home, a foot behind me, quiet and steady and sure.

I was grateful for it then. I wasn't later.

One of us should have stayed.

LATER, MUCH LATER, I WOKE IN MY BED FEELING LIKE I'D drunk three whole bottles of champagne and then broken into a government building with a flamethrower.

I hadn't, though I knew what that felt like. I was a different sort of wrecked.

Watson was propped up beside me, his fingers in my hair, his other hand turning the pages of a book. *The Good Soldier*, I saw. He was nearly finished; hours must have passed. The sky outside was dark.

"Did you hear something?" I asked him sleepily.

"A knock, maybe?" He looked down at me, pulled a strand of hair from my eyes. "But it's been thundering outside. Kind of hard to tell."

There it was again—*rap, rap, rap*. An argument muffled in the hall.

At that, Watson was on his feet. He opened the second drawer of my dresser, pulled out my knife, and stalked out of the room without bothering to do up his shirt.

People were shouting.

Then I was awake, too, putting on clothes as Mouse dashed for the safe, quiet space under my bed. I picked up a blanket from the floor and threw it around my shoulders and followed.

"—she's dead," Rupert was saying in the living room, his hair plastered to his face. It must have been raining quite hard; water was leeching out from his boots into the carpet. "Dead. And I saw it happen. We all did."

At first I thought he meant Anwen, but no—she was there behind him in a translucent rain slicker, a lace dress beneath it, her face drawn and thin. Theo, behind her, was shutting the door. Under his arm was a bottle in a brown paper bag.

"Dead," Rupert said again, and he sat right there on the rug, his back against the door. "I can't believe it."

"And Rupert—*Rupert* is playing Hamlet," Anwen burst out, as though it were the worst thing of all.

thirteen

"Nobody say anything else," Watson said, heading into the kitchen. He dropped the knife on the counter.

"Were you making something?" Rupert asked, confused. "Cooking shirtless can be sort of dangerous—"

"Rupert," Anwen said despairingly, and then burst into tears, turning her face into Theo's shirt. He recoiled slightly, and then brought his hands up to her shoulders. Rupert, chastened, stared at the floor.

In my experience, the teenage brain tended to go one of two ways in the aftermath of tragedy: one became either the animal or the child. Giving these three orders right now would satisfy that second impulse. And, under the guise of taking care of them, I might be able to ferret out some information.

"Jackets," I said, and as they shucked them off and hung them in the entryway closet, Watson came from the kitchen with three glasses of water cradled between his hands. "Shoes, too."

Once the water was distributed, Watson produced a stack of fresh towels from the bathroom and handed them out, and the three of them gathered shakily on the couch.

I sat in the leather club chair, tossing the end of my blanket over my shoulder. Watson perched on its arm. "What on earth happened?" I asked. For Theo's benefit, I kept my voice at its natural register, though I was certainly not going to play this round as myself.

Blindly, Theo drained off his water, then fetched the bottle from his paper bag, affecting a mad scientist's squint as he refilled his glass with brown liquor.

"That," Watson said, "is a lot of rum."

"That," Theo said, "is the point," and took a gigantic swig, then sputtered. Anwen reached to take the glass from him, but he batted her away like a child.

"Please forgive Theodore's theatrics," she said. "Dr. Larkin is dead."

With a low groan, Rupert buried his face in his hands. Theo tossed back his rum.

Watson shot me a horrified look, and I reached out to take his hand, to steady myself as much as him. One would think, perhaps, that recent years would have hardened me to the possibility of death. But Dr. Larkin hadn't seemed in any danger. She'd been a harried academic at my uncle's party, asking for my help to protect her students.

Though part of me was reeling, another, abstract part knew that it was important to catalog Anwen's and Theo's and Rupert's reactions before they could begin to paper them over with what they wanted me to see. But grief did strange things to you. Made you see yourself at a distance. Theo's drinking was clearly taken from something he'd seen onstage, or in a movie, a portrait of a young man prettily losing control; perhaps he'd had practice in the weeks after Matilda's disappearance. Anwen's grief was laced with the resentment I'd still yet to see her shake.

Rupert? His seemed genuine, which in its own way made me suspect him more.

"What happened?" I asked quietly, though more than that, I wanted to ask, *why did you come here first?*

Theo tilted his head to the side, locking eyes with mine. "Tonight, while she was onstage, explaining to us the idea of betrayal in *Hamlet,* a light fell out of the grid."

"Oh my God," Watson murmured. "Onto her?"

Anwen nodded. My heart seized, but I said nothing more. I owed it to Dr. Larkin to stay silent, to let them talk.

"We were all watching. We were all there." Theo scrubbed at his face. "People were screaming. Running out of the theater like there had been gunshots, or like there was a fire . . . no one went up to help her, so I climbed onto the stage and I got down there beside her and I didn't want to move the light in case—in case—you know, on the television shows, they tell you not to move them—"

"You did the right thing, mate," Rupert said, reaching out to touch Theo's knee.

He batted away Rupert's hand, struggling to sit up on the couch. "And because I was up there when the police came, they took me back to the station and questioned me. Some bitch of a detective named Sadiq, she went at me for hours. *I* had been the last person to see Matilda before she disappeared. *I* had been unhappy about her casting. *I* had been onstage when Larkin was—was—and because these things keep happening around me, because my life *sucks*, I keep being the one they go after." With shaking hands, he tried to topple more rum into his glass.

"Stop, Theo," Anwen said, though I didn't know whether she meant the drinking or the talking.

"We need to get some food into him." With a sigh, Rupert stood and padded over to the kitchen. "Is it all right if I raid your fridge?"

Too much was going on. Was he moving away to hide his reaction?

"Was there anyone near the lighting grid?" Watson was asking Theo. "Do they have any suspects?"

"Why does your fridge smell like anchovies?" Rupert asked, popping his head over the door. "Why is it filled with toasts? Were you having a party?"

Watson shrugged. "Maybe. Or is this a wake?"

"Theo?" I prompted, "The lighting board," but he was staring somewhere over my shoulder.

A sharp lash of thunder outside, a burst of wind. In the

kitchen, Rupert set out trays on the kitchen island, bottles of juice, the rest of the Diet Coke.

"I'm starving," Anwen said, jumping to her feet, "and I can't talk about this anymore, not now. I've been with the police for *hours.*"

Theo followed suit, rum in hand, and the three of them together made short work of the rest of the breakfast I'd made for the week. I watched them gathered around the kitchen island, their heads bent, the three of them silent as they ate. Apparently, their animal brains had won out.

I looked up at Watson. He looked down at me. "It's a party," he said in an undertone, and kissed my forehead.

"It's a party," I said grimly. "Why are they here?"

"I know one way to find out." He looked up, his mouth in a tight smile. "Who wants to do shots?" he called. "Theo, you're hogging that rum."

Theo flipped him off, mouth full of toast, but Rupert, ever obliging, was pulling glasses from the bar cart as though he'd lived in my flat for months. Anwen had already drifted over to sit at the table with her makeshift cocktail, stealing little sips of it. She traced a pattern on the floor with one sock foot.

The night went on like that, in fits and starts. Watson poured a round of shots, mine into the glass I kept in my fist so that no one could see that he'd given me only a splash. I understood the plan he'd come up with: it was simple, really. *In vino veritas.* If we could get them drunk, we could maybe get them to talk, and if we had to burn Watson on the pyre as well—

Well. At least alcohol was flammable.

There was a second round, and a third, Watson bellowing out the numbers like he was the sort of rugby asshole that we'd always avoided back at school. He fit the part, confidently broad-shouldered, slim-hipped (I had been thinking much more about his body lately, *nemo malus felix*); he performed his role with vigor, and soon enough they were all soused.

We'd turned on the lamps against the dark, and they cast strange shadows across the room. Rupert's nose went peakier still, and Anwen's chin disappeared as she ducked it, studying her hands, picking her cuticles. I was surprised by how cowed she was tonight, how she'd been holding herself apart. The only way they'd have known about my flat would be from her: she'd been here only yesterday. Rupert had made some throwaway apology about barging in on us, and Theo had said hollowly, "Where else could we go? The dorms? A *pub*?"

"Everyone else was going to The Bell and Book to, you know, grieve—"

Theo slammed his glass down on the table. "People repeating the same horrible patterns. Someone else is going to get *hurt*."

"Hey." Anwen glanced up. "We don't have to talk about it."

"I know we don't, but I *want* to—"

"You haven't told me anything about this spring," she said. "How was Boston? How was your last semester of school?"

"School?" Rupert asked. He glanced between the two of them. "You two haven't talked about it? I thought you'd been in touch."

Anwen swallowed. "I mean—"

"Oh, *school,*" Theo said, fury lurking at the corners of his voice. "School. Yes, let's not talk about Larkin. Let's not talk about this summer. Why would we need to? It's not like *last year* had anything to do with it—"

"Theo," Anwen said, hands up, "I'm sorry, I didn't mean to pry—"

"Pry?" Theo laughed. "How is it prying? You and me are *friends,* Anwen, remember? Remember when my girlfriend broke up with me last summer, because she thought I knew why people were being attacked and wasn't telling anyone. Who knows where she got that idea. Oh, and then she *disappeared.*"

At that, Anwen stopped breathing. For a moment, only, but I was watching for it.

"And so after that I went home, where no one knew anything about it, and no one would talk to me about it. Including my parents. So fuck them. I did a lot of this"—Theo lofted his glass full of rum—"and cutting class to go boxing with Gael and like, fuck around downtown, and so I got a bunch of Cs in the fall. But fuck it, Laurence Olivier didn't have to do AP fucking Physics so why should I, especially when I was going to acting conservatory in the fall?" He looked around the room. "*Tell* me."

"I can't," Anwen said softly.

"So then my mom talked to the Boston Players Club about giving away my part in *Curious Incident of the Dog in the Night-Time*—"

"Oh God, Theo—"

"—the *lead,*" he bit out, "which I had auditioned for in the months after I got home from *Matilda disappearing,* but why does that matter? My parents said I had to focus on my grades, which didn't matter, because *senior spring* and the Guthrie conservatory program emphatically *did not care.* So I understudied instead. Understudying's the same, right? Totally the same. So yeah, Anwen, my spring was great. Fucking awesome."

"That's cold, Theo," Rupert said, and he sat down next to Anwen on the rug, tucking one thin arm around her shoulders. "She didn't deserve that."

Theo stared at them, then viciously bit his lip. "Fine," he said.

"Do better than that," Rupert said, with an edge I hadn't seen before.

"Fine," Theo said again, and then, "fine. I'm sorry. Look, I wouldn't've met Gael if—if Matilda hadn't ended things with me. Her disappearing . . . I couldn't do anything about that. But it was all I could think about. The only thing, figuring out where she'd gone, that maybe she'd given me some clue and I'd been too stupid to see it for what it was, and then, these last few months, thinking about coming back here . . . I kept thinking, and it was so stupid, but . . ."

None of it seemed rehearsed. It looked and sounded genuine—the confusion, the grief, the sad, soft eyes.

But I had seen Theo do Shakespeare that afternoon. I knew what he could do with words.

"You thought maybe she'd come back," Anwen murmured to him. "Like magic. Maybe you'd both come back here, to

Oxford in the summer, and it would all be the same as it was."

It was a wild thing for her to say to a boy in the throes of grief. I expected him to fire back with renewed outrage. But Rupert hung his head, and Anwen turned to tuck her face into his shoulder, and Theo stared up at the ceiling, the vein in his neck still showing, and I watched in fascination, the three of them rearranging their dynamic once again.

"What was it like?" Watson asked, pulling a leg up to his chest. "Last summer?"

"It was—" Anwen sighed. "I don't even know where to begin."

But she did begin, and Rupert picked up when she trailed off, and even Theo, finally, joined in, his head tipped back on the couch, words spinning up into the air. The three of them together on the floor of Theo's room, Anwen hemming a skirt she'd bought at a charity shop while Rupert read his economics textbook out loud, asking, periodically, if he had in fact forgotten how to speak English or if the author had. The first time they'd seen Theo perform, not onstage but in the bathroom of their suite, jumping up to balance on the clawfoot tub while he did a blistering monologue from *This Is Our Youth*, Rupert throwing popcorn at his face to see if it would faze him. It didn't; Theo caught a kernel in his mouth and yelled so loudly in triumph that their downstairs neighbors hammered at the ceiling with a broom. The second week, when they discovered they could take out punts from the boathouse, Anwen had brought a Bluetooth speaker and played experimental jazz as Rupert maneuvered them through the River Cherwell. They did it every afternoon, the three of them on the water, the three of them at their Italian restaurant, the rituals they developed by accident and then held to because they were theirs. Anwen adding ruffles to her socks, adding a lining to a coat, buying silk scarves from Oxfam and making them into pocket squares for their blazers, all three of them, in complimentary shades of green, paisley. And nights, then, at the St. Genesius theater, where Theo met Matilda.

"We can show you videos," Rupert said, tugging his phone from his pocket. "I took a few last summer, back before things went wrong."

Theo turned his head. "Go on," he said hoarsely. "Show them your evidence."

Watson and I exchanged a look.

There it was. Why they had come to us first, before they had even gone home.

We knew the two of us weren't entirely anonymous; even before the Lucien Moriarty case ended up in the tabloids, our last names made us conspicuous targets. And it wasn't precisely a secret that I'd been brought in by Dr. Larkin to help.

But I didn't want them to think of me as a detective. Not yet. I wanted them to think of me as a friend. To *confide* in me as a friend.

"I'd love to see her," I said quietly.

"Aha," Rupert said, scrolling. Watson pulled his chair forward. "Here's a good one. At the Parks, last June." He held the screen out between us.

The camera shakily panned over a long grassy expanse,

trees shimmering in the distance. The light was red and soft, as it was the hour after sunset or before sunrise. Anwen came into frame, her hair an exuberant mess. She held a hand over her face. "Rupert, don't, I'm a shambles," she said, laughing, and the camera jerked over to Theo. He was bundled in a letterman jacket, too big for him in the shoulders, and he was turned on his side with his arm thrown over—

Matilda.

"Rupert," she sighed, stretching her arms over her head, "what are you doing?" There were the remains of a picnic basket beside her: cupcake wrappers, a few empty bottles of wine. They'd been drinking.

"Making something to watch later," he said. "Tell me a secret."

(Anwen and Rupert, on my uncle's sofa, exchanged a significant glance. Was this the video they thought they'd show me?)

"You first," Matilda said sleepily. "I've been in the sun all day. I'm wiped clean."

Rupert, always obliging: "Sure," he said. "Let me think. Hmmm . . . ha! How about, when I was twelve, do you know what I asked for, for Christmas?" A triumphant pause. "Backup singers!"

Anwen giggled, pulling at a bottle of wine. "Too many music videos."

"It's not a secret," Matilda's voice said, and she pushed herself up on her arm, her dark eyes knowing. "A secret is something embarrassing. Something compromising, something with *power.* Secrets are what we make art from."

Theo couldn't tear his eyes off her.

(I understood it. Her words were pretentious, but the way she spoke them—slowly, deliberately—all I wanted was to look at her. When Rupert's camera panned back to Anwen, I made a tiny sound of disappointment.)

"You can't make art from my secrets," Anwen said, in an attempt to match Matilda's tone.

"Oh?" Matilda, off-screen. "Mine aren't *my* secrets, you know. I keep everyone's secrets. Rupert's. Theo's. My parents'."

"Your parents have secrets?" Theo asked. "Mine just go to work and go home. Like machines."

"My mother didn't, but now she's dead," Matilda said in a singsong voice. "My father spins his art from secrets. And my stepmother has *none.*" She started laughing, a low, throaty sound, and Theo tugged her to him.

"You've been drinking, lady," he said, but her laughter was contagious, and he joined in.

"I've been drinking *so much,*" she gasped out. "Am I just talking nonsense?"

"Yes," Anwen said, with a laugh that sounded forced, and she reached up a hand for Rupert's camera. "Give me that," she said, "and get a beer. We need to catch up."

The video ended.

I was starting to get a better idea now.

"She had a way of rearranging a room," Anwen was saying, "just by sitting there, making some people nervous, making some people . . . excited, and it was because she was so watchful." She looked over at me. "You have a little of the same quality."

Theo's eyes opened.

Matilda, Anwen had said yesterday. *It's all her fault.* It would do me no good to repeat it now; the three of them would clamp down, the scene would devolve into chaos.

"It's not that I mind you guys being here," Watson said carefully, "but . . . why? Why come to our flat?"

"I'm not an idiot," Theo said suddenly. "You're James Watson. She's Charlotte Holmes. I've read the news articles. I *get* it—"

There it was.

"Oh, come on," Watson said, leaning forward. "There isn't anything to get."

But he barreled on. "You wouldn't be here unless there was a mystery to solve. That's what you *do.* I read the *Daily Mail* article, Jamie, after I met you—I thought your name had sounded familiar." He glanced over at me. "I'm keeping my ears away from her, for starters."

"Thanks," I said. "I do get tempted."

"We're here because we want to go to university," Watson said, standing. He was steady, sober. I wondered how much he'd actually drunk, how much he'd stealthily poured into the planter in the corner. "Charlotte's been here since the winter, living with her uncle. This is *his* flat. And I'm here because I want to be with her. Full stop. I'm sorry to tell you this, and I'm sorry all this shit has been happening, but we are just trying to live our lives."

He said it so firmly I nearly believed it. It might be worthwhile to get Watson some acting lessons; who knew what he could accomplish then?

"But that's—" Anwen struggled for words. "We need your help!"

"I thought you came here because Rupert was somehow cast in a lead role," Watson said flatly.

Her lip wobbled, and she buried her face into Rupert's cardigan. "Real nice, Watson," he said. "We don't know what to do next. This is the second time in two years that we've been in the wrong place at the wrong time. It doesn't look like coincidence anymore."

"We were in with the police all night." Theo took a swig of his drink. "And when I got home, I had an email with the cast list. They're going to put on the fucking show. And—and Rupert—"

Rupert sighed, his hand on the back of Anwen's head as she hiccupped. "And Dr. Quigley, bless his stupid heart, insisted that everyone in the theater audition because there was a 'paucity of male actors,' and when he hauled me up there, I reminded him that I didn't have anything memorized, so I just read one of Hamlet's monologues from a book."

"Straight-up 'To be or not to be,'" Theo said, "and you killed it." And despite everything, there it was—that thread of appreciation for even his competition's talent.

"I just channeled you," Rupert protested.

"Really, Rup," Anwen said. "I know it was a lark to do it, but—"

"But what?" he asked, his shoulders beginning to rise.

"But you don't want to be an actor," she protested. "Is it really fair to take the role, when Theo didn't even get to perform this spring? You heard him talk about his part in Boston!"

"I'm sorry about that," Rupert said quietly. "But what does it have to do with me?"

"Stop it, Anwen." Theo pushed himself off the sofa. "I'm Polonius. It's a good role, though not exactly what I wanted, and—and, well."

"What?"

He shrugged, shuffling off to the bathroom. "And Charlotte, you're understudying Ophelia. Not sure how that one happened."

At least I had an answer prepared. "I ran my monologue for Dr. Larkin yesterday," I said. "I wrote her this afternoon and told her I wasn't well, so she must have counted that as my audition."

"There weren't a lot of female roles this go-round," Rupert said. "Good work." Anwen had stilled against his chest.

Watson put a hand on my shoulder. "We should all sleep," he said. "Get a handle on things tomorrow. I'm sure you're all wrecked."

"And the police have an appointment with me in the morning," Rupert said, as Anwen drew away from him slowly. He helped her to her feet, and she held on to his waist, a throw blanket dangling from one hand. Rupert took it from her, laying it with extreme care on the velvet sofa.

"Shall we?" she asked him softly. "I'm knackered."

He looked unaccountably—or, rather, accountably—thrilled. Without waiting for Theo, he took her by the elbow and steered her down the stairs.

Before she changed her mind, I thought uncharitably.

"Anwen forgot her raincoat." Watson looked down at me. "You okay?"

I didn't like being handled as though I were glass. I was aware, however, that I still felt quite a bit like glass. "Tired," I said. "I've taken notes for hours in my head. It'll take some sorting."

Theo stumbled back into the living room. He flung out a hand against the wall for balance. "Figures. They leave?"

"They left." Watson peered at him. "You okay, man?"

"Fine. I'm fine, I—" He put a hand to his stomach.

"Not fine," Watson said, and when he took a step toward him, Theo took one back.

"Don't trust her," he burst out. "Don't trust Anwen. She's not who you think she is, and I—oh God," he said, and he ran into the kitchen. I flinched half a second before it happened: him retching into the kitchen sink. Watson ran over to help him. The sound of running water, of coughing.

I had, thankfully, already done the dishes.

"You," Watson said, steering Theo back toward the sofa, "sleep here. Bathroom's that way, you know that. I'll get you water. Shoes are off? Good. Lay facedown. Good man."

Within moments, Theo was snoring. "I'll kip in the chair," Watson said, throwing the blanket over him. "I'll check in every few hours, make sure he's all right."

"Your accent is back," I said, charmed despite everything.

"My accent?" Watson smiled. "I didn't notice. Do you like it?"

"Like home," I told him. "Always like home."

He put his arms around my waist. "Anwen, huh."

"Anwen," I said. "Or Theo. But more than that—I have so many questions. The precollege suites are for four people, not three. Who was their fourth, last year? Why don't they mention him?"

Watson lifted his head to look at Theo, prone on the couch. "Some poor fucker who tried to stay out of their way? The three of them are a drama tornado."

"Perhaps, but it's something to look into."

Dr. Larkin's death. Matilda's disappearance. I couldn't see a way the two couldn't be connected. I couldn't see how these three maddening people weren't at the heart of it.

"I'll go see Sadiq in the morning. Please don't let Theo choke on his own vomit."

"The romance," Watson said. "It never dies."

fourteen

It was some time before I fell asleep.

When Dr. Larkin had originally approached me, her worry had been for the health of the Dramatics Society, not her own. She'd wanted her position back as their director, of course, and she'd wanted the attacks to stop. But her main concern had been not knowing who the true target was, whether it was her, her students, or—as tonight's murder suggested—the institution itself. The killer had had all of last summer to do away with Dr. Larkin, but they waited until now to try. Tonight's "accident," then, was meant as a warning—but to who?

Really, I was searching for the identities of both the culprit and the target, which put me out. I was used to having mystery at one end of my case, not both.

One detail I found interesting: a light had fallen from the grid the summer before, though no one had been injured. This killer's bag of tricks, then, had a bottom. It would be worth nosing around the theater's lighting rig in the morning.

I didn't sleep well. As a child, I found the notion romantic, staying up sleeplessly recounting the day's events. But the world goes warped and strange in the hours before dawn, as the birds, with their voices, remind you how they spend their days loitering above, unseen.

A stranger was sleeping in our living room. My uncle wouldn't be making eggs on the stove. The boy I loved slept away from me, and I resisted the selfish urge to creep into the other room to wake him, to see what secrets I could glean from him in the dark.

Am I still interesting to you, now that you finally have me the way you wanted? Or, *Now that we aren't running for our lives, is this still enough to keep you?*

Around four, I gave it up. The refuse trucks had begun down the road, and I could smell the morning cold and sharp through the window. I put my cigarettes and a pair of tweezers in the pocket of my robe and took my bag to the living room.

"Jamie," I whispered, rousing him in the armchair. He'd been sleeping all twisted up and tangled; he wouldn't be able to turn his neck in the morning. "Go to bed. I'll look after Theo." He mumbled something like *thank you* before he made his way to my bedroom, and I took up his post watching Theo drool into a towel he'd balled up into a pillow.

As he slept, I unloaded the scraps I'd collected the last few days—the newspaper pages from the bus, the note from the theater door—touching them only at their edges. Then I went to Anwen's translucent mackintosh in the closet, and, using my tweezers, retrieved the papers I'd seen in the pockets. Two were receipts, from Blackmarket café and from Pret A Manger, and the last a wrapper from a candy bar. On the coffee table, I lined them up and then turned them over, tweezers in hand.

There. In pencil, on the back of the Pret receipt, a series of numbers. I held it up in the dark: *II.ii.87, IV.v.27, III.i.132.* Immediately, my brain began running them through as code. Roman numerals corresponding to certain letters? Periods indicating new sentences? Anwen was far more complex than I'd thought.

On the sofa, Theo muttered in his sleep, and I placed an unlit cigarette between my lips and settled in to solve a long, satisfying problem.

It was a full two minutes before I realized she'd jotted down a list of monologues. Act number, scene number, line number—the best pieces to audition for Ophelia, listed out in her spiky hand.

Fine, then. I'd use this list for its intended purpose—squaring the handwriting against the note from the theater. *I'm in the sound booth upstairs. Meet me there?* it read, so both samples at least used the capital and the lowercase *I*. But there was no similarity, neither in shape nor in pressure points, the places where she'd set down and lifted her pen as she wrote.

Theo muttered again, and my eyes lit on his messenger bag, toppled over on the rug next to his shoes. But a cursory examination of its contents proved only two things: one, he was a meticulous notetaker in his theater history lectures, and two, he hadn't left the note on the theater door. The handwriting wasn't a match in the slightest. I tucked his notebook back in his bag and stretched, feeling a satisfying pop in my shoulders.

The newspaper took only a cursory glance. What I wanted was on the second page of the culture section, in a little column at the bottom. It was an item on this summer's production of *Hamlet*—a blurb, nothing more—and a brief profile of Dr. Quigley. Twenty-nine, a London native, educated at St. Genesius ("which makes this new position a homecoming!"), danced, surprisingly, in the chorus of *Billy Elliot* on the West End straight after university. Then came graduate school, and his new position. "My sister was an actress," he'd told the paper, "and so I grew up in the theater. There was nothing else I'd rather do."

Than act? If that had been his goal, his role with the Dramatics Soc was a demotion. That would make him bitter, certainly, but how could that have led to Dr. Larkin's death?

I became aware of Watson in the bedroom doorway, and looked up. "I can't sleep," he said, rumpling his hair.

"I couldn't either."

He smiled a little. He was still a bit drunk. "You look so picturesque, out there. The moonlight on your hair. It hurts a little."

"I'm only working," I reminded him. "Nothing more."

"There's always more, with you."

Once, Watson had liked to tell stories about the two of us in his head, and in those stories, the girl who looked like me, who had my name, had reasons for her behavior far crueler and more romantic than mine had ever been. When we first met, I had only been trying to survive. And he had snuck in, somehow, when I was at my lowest, and now I didn't know myself without him. His steady hands, his quick wit. How we were telling a new story, and I was holding the pen.

"Come to bed," he said, and after a moment, I did.

WATSON WAS STILL SLEEPING WHEN I LEFT TO KEEP MY appointment with DI Sadiq. The morning was colder than I'd expected, and I was thankful that I'd brought along my leather jacket. Unlike in the States, where whatever I'd had on was a notch or two stranger than the camisoles and cardigans the other girls wore, here I felt as though I made sense against the scenery. I paid attention to this sort of thing, to whether I could be picked out easily in a crowd, and oftentimes I'd change the way I presented to more easily maneuver through my day. Girls do this; boys do this; everyone does, really. I monitored how I felt in the world as a sort of barometer for how I felt about myself.

Would a Holmes go out in a moto jacket and velvet loafers? No. Why on earth call that much attention to oneself? I was meant to sketch in the rest of the world, leaving myself a perfect blank.

But still—I liked these loafers.

I made a point to walk by the St. Genesius theater, but the

doors were cordoned off with police tape. A lone PC leaned against the railing, scrolling through his phone. While I'd made myself known to Sadiq, I didn't think that I could talk myself into that theater without a number of tricks that I was too tired right now to try out. Still, I wondered about it as I walked to the police station: the wall by the dressing rooms in the basement, how I could hear the sound coming through. There was another way in, I was sure of it.

I made a quick stop at Blackmarket before I took the bus to the police station. There, I didn't ask for DI Sadiq. Instead, I said that I had an appointment, that I had been at the St. Genesius theater yesterday (all truths, far easier to sell than lies), and was ushered to a bench outside the squad room.

It wasn't empty. Three people I recognized from the auditions yesterday sat there, two girls and a boy. One of the girls gave me a walleyed once-over as I sat down; she was Keiko, the girl who had been so excellent at her audition yesterday. I didn't recognize the other. She was crying into her hands.

"This is so messed up," I said quietly.

Keiko sighed. "That's an understatement." She eyed the carrier on my lap. "Bringing them coffee? The police?"

"No, I thought—I thought I might see Theo and Rupert and Anwen here," I said, shimmying one of the cups free. "But they're not, so I guess I have some spare lattes. Do you want one? They're all mochas or vanilla. I thought some sugar might be on order."

The girl accepted it and took a sip. "I'm Keiko," she said.

"Charlotte," I said, and silently handed over the other two

coffees. The second girl didn't stop crying as she cupped it between her hands. "Have you heard anything? Did they catch the killer?"

"No," the boy said. He made a face. "They're still out there, somewhere, deciding which one of us they're going to kill next."

A bit dramatic, but I could see his point. "I'm new this year," I said. "Were any of you here last year? Shouldn't somebody have warned us if this stuff was happening?"

"Finley wasn't here," Keiko said, looking at the other girl. "I was. Do you know if they found an orchid at the crime scene?"

"An orchid?" I asked, widening my eyes.

"And the footlights—did you see the footlights? They flashed twice before the light went crashing out of the rig."

Finley took a deep, shaky breath. "I saw it," she said. "I thought there was a power surge. Especially when the light fell right after. It was blinding. I thought there had been a bombing, or that everything was going to explode."

"Someone was signaling someone," Keiko said. "To move out of the way. To act. That's my thought."

She was a clever girl, but I was more focused on my not having been told about this last night. I made a note in my mind, category *bullshit*, subcategory *things being kept from me.*

"Can you all stop?" the boy asked, looking down at his shoes. He was small to begin with, but the slump of his shoulders made him look even more diminutive. "It's not like we're going to figure it out. I don't even want to try. People are dead, and they're missing, and it's not safe to even think about it."

At that, the door to the squad room opened, and the PC

from yesterday came out with a clipboard. His eyes narrowed when he saw me, but he only said, "Sebastian Wallis," and the boy gave us all a miserable look and followed him inside.

The name from the file. The other friend who had gone drinking with Anwen and Theo and Matilda and Rupert, the night that Matilda was attacked.

Keiko watched him go with an unreadable expression. "I wonder where they dug him up from," she said, taking a sip of her latte. "He didn't come back this year. Thanks for the coffee, by the way."

I nodded. It had done what I'd hoped it to.

A SHORT WHILE LATER, DI SADIQ CAME OUT TO PULL ME into an interrogation room. It was one of the purposely horrible ones: chairs with uneven legs, a low whine emanating from the high-mounted speakers.

"Sorry," she said, sitting down. "The 'comfortable' rooms are all taken right now."

I eyed her from the doorway.

She laughed. "I'm not interrogating you, Charlotte. You know procedure well enough—I'm not cautioning you, I'm not turning on the cameras. To be honest, I'm in need of some help. You were in here just yesterday to remind me of this case, and now we have an Oxford don down."

"Down." I eased myself into the chair across from her. It wobbled. "That's a euphemism."

Sadiq smiled a bit. "That's really all I can say."

It was a fairly common trick: tell the suspects the victim

was dead, and they could be moved to confession through guilt and shame; tell them she was still alive, just in a coma, and they could be moved to confession through the fear of her waking up. I wasn't sure what game Sadiq was playing. In the end, it wasn't my business.

"I've spoken with the fellow who does tech for the St. Genesius theater," she said. "Unfortunately, late last year after the light fell onto the stage, he led a workshop in proper lighting safety—how to rig a light, how the board works. All the members of the Dramatics Society were required to attend. Any of the returning students would know exactly how to make a light fall."

"And the tech himself?"

"He's been in hospital the past few days with pneumonia, which is an alibi if I've ever heard one. I spoke to him by phone today. Dr. Quigley had volunteered to run basic tech while he was out. We're investigating both further. How about you? Dug up anything?"

"I had some interesting visitors late last night," I told her, and described the situation in detail. The important details, that is. I finished by relaying Theo's warning about Anwen before he ignominiously passed out on my sofa.

"Facedown, I hope," she said, taking notes.

"Facedown." I grimaced. "He was still sleeping when I left. Honestly, they're all so private, even Rupert, but there's something one of them needs to confess, and the rest suspect it. They wouldn't keep pulling in Watson and I otherwise. They can't stand to be alone with each other."

"Have you tried isolating any of them? Asking questions?"

I shook my head. "They'd rabbit. No, I have to let them come to me. They know my history. My . . . profession. I can't just innocently inquire about their lives, at this point."

"So you're only quasi-undercover, then."

"I'm not undercover at all," I said after a moment. "Quite honestly, I'd wanted to take some summer classes and go punting with my boyfriend. And now . . . well, I should be in my chemistry tutorial."

Sadiq whistled. "They don't take well to being blown off, your tutors."

"No." An understatement. "Anyway, I know better than to ask you what you've learned this morning. This isn't a collaborative exercise. But I hope you don't mind if I ask if you've followed up with Matilda Wilkes's father?"

Sadiq sighed. "I tried their home number twice. The mother rushed me off the phone both times—she wants nothing to do with us 'unless we have firm information.' And as for the father—well, you have a message waiting."

On her phone, Sadiq pulled up her voicemail and set it to speaker.

"This is George Wilkes, returning a call from a Charlotte Holmes. I hope you're following up as to my daughter's disappearance. I've been traveling for work but am available off and on these next few days . . ."

"Interesting," I said, playing it back again, listening for the nuances in his voice.

"I know. A different tack than his wife's. Though it makes

sense, if she's a nervous wreck. Wants to shove it all under the rug while he wants answers." Sadiq tapped her pen on the table. "Anything else you want to share?"

"You're bringing in Rupert Davies and Anwen Ellis this morning, yes?"

"An hour from now."

I thought for a moment. "Is there anything you can do to upset Anwen? Something that perhaps implicates Rupert, so she wouldn't go to him for solace?"

Sadiq thought about it, a smile pulling at the corners of her mouth. "You're not a terribly nice person," she said finally.

"No," I said. "I'm not."

"As long as you can admit it. I'll see what I can do."

"And one last favor?" I asked, handing her back her phone.

She slipped it back in her pocket. "Depends."

"How good are you at making a scene?"

"Hmm," she said. "Most likely not as good as you are."

"I TOLD YOU, I DON'T HAVE TO TELL YOU ANYTHING WITHout a lawyer!"

Sadiq stormed out after me into the hall. "Then get a lawyer," she growled, pointing a finger between my eyes. "You're going to need one."

The finger was a bit much, but her tone was actually quite believable. "I'm not guilty!" I let myself spiral up into panic. "I've only *heard* things, I haven't done anything myself! How could I—last year I was in New York!"

"Someone has died," Sadiq said, advancing on me. "If you

don't tell us what you know, there will be *consequences.* Don't leave town. We'll be picking you up tomorrow, if we aren't at your door tonight."

At that, she slammed her way through the door back to the squad room, leaving me, lost and forlorn-looking, to gape after her.

(Really, I was proud. She wasn't a bad actor. And I knew the lines I'd given her were realistic, as Detective Shepard had once used them on me in earnest.)

"Um," a voice said. "Are you okay?"

A boy was behind me, frozen in the door of his interrogation room. One of the comfortable ones, from the look of it.

"Oh my God," I said, wiping at my eyes. "I'm sorry. I didn't see you there."

"No—I, uh. They, like, threw the door open and told me I could go, but then you were, um. Out there."

As she'd promised, Sadiq had excellent timing.

"Can you walk me out?" I said to Sebastian Wallis. "I feel sort of shaky."

He agreed, swinging his bag over his shoulder. I kept my head down until we made it clear of the front doors, and then, halfway down to the street, I swayed a little, clutching at the railing.

"Hey, hey, hey," he said, grabbing my arm to steady me. "Slow down. Do you need to find a place to sit?"

I didn't. I needed to ride the momentum all the way out of the police station to a place where this boy I'd just met would give up some of his secrets.

He shaded his eyes, looking up the road. "We're not far from Magdalen College," he said, "and past that's the botanic garden. Have you been? It's a good place to collect yourself. I used to go there last year when I needed to . . . escape."

We wandered up the bridge, the spiny thrust of the Magdalen Tower in the distance. The small talk we were making was exceedingly small: where I'd grown up, where I'd gone to school. I didn't lie, but I also didn't provide too much information. (These days, my surname was too much information.) He told me more or less the same. He'd grown up outside of Bristol, and it was where he was this summer, scooping ice cream at a shop before he went off to Bath Spa to study communications.

"I took the train in this morning. I got a call late last night from the detectives that they wanted me back in, that Dr. Larkin . . ." Sebastian swallowed. "I'd known it wasn't over, but I hadn't expected *murder*."

I let the silence hang between us. "I'm worried," I said finally, as we approached the ticket window. There was a short line, as it was a weekday: a girl in a Ramones shirt, a man wearing a baby in a sling, juggling her as she fussed. At the gate, we showed our student IDs—Sebastian still had his in his wallet from last summer—and paid. "My boyfriend is living with these Dramatics Soc kids, and there's something off about them."

Sebastian slowed, then sped up, shouldering past the people ahead of us. I followed. We ducked through a wrought-iron gate and into one of those wonderful wide-open spaces that

Oxford had in abundance—an expanse of vivid green wound through with walkways, and beyond, a hedge maze. Watson would tell you more, I'm sure, but I wasn't considering the flora.

A fountain burbled water up into the air, and I cut across the grass toward it. After a moment, Sebastian followed.

"Is that what you were talking to the police about?" he asked, sitting beside me on the wet marble. "His roommates?" I nodded.

"Are they . . . Theo Harding? And Rupert Davies? And Anwen Ellis? Just by chance?"

I nodded again.

"Huh," he said, and I said nothing.

The fewer words while drawing someone out, the more you were often given in return.

Sebastian Wallis held out a good long while. He was a small boy—small feet, small ears, a small upturned nose. He had a sprightliness to him that suggested its root word, *sprite,* and I wondered if he had been cast as one of the fairies in *Midsummer* before that production had fallen apart. I'd been surprised by his burst of fellow-feeling that had led him to suggest gardens; the most I'd hoped for was a brief conversation on the street, a suggestion of the next tree I needed to shake. And yet he'd led the two of us here, and nothing about him suggested malicious intentions.

He had something he needed to say. That was a commonality I was finding amongst the players in this case—this need to *express,* to *speak,* to be *seen.*

Sebastian squinted straight ahead, massaging his small

hands. "I can't tell you much," he said. "Especially since the police still want to talk to you. If I've learned anything, it's that there are consequences for doing the right thing."

I nodded. I, too, was familiar with this lesson.

"Last summer, they wanted nothing to do with me. I wasn't rich, or some artistic genius, or a hot girl. I was just their stupid suitemate who worked theater tech and stayed out of their way." He stood. "The day after Matilda disappeared, I was in Anwen's room, and I had this . . . feeling. I looked around. I found some . . . weird things in there. Have you been there yet?"

"I haven't been to the dorms yet," I said, cursing myself. Why on earth hadn't I gone there first? "My boyfriend's been staying with me."

The stakes had shifted only last night. It wasn't even noon. And still it felt like I was running out of time.

"It doesn't matter now," he said. "Matilda's gone for good. Dead. Locked in someone's garden shed. Who knows. And everyone else . . . they'll just drop one at a time, until there's no one left."

Above us, the sun took its watery light behind a cloud. In the sudden wash of shadow, the birds went louder, louder, calling for something that refused to answer.

"Go look in Anwen's room," he said, already walking away. "Then get your boyfriend out of there."

fifteen

I SAT IN THAT GARDEN LONGER THAN I'D LIKE TO ADMIT.

Meet me in the main quad, I'd texted Watson, and he was there as I made my way over the freshly trimmed grass. He nodded his head toward his building, and the two of us ducked inside, out of the late morning.

"I thought I was going to the station with you," he said, holding the door.

"You were sleeping," I said. He was put out, I could tell, so I continued. "You were very handsome while you were sleeping."

His lips quirked. "Too handsome to be useful?"

"One can't have everything," I told him, and he caught my hand and squeezed it.

"It's fine. It gave me a chance to talk with Theo this morning, over coffee. I pressed gently on the Anwen thing from last night, but he's all clammed up. He changed the subject to orchids."

"What about them?"

We'd reached his stairwell and paused at the door; his common room was within earshot.

Watson adjusted the straps of his backpack. "Well, we haven't really considered the . . . *finickiness* of orchids."

"'We,'" I scoffed. "*I* certainly have. Did you know that only older forests grow the sort of fungi that feeds the variety of orchid called *Goodyera pubescens*—"

"You're making that up."

"I promise you, I'm not making up mushroom facts for your amusement."

"*Pubescens*? Pubescent orchid?" He snorted. "Has it grown a little stupid mustache? Does it skateboard?"

"Watson."

"You were the one suggesting that I haven't stopped to consider one of the key aspects of this case—"

"You hadn't," I said mildly.

He groaned. "So, this morning, Theo and I were talking, and like . . . right, some of them only eat really old mushrooms. You have to feed some of them with an eyedropper. With honey. Some of them can't deal with shade *or* sun. And they're bloody expensive. It's not like there's just a garden patch of these that the Orchid Killer—"

"Has he been officially promoted from Orchid Attacker?"

"—that the Orchid Killer is harvesting them from," Watson said. "Someone is spending a lot of time in a greenhouse, or stealing them from someone who does."

"Well," I said. "When that sheet-ghost fell on me, the culprit thought it funny to hang an orchids *calendar* beside the door. Someone didn't have access to their flowers anymore. Or we're dealing with someone else entirely."

He shifted his weight foot to foot. "I brought my backpack," he said. "I can act like I'm here to switch some stuff out, though almost everything I own is over at your flat. Is there anything you need me to do?"

"If Theo or Rupert is home, we'll need to roust them from their rooms. I don't want any witnesses."

"Gotcha," he said, and opened the door. "After you, pumpkin."

The rooms in St. Genesius were arranged this way, in stairwells that connected a small number of bedrooms to a common area with a kitchen and a few worn-in couches. We came through the kitchen first, which was unoccupied, though an electric kettle was switched on on the counter. The shelves were largely bare, as you'd imagine from summer students in undergraduate housing, but a sad-looking little saucepan was drying upside down next to the sink. Quickly, I searched the cabinets for a pair of drinking glasses, and we headed upstairs before someone could come down to find us.

We stopped off first in Watson's room so he could drop his empty backpack. I took a minute to marvel at the space he'd been given. Tall ceilings that sloped with the ceiling of the turret. A full-sized bed, chairs and a coffee table, a pair of casement windows that overlooked the St. Genesius chapel. The walls were plastered white. A fireplace at the far corner was heaped with wood, and I walked over to touch it. It looked a hundred years old.

Watson leaned against the wall. "I want to use that to dramatically burn a letter at least once before this program's over."

"Fireplaces," I informed him, "are wasted on teenage boys."

"I'm not arguing with you there." He dropped his voice. "They requested the same rooms they'd had last year. Theo's to the left, Rupert to the right. Anwen has the little room at the very top next to the bathroom."

I handed him one of the drinking glasses. "You take Theo," I said, and put the mouth of mine against the closest wall.

"Really?" he said, interested. "This works?"

I held a finger up to my lips, leaning forward and backward until I came across a decent spot to listen. I could hear the radiator rattling away, the creak of a window sash in the slight wind. After a few minutes, I straightened.

"Nothing," I murmured, and joined Watson at the other wall. His brow was furrowed with concentration; he was still moving the glass against the wall as one would a stethoscope against a human chest. But if Theo were in there, he was sleeping. The only sound either of us could hear was the quiet chatter of the students on the quad, someone beginning to strum a guitar.

"Upstairs," I said, and Watson followed.

There, I put my glass to Anwen's door, but her room was

quiet except for the whirring of her fan, something I noted uneasily. White noise; I couldn't listen around that. The door was locked—another difficult detail to explain away if we were caught inside. Sighing, I pulled my picks from my bag and got to work.

"To think," Watson said, "I used to wonder why girls carried purses."

"We need somewhere to keep our mace." I smiled as the lock shifted and gave under my hands. "Will you keep watch on the landing? Think of some suitable explanation if we're caught."

He leaned to look inside. "As long as your plan isn't to go out that window," he said, taking in the fourth-story view.

"My father trained me for every eventuality," I said, and left the door cracked as I slipped inside.

While Watson's cavernous room was as bare as when he'd moved in, Anwen's was small and alive. At first, I had the confusing impression that I'd stumbled into a spiderweb: her walls were electric with ragged, moving white. I moved closer, extending a hand, and as my hand touched the wall, my eyes finally recognized a pattern. A series of patterns. She'd hung layers and layers of vintage lace, cut down to handkerchief squares, and pinned them with wooden clothespins to wire that she'd extended across the wall. Her windows had been left open, and the breeze coming through shuffled and reshuffled them, lifted the fringe on her window seat cushions.

There wasn't much else in that space. A twin bed, heaped in light blankets, with a stack of pillows arranged for reading. A desk, bare but for the oscillating fan I'd heard outside. A shelf of books above it. (She hadn't left her laptop, though I didn't imagine I'd be able to crack into it in the time I had now.) And a wardrobe that spanned the length of the remaining wall, stuffed so full that its wooden doors wouldn't latch across its contents.

I opened it with care.

This, I realized, would take longer than five minutes.

I'd known Anwen had designed costumes, made her own clothes and bits and bobs for friends; I'd taken the lace wallpaper she'd concocted as a tasteful way of storing a number of fabric samples. But still the closet in front of me was shocking in its exuberance.

Before I did anything else, I snapped photos with my phone to keep as a reference. And then, in the quick, neat-handed way I'd been trained, I removed the evidence and cataloged it on the floor.

A peacock-blue silk dress with a drop waist and a rhinestone-embellished Peter Pan collar. A vintage 1960s majorette costume, with full skirt and brass buttons. A marabou-feathered flapper dress with a belt, and behind it a second, identical, except made up in red instead of champagne.

It was wild, all of it, more costumes than clothing, and I could feel my deductive faculties rioting against the restrictions I'd placed on myself. I badly wanted to hunt for patterns, to figure out the girl from the clothes. Instead I forced myself to focus on minutiae: Did these have designer labels? Was there any hint that they weren't what they seemed to be, a closet full of vintage "finds" assembled with a sniper's accuracy—were they instead purchased at huge markup from a London resale shop or similar?

Nothing that I could tell from my cursory inspection. I was furious that I didn't have more time, not the least for myself. My profession calls for me to be an artist of a different kind, and below my searching hands were a hundred different selves I could slip on to wear like weapons.

But I'd taken too much time already. Before I returned each piece to the wardrobe, I examined it thoroughly, then around its sides and back; had it held secrets, I would have found them. Cursing quietly, I put back the clothes the way I'd seen them and shut the doors.

I could hear Watson lean heavily against the wall.

"No one's coming?" I asked.

"We're clear," he said.

I opened the drawers under the bed (a pair of jeans with the tags on, tights in their packaging, black boots shined to a polish), the drawers to the desk (a jewelry box, locked; a notebook with pages trimmed in rose gold—blank; three blue pens—new; a cloth bag full of ribbons; a pair of sunglasses). Her toiletries would be in the bathroom.

Shutting the final drawer, I realized that there wasn't a single thing in this room to remind Anwen of a place outside its walls.

No photographs. No cards from friends. No notes, no ephemera, no trinkets. Nothing that had the slightest bit of wear, the slightest bit of story. Nothing but those clothes.

I wasn't unfamiliar with this aesthetic, or with how it unnerved me. There had been girls back at Sherringford who kept their rooms like pristine film sets for their Instagram shoots. I don't doubt that this made them happy. I understood, too, that a six-week summer program like this wasn't necessarily long enough to want to bring your whole life along. But as someone who spent her life reading history into trifles, walking into a room washed clean of its owner made me feel as though I'd stepped right through a ghost.

I moved through these thoughts quickly as I stood at the window. Sebastian Wallis had told me to check Anwen's room, and I had. It was, indeed, strange, but it wasn't as strange as his terse warning had implied.

Below, the quad had emptied out, students having rushed off to lunch or to their next lecture. All except for a brunet boy ambling along the path that bisected the lawn, his hands in his pockets. I knelt on the window seat and put my head out to make sure of who he was.

"Watson," I said, turning. "Rupert's on his way."

"Hurry up, then," he whispered back.

I leaned back to put a foot down on the floor when I heard the window seat groan below me. Frowning, I stood, pushing off the pillows, the raw-edged silk covering below them.

The seat was a storage bench.

I'm not sure what I expected; largely, I try not to expect anything at all. Life is emphatically disappointing to those who expect it to be otherwise. Still, I was put out to find another stack of improbable clothing folded neatly in a series of garment bags.

I unzipped them, quickly, one by one. Velvet shifts; wide-legged corduroy pants; a faux-fur jacket with oversized lapels. Winter clothing, all of it too unseasonable to wear. It was odd for it to be here, but not incredibly so—she might have a job away from home between the end of her time at Oxford and when she began at Cambridge; she might not have storage at her house; she might be estranged from her family, as I was, and not welcome to keep her things at their house.

I was tucking the final piece back into its bag when I felt a sharp prick in my finger. A pin, most likely. I stuck my finger into my mouth and attempted to wrestle the coat back in one-handed. I had no intention of leaving bloodstains.

"Holmes," Watson said, low. The stairwell door had just slammed shut.

"Just a moment," I said, leaning forward to straighten it with my elbow. My brain was listing away what it saw, the way it always did: the cut of the coat, the name on the lapel (Guy Laroche), the bit of stitching that had come undone in the lining, the—

The name penned onto the label, in the tiniest possible handwriting.

Larissa.

Footfalls up the stairs, slow ones.

"Holmes," Watson said.

Cursing, I lifted up the garment bag and checked the one

below. The corduroy pants. A different store on the label. The same name on the tag.

Larissa.

The dresses, the silk blouses, the cashmere sweaters—the name, or the initial. *Larissa; L; L.*

"Hallo!" Rupert, calling from downstairs. The kitchen. "Anyone home? I'm making popcorn! Beastly time with the police . . ."

I dropped the window seat and threw the cloth over it, the pillows. There wasn't any time, I knew that, but I threw myself on the wardrobe anyway. The clothes inside were packed together too tightly for me to separate one-handed—even if my one hand wasn't bleeding.

Moments. I had moments. I shucked off my jacket, then my shirt, and I wrapped the material around my hand to keep from leaving marks with my bleeding fingers.

There—

The majorette outfit: *L.* The flapper dress: *L.* The blue silk: *Larissa.*

"Anwen?" His steps were coming up the stairs now; I could hear the popcorn swishing in the bowl. "You here? I know you were upset . . ."

Shaking his head violently, Watson backed into the room on his toes. His eyes widened when he saw me. *You're in your bra!* he mouthed. *What the* hell, *Holmes—*

I gestured frantically with my bleeding hand.

"Anwen?" Rupert was almost on us.

"Goddammit," Watson said, out loud, and kicked the door

shut with his foot. He grabbed his T-shirt by the collar and pulled it over his head.

"Oh!" I said, surprised. "I get it."

"Do you, now," he said, a bit hoarsely, and took my hips in his hands, pulling me to him. His pulse was quick, his eyes gone black with fear or with something else, and in the moment before Rupert could open the door, Watson pushed me up against the wardrobe and put his lips to the hollow of my throat.

The door swung open.

"Shit, shit, shit," Rupert said. "Guys! Shit!"

With a clatter, the bowl of popcorn overturned on the floor. Watson stumbled backward, and I spun to face the wardrobe.

"What are you guys doing!" he yelled. "Guys! Why are you naked!"

"I mean," I said into the wardrobe door. "The usual reasons?"

"I'm so sorry, dude," Watson said, reaching for his shirt.

Rupert dropped to his hands and knees. "Your room is *downstairs*," he said, picking up handfuls of popcorn and throwing the kernels back into the bowl. "Ugh, it's all covered in dust now."

Watson got down to help him. He glanced up at me, a clear *your move*.

"I know, but Jamie's room was locked, and he forgot his keys," I said sheepishly, "and my uncle is at my flat and so we came here, and . . . things just kind of got out of hand?"

"Right," Rupert said. "Obviously."

"We were in the bathroom," Watson said, "but we heard you coming up and she panicked and ran in here and I just kind of followed." He dusted his hands off and gave Rupert his most winning smile.

Rupert picked up the bowl, rattling it nervously. "I'm sorry. I'm being a grouch. Anwen would have a little bit of a fit over this if she knew, so let's not tell her, all right? I'll sweep up here in a moment."

"Bad day?" I asked. I was still pressing my front into the wardrobe.

He glanced up at me, colored pink, and snapped his eyes back to the ground. "How about—ah. How about we talk about it downstairs? I'll make some more popcorn!"

"That's a great plan," Watson said, clapping him on the back. "Charlotte and I will be right down after we've . . . recombobulated."

As Watson and I dressed, I listened carefully to Rupert descending the stairs. And there it was, what I'd expected: the slightest rattle as he tried the handle on Watson's door. Making sure it was, in fact, locked.

Of course, since I am the girl I am, it was.

sixteen

"That was your brilliant plan?" I whispered. I turned my T-shirt so the spatter of blood faced my back, then slipped my jacket on over the top.

"You," he said, sitting on the bed, "were in a state of *déshabillé.*"

"Since when do you speak French?"

"I did suffer through two solid years of class with Monsieur Cann," he said. "I wasn't sleeping the *whole* time."

"No, of course not. You woke up during the lesson on how to describe the scandalously underdressed."

"I also know *in flagrante,*" he said, "and *coitus interruptus*—"

"That's Latin," I protested, but he was laughing.

"I hope it was worth it." He swept a hand across the room. "Did you find what you needed?"

"I always do."

Watson's eyes crinkled at the corners. He didn't pry further. How glorious that was; it gave my mind time to sort and contextualize what I'd found. "Come on, then," he said. "Rupert's waiting for us downstairs."

In the kitchen, Rupert had a bag of popcorn spluttering away in the microwave, and the kettle was already boiling for tea. "Forgot to turn it off when I went to the shops," he said. There was a string bag full of vegetables on the counter. "Thought I'd make something nice for dinner, for a change."

"That's hard to do on a hot plate," Watson said, settling down at the table.

"I know." From the cupboard, Rupert took down a trio of mugs, horrible novelty ones, WORLD'S BEST GRANDMA written in red and another with a penguin-shaped handle. "Anwen and I had a hard morning, though, and I thought maybe she'd like something home-cooked for a change. Just a stir-fry. Nothing complex." He bit his lip. "Have you ever made a stir-fry?"

Watson's eyes darted from Rupert to me. I'd never profess to reading Watson's mind—I am not actually psychic—but I knew him well enough to guess what he was thinking. Wondering if I wanted to take the lead. I shook my head slightly.

"I think I could help you figure it out," he said. "Unrelatedly, adulthood kind of sucks."

Rupert set a mug in front of Watson, one in front of me. "I don't know if our version does, actually. There are so many different kinds of adulthood—only depending on yourself for your survival, or supporting others with a small salary, or doing work you aren't equipped for, or that you're far too *over*-equipped for . . . responsibilities that we most likely won't see, as Oxford students, for some time. We're privileged. It's best to be aware of that. If my worst problem is that I don't know how to cook . . ."

"Are you close with your parents?" I asked as Watson fetched the popcorn from the microwave, holding the bag at its edges.

"Fairly close," Rupert said. "Closer with my father than my mother. She runs the bulk of the business, you know. Wasn't the case when they met—they married while my father was being groomed to inherit the company—but she has a head for it that he doesn't."

"So she's in charge, then?"

"Right. And my father manages more of our day-to-day lives. I mean, I imagine he still does. I've been away at school for a while now." Rupert shrugged. "I've never really understood businesses that pass down through a family. Financial reasons, sure. Fine. But it's almost a kind of erasure, don't you think? What if you could've cured cancer, or something, and instead someone before you were born decided you should make spreadsheets all day?" He jerked the bag open, and steam poured out. "For some reason they think I should step up, when my father got to dodge the noose. Bicker on the phone with bankers. Chase down payments from far-flung members of the royal family. Have you ever *tried* to get a royal to settle a past-due debt? Speaking of blood from a stone . . . of course it was just oversight, but . . ." His ever-running engine finally ran out of steam. Sighing, he stuffed a handful of popcorn into his mouth.

His interview at the station this morning had rattled him. It was either that, or this is what Rupert was like away from the stifling presence of his friends: a thoughtful, anxious sort, someone whose mouth raced ahead of his brain. Still, I knew something about family businesses and unrealistic expectations and how those things could wear on you. "That's hard. I hate that feeling. What would you be doing otherwise?" I asked. "If you weren't working for your family?"

He shrugged, chewing. "Theater?" he said finally. "I still can't believe that casting. Of course, it's not like the play will run now, it's all moot . . . but to think that I could do Hamlet. *Here.* Last summer, I only helped out in the sound booth."

"That's not easy," Watson pointed out.

"It is if the tech in charge won't let you do anything. It was clear they'd just made space for me so I could hang around with Anwen and Theo. Kind of them, but a bit condescending." He pushed the paper bag to the middle of the table, and I picked out a few kernels, held them in my palm. "I hate it, you know," he said, looking at my hands. "That feeling of being . . . unneeded."

Sebastian Wallis had said more or less the same thing earlier. What was it, I wondered, about Anwen and Theo, their bright exclusivity, that kept even their best friend on the outskirts? And despite all that, Theo despised something about Anwen, something he couldn't bring himself to say out loud.

"You've escaped them, though," Rupert was saying. "Your family."

"Have I?" I asked, with a tight smile.

"Sure," he said earnestly. "Of course you have. You aren't studying . . . whatever you would study to be a detective."

"I'd be at training college," I told him. "You begin as a uniform. Work your way up. Unless you're my bohemian great-great-great-grandfather a century or so ago, in which case you do two years at Oxford, leave for unknown reasons, and take cases from Baker Street. But no. I'm not studying any of that. The more time I spend doing detective work, the less that I like it."

"Really?" Rupert asked, interested. Watson was watching me intently. "What don't you like?"

I was treading uncertain ground here. This wasn't new, of course. My work often called on me to be a chameleon—my shape stayed the same while my skin began to shift colors.

I've said before that the way to convincingly lie is to be convinced of what you're saying. In the moment, you need to believe it. Thoroughly. To wit: in order to convince Rupert to trust me enough to come clean about his experience this morning with the police (and in doing so, unintentionally give up information he'd kept from them), I would need to persuade him that I, like him, wanted to escape my family business (detection).

Why was this complicated?

Because, perhaps, after escaping my family, after using my skills to escape Lucien Moriarty (if barely), I was finding that, maybe, I *did* want to escape my family business. At least this version of it. At least for a time. In order to uphold the law, I had to continually break it, and while I didn't have personal compunctions about breaking into someone's dorm room to sack it for clues, or to lie to someone to get them to tell you the truth, the more I did it, the more I started to lose the plot.

Perhaps I wanted to be a chemist. Perhaps I wanted to be a gardener, or jewel thief, or a beekeeper. Perhaps I wanted to be a detective after all. But three months ago, I was an invalid, and three months before that, I was on the run from someone who wanted my head on a platter.

All I knew was that I wanted Watson with me. But I also knew that the girl with informant status with the Thames Valley Police and a lockpicking kit in her purse was infinitely more compelling than the girl I was becoming now. Someone who wanted to eat Nutella toast on the sofa while rereading the encyclopedia article on waxwings, because she thought she'd seen one in the garden.

That girl wasn't nearly as compelling. Wasn't as clever or as dangerous. Wasn't the kind of girl you followed anywhere.

I wasn't giving Watson enough credit. I knew that. It didn't stop me from being afraid.

"Interrogations," I was telling Rupert. "I don't like them. The detective's allowed to keep you there for hours. Leave abruptly. Come back. Dig into the most private parts of your life. Lie to you about your lover seeing someone else behind your back. Insist you were somewhere you know you weren't and then convince you of it. Confuse you. Frighten you, badly, start you babbling. Or make you think that they're your best friend, that they agree with everything you've done. That they understand the part of you that killed that girl, that she had it coming, yeah? The way she was looking at that other guy. Offer you coffee, then take the cup 'to throw it out for you' so they can test your saliva at their lab. All of it . . . the way the police operate is so foreign to me. It isn't how my family solves crimes. I was taught to treat the suspect's confession as a sacred act, as someone bringing you an offering. The two of you could decide together what you did with it."

My feelings on interrogation practices were far more complex than this little speech suggested. These methods were the kind that found missing girls like Matilda Wilkes. That said, there *had*, in fact, been many times when Sherlock Holmes had heard his culprit's story and decided to let them escape into the night, rather than sending for Scotland Yard.

Judge, jury, stay of execution.

My father and my brother took a page from this book, but their decisions tended toward the bloodier side.

Luckily, Rupert couldn't see inside my head. He was nodding along, as I knew he would. "It's all mind games. And these are the people who are supposed to protect us? Please."

Watson stretched; his back popped. "Trust me, Charlotte and I have been there. You should've seen the shady shit the American cops pulled on us, during the first investigation we helped solve."

"It's just unfair," Rupert said. "They separated Anwen and me and I could hear her crying in the next room. And the detective, she was asking all these questions about last year. I could tell she didn't like my answers, but I was telling the truth! What do you say to that?"

"Double down," Watson said. "You know the real story. Don't let them bully you into admitting to things you didn't do." He talked like he was rubbing Rupert's shoulders in a boxing ring, playing to his sense of urgency.

"It wasn't even my story," Rupert said, voice rising. "It's like they were trying to . . . write me into something I didn't know about. They kept asking if I'd spoken to Matilda!"

"Have you?" I asked.

"No!" he exploded, and there it was, the payoff. "No one knows where she is! She was *Theo's* girlfriend, she was cold as ice, and even if none of that mattered, she's *gone*! Anwen tried to send her a text last night about Dr. Larkin . . . none of us were thinking straight, and I don't know, maybe Anwen forgot for a moment that Matilda was missing, and the police *won't let it go*. Like that weird slipup means that she kidnapped her. Or like she knows that she's alive, that she just ran away." Rupert slammed a hand flat onto a table, a gesture so out of keeping with his usual bumbling pleasantness that Watson jumped. "They're upsetting Anwen. They can't do that."

The phrasing was odd. *They can't do that*. Because they're adults and should know better? Because treating Anwen this way would have consequences?

What consequences?

I stood and put a hand on Rupert's shoulder, taking my mug to the kettle for more hot water. Now that Watson had him going, it was best to let him take the lead. "Are you worried Anwen's going to bolt or something?" Watson asked. "It seemed like, last night, when you left together . . . was there something going on?"

"She went to take a call right after we got outside," Rupert said miserably. "I waited up for her, but it was hours before she got home. Hours. I tried texting her. I waited in the kitchen so I could tell if she'd gotten home safe, but . . ." He looked from me to Watson and back again, not wanting to ask, and then he steeled himself and said, "She came back up for Theo, didn't she."

"Actually, no," Watson said. "Theo passed out on our couch. He was there all night, we had breakfast together this morning. I think . . . Anwen was somewhere else."

Rupert bobbled his head up and down a few times, like a ball floating in a bath. "Okay," he said jerkily. "Well. Good thing I told the detectives she did, then. That she went back and shagged him senseless. I told you, they wanted me to confess to something, they kept *digging*, and that was what I gave them. And it isn't true? Good thing I *embarrassed* myself in front of them. No. It's fine. I—"

"Rupert—"

He blew out a deep breath. "I'm worked up about nothing," he said. "She'll have a reason." I could tell he believed it. "A good one. I'm just being a baby. But yeah. Yeah, I should look up some stir-fry recipes. I'll be fine, Jamie, won't need your help. Good. Excellent. I should get to it—I'll go ahead and see you all later—"

That was all we were getting from him today, that much was clear. Still, I watched him for a minute from the hall. Pacing, searching through recipes on his phone, heating up the sad little hotplate. His sweet, delicate face, his pointed chin, the slub neck of his too-expensive T-shirt.

Though I knew it wouldn't matter, I hoped that his stir-fry turned out brilliantly.

"Anwen," Watson said, as we walked out onto the quad, some distance from their open windows.

"Anwen," I echoed. "Always Anwen. I have a few thoughts about our next step . . ."

But he was shaking his head. "Love," he said—that word was new between us; I watched the way he said it, the slope of his shoulders, the slight step toward me—"I have a story due, beginning of next week, that I haven't even started. I'm going to explore the Bodleian Library, I think. Find a spot to sit in there where no one has written anything brilliant before."

"It's a very old library," I said. "In Oxford. You might be setting yourself up for failure."

"Nothing new, then," he said.

"No," I agreed.

He snorted. "You're awful."

"Yes, but you're a bit silly." I took a step forward, and only then did I realize I was presenting myself to be kissed. I tried very hard to keep from blushing.

But Watson leaned down to brush his lips against mine.

As he pulled away, I found myself listing forward, wanting more, wanting to follow him home like a shadow in the night. "No one," he said softly, "sees you like . . . like this, do they?"

"You do," I said, though for how much longer I couldn't say.

seventeen

As I walked back to my flat, I took my phone off silent and saw that I had a number of missed calls. Two messages. The first, from my aunt Araminta: "Lottie, hello. Leander tells me he's spoken to you about my upcoming visit. I'm calling to say that my plans have changed; one of my potential clients has rescheduled for tomorrow, so I'll be coming in tonight on the six forty-two from Eastbourne. I won't be in your hair, of course, but I'd like to see you and your friend for dinner. Or perhaps a coffee? A drink? Ah. Perhaps I shouldn't be suggesting that? . . . Give me a call . . ."

The second, from DI Sadiq: "Holmes. Got a call back from George Wilkes. Told him about Larkin, and requested his presence at the station to go over some information. He's on his way from London, but he won't get in until tomorrow afternoon, when I'll be off shift. Maybe you and I can work out a time to talk in the morning, run through any questions you think are pertinent?"

I confirmed with Araminta for tonight; I confirmed Sadiq for tomorrow morning. I texted Watson about both, and then caught a bus home to clean up the flat before my aunt arrived and drew conclusions, accurate or not, about her niece's lifestyle.

There really had been a lot of rum last night.

As I did the washing up, I ran through the list of investigative avenues I hadn't yet gone down. Though I'd done cursory social media searches for everyone I'd met in this case, I hadn't found anything more compelling than some general (quite natural) alarm about the attacks. Had I the resources, I'd be pulling phone records and sorting through suspects' email accounts. But outside of DI Sadiq, my brother Milo was the only one I knew with that ability, and I wanted him and his methods nowhere near this case.

Again it struck me, the difficulties of participating in a full-scale investigation of this kind with one hand tied behind my back, as it were. As I scrubbed another glass tumbler, I thought about what I'd told Rupert. How my forebear had said, to wit, *fuck it all*, and abandoned university to take cases from his armchair. Only those cases that were otherwise overlooked. Only those cases that only he, and he alone, could solve.

Oh, it was tempting. Wildly tempting. I turned the tumbler

in the light, looking for spots then scrubbing it again, and I told myself I wouldn't make any decisions, not yet. Not when I had a case to wrap up and a flat to clean.

An hour or so later, I took my cloth bags down to the market to replenish our pantry. Our "guests" the night before had cleaned us out, and I wanted to be a good host for my aunt, as well as cover my own ass, as it were. I'd texted to ask Leander when he was planning on coming home, and I hadn't yet had a response, but it was better to battle two thousand armies in the driving rain than to face Leander Holmes having eaten all his Jaffa cakes.

I finished my shopping an hour or so before Araminta's train was set to arrive. Rather than heading straight home, I found myself taking a path through St. Genesius College. It was blocks out of my way, but the day was cool and clear, and I enjoyed the swing of the heavy bag along my side, the tap of my boots on the pavement. The theater, when I passed it, was bare of the blockades and tape the police had put up that morning.

A constable was sitting on the marble steps, extravagantly bored.

Despite the incredible leeway DI Sadiq had been allowing me, my status as an official informant didn't let me into crime scenes, and I found myself increasingly in no mood to bluff my way into places I shouldn't be. Still, I checked my watch. I had the time. I tucked my bag under my arm and moved with purpose, past the constable on the steps, along the brick path that wound around the theater.

The other day, as I'd explored the basement, I had heard wisps of sound coming from the street. There had been another way in; surely Sadiq's team had found it as they'd locked down the building. As I walked, I traced the foundation of the theater with my eyes. As I'd suspected, it had been built on a hill, and the lower level was exposed around the back, covered in trailing vines.

There was a pair of high windows covered in intricate grating, too small for anything but a squirrel to sneak through; there was a metal folding chair and an ashtray heaped with cigarette ends from whatever uniform had been out here last night. There were no doors, at least not that I could see, but there was also no one around. It was a matter of a minute's search with my hands to find the utility door, hidden under the ivy like something from a children's story. I made short work of the lock, but the door was surprisingly heavy. I had to brace my feet and power through it with my shoulder, and behind me the ivy swung out like the hem of a long, strange skirt.

I thought again of Anwen and her strange collection of clothing, piled in her wardrobe like outfits pulled off a paper doll.

With a growing sense of disquiet, I pressed my hands against the door until I felt it latch.

Then I turned, only to rear back directly into the door.

A forest?

I had stumbled into a *forest*, somehow, the trees all hung with lanterns, the branches bending down like the longest fingerbones. Before me, a fir tree, another, a stone house in the distance. I reached out carefully, and as my fingers brushed against cloth, I pieced together what I was seeing.

Canvas. It was a set. I was at the end of an unlit hallway that had been used to store the backdrops from productions past. Shaking my head at myself, I hefted my cloth bag over my shoulder and picked my way through the landscapes before me.

A desert, lovingly rendered by someone who had never seen a desert, festooned with the required glimmering oasis in its distance. A Romanesque colonnade, the long rows of columns stretching out to disappear in a fountain. I ran my hand over its smooth surface. Wooden benches; a gilded throne on casters, paint chipping around the lions' heads that made up its armrests; a streetlamp, patinated as though it had come straight out of Victorian London, leaning against a wall.

This maze of places and props was so dense as to block out any light that might have leaked in around the door. But the path I was taking . . . I wasn't the first one to do it. Someone had picked their way through here before.

I took out my phone and switched on its flashlight, training it on the floor. Scuffed linoleum. No way to check for prints. But there—and there—and there. Petals. Dried up on the ground.

Fallen from an orchid handled too roughly in the dark.

Quickly, I stooped to take photographs, but I left the petals where they were. Tomorrow, if I was feeling particularly invincible, I would pass the photos on to Sadiq for her own purposes.

With my phone out, I checked the time again. Half past five, and nothing frozen in my shopping bag. Since I'd made my way into the building, I decided to satisfy my curiosity about the lighting rig. I crept out slowly from behind the final backdrop (a confectioner's shop, painted kindergarten-bright) and to the bottom of the stairs that led up to the stage.

Voices up above. Quiet ones. Assured. A team from the Thames Valley Police, perhaps, collecting evidence. But as I turned to go, I heard a man's frustrated exclamation, a foot slammed hollowly against the stage's sprung floor. I eased my bag onto the floor, then slipped up the dark stairs and backstage, taking care to keep out of the light.

A blond boy, tall and broad-shouldered, his arms crossed as though he was hugging himself. Theo, his face a mask for all it showed, and across from him, a man with his back to me. Graying hair, expensive shoes, trousers tailored far more fashionably than I'd have expected for a man of his age.

When he spoke, he spoke the queen's English. An accent native to nowhere. It had to be bred into you. "I've been waiting," he said. "In your position, it's poor form to keep someone waiting, especially when you demanded to meet them."

"You didn't say you'd be getting in so early," Theo protested, and something—the note of fear, his half step backward—urged me to take out my phone to film the rest of what I saw. "Besides, I had to talk my way past the officer out front, and that took forever."

"What did you tell him?"

Theo lifted his chin. "That I'm directing the production of

Hamlet that's going up next month, and that I had to meet my costume designer inside. What did you tell him?"

"Does it matter?" The man scoffed. "The school won't allow you to run this production."

They were speaking very quietly, but the acoustics caught their words and carried them into the corners of the building. Beyond them, in the auditorium, the seats unrolled up and out into the shadows.

"I talked to Quigley today. They canceled the production this morning. But I told him I'd do it myself. Without their help. And he told me—and I quote—'Do what you want, it's your funeral,'" Theo said. "Mature of him, huh? And I can't get anyone else to answer my emails. They're all too concerned with saving their own necks to lift a finger for us. But I can't waste this summer. I *can't*."

"From what I understand," the man said coldly, "you'll be at conservatory this fall. Why does this matter?"

Theo stared him down, his brow hardening. I remembered his easy grace during his audition, the force of his presence. I could see him bringing those things to bear now.

"You've never understood," Theo said. "You've never understood. Matilda told me that about you, you know that? You make this big deal about being this insider, this true *artist*, but the work you've done was never onstage. You never *breathed* it the way we did. You never really understood the alchemy of it. Your blood turning to something better, right there on that stage. We make our art from ourselves. We're the musician *and* the instrument—"

"Oh, for God's sake, do I have to listen to this pretentious nonsense—"

"Yes," Theo said, his voice breaking. "Yeah, you do. Because I got a call last Christmas from my girlfriend. My *ex*-girlfriend, I guess I should say, because she broke up with me the night before she 'disappeared'—"

"How is that any of my business?"

"—because she insisted that I knew why people were being hurt. Why did she think that? Fuck if I know—not like I could ask her, because again. She *disappeared*. Until Christmas day, when I got a call from Matilda's cell. I picked it up, and I just heard her breathing—"

"What a sad fantasy," he said.

"*—until* she said my name. She said it twice—*Theo, Theo*—and then *help*. And then it sounded like the phone was being wrestled away from her. The line went dead." Theo stared at the man, anguished. "How can I say this and have you not care? She could be chained up in some pervert's basement! She could be anywhere, *horrible* things could be happening to her, and you don't care—"

As he'd been talking, the man had begun to pace a tight, controlled path, back and forth in front of Theo like a tiger. And at that, he exploded. "You don't know a *thing* about this, boy. You're just some American piece of trash she picked up last summer! Our daughter, always hauling home the charity cases, I was used to that. But never someone like *you*. Do you know what she told me, so defiantly, before we came out to see her show last summer? 'You're going to meet Theo, my boyfriend, he's *bisexual.*' So smug, as though she'd invented acting out to get your parents' attention. I don't care what you do in bed, that's none of my business, but I told Matilda, he'll do that nowhere near my daughter—"

Theo had gone entirely white. In my hiding spot, I felt my hands begin to shake. I knew, intellectually, this kind of prejudice existed; I had seen it spewed about online, in the news, seen it bandied about like it was divine will to discriminate.

I had never seen it delivered at such close distance, with such personal hatred. I thought of my uncle Leander, and my hands tightened on my phone.

"—and so when she disappeared, I knew why. Because of you. Because of what you did to her, you—" He cut himself off with a curse.

"What did I do?" Theo said. It was almost a howl. "What the hell did I do?"

"We knew enough to tell Matilda that she was headed down a dark path," Wilkes said. "And she decided to run rather than stay with you. So there's your mystery solved. Are we finished now?"

"You're a bigot," Theo said, with a hard-fought calm that I admired. "And you would rather imagine that I had something to do with her disappearance than take this *gigantic* lead I'm handing you. I don't trust the police. They want to pin me down for this. But I thought I could trust you."

"You imagined that phone call," George Wilkes said stoutly.

"You're a selfish little boy, trying to make this all about you. My daughter is missing, and you're making light of it for your own perverted purposes."

At the top of the stage, a door opened. I wanted badly to lean out to look, but I stayed where I was.

"*Imagined* it? I . . ." Theo dragged his hands through his hair. "What are you not *telling* me?"

"It sounds like," a voice said, carrying down from the back of the auditorium, "the two of you are done discussing school business, or whatever it was you said you were doing. Both of you. Out. I don't want to ask twice."

"Yes, Officer," Theo said, and with a final loaded glance at George Wilkes, he hopped off the stage. I ended the video and shrank back farther into the darkness of the wings, and not a moment too soon—George Wilkes cast one final, dismissive look around him before he passed out of my sight.

And as for Theo?

I was hard-pressed to see him as the guilty party, anymore.

I WAITED TEN SILENT MINUTES BEFORE I PADDED BACK down the backstage stairs into the bowels of the theater. After I'd made it out the utility door, I trotted out to the high road, my shopping bag over my arm. A girl on her way home to make dinner, nothing more.

Once I was safely in my flat, I texted DI Sadiq the video. Then asked, what is George Wilkes's profession?

Theatrical costuming, Sadiq had said. Will review this before tomorrow. Thanks.

I thought, again, of Anwen's cabinet of curiosities, of Theo texting her last Boxing Day to demand what she knew. I thought of George Wilkes's fury at his helpless daughter. I thought of the stage light falling out of the sky like a bomb, and then I cleared the kitchen counter and laid out an elaborate cheese plate, because I was an adult, or at least, I was pretending to be.

eighteen

I SENT WATSON TEN QUID FOR A CAB, AND THE VIDEO I'D taken in the theater. Watch on your way over, I said. I want your opinion.

I live to do your bidding, he responded.

Thanks, I said. Pumpkin.

It was a twenty-minute walk from the station to my door, and my aunt had always believed in a "constitutional" after train travel of any length, which meant that she would arrive, with military precision, at two minutes past seven.

And she did. When she let herself up into the building, I was waiting at the door to our flat to take her jacket.

In appearance, the Holmeses fell into one of two camps:

those with a severe, clean-lined beauty, and those who looked like badly boiled eggs. In her youth, Araminta had been the former. I had seen pictures of her when she'd worked as a codebreaker for the Home Office: a tumble of black curls, her eyes glittering like jeweled knives. But in recent years, her face had begun to give way to gravity (we all do, in the end), and now the long bags underneath her eyes made her look startlingly like my great-aunt Mildred. She was slim, in sensible shoes with a sensible suitcase, but despite her neatness, she looked years older than the last time I'd seen her.

Though, when I thought about it, it had in fact been . . . years.

"Lottie," she said, wheeling her suitcase smartly against the wall. "Let me have a look at you."

I stepped forward to present myself. (A small, horrified part of me wondered if this had been what I'd done this morning to Watson—presented myself for inspection, as I'd learned growing up.) For a long moment, she studied me with those cut-glass eyes she'd had as a girl.

"You had a party last night," she said.

"Of sorts." I'd known there was no point in cleaning up. "You're not going to make me work out how you knew, are you?"

Araminta snorted. "I'm not your father."

"Thank God for small mercies."

"And this—" She swept past me into the flat, and I could hear her judgment as she looked it over. Its overstuffed chairs and bookshelves, its bright throw blankets, its *television*. "This is quite nice, actually."

I blinked. "I think so," I said cautiously.

"You seem happy," she said over her shoulder, as she floated into the kitchen like the indefatigable ship she was. "Your boyfriend—James—he stays over most nights?"

I followed behind her, trying not to stomp my feet. "Jamie. Watson, rather. And only since Leander's been out of town."

Watson, in his previous accounts of our "adventures," has spoken of the frustration inherent in holding a conversation with someone (ostensibly me) who knows all your secrets at a glance (I don't—well, not always). He'd said once it was like playing chess one-handed. I disagree. I can play chess perfectly well one-handed. Conversing with my aunt Araminta was, at times, like playing speed chess with both hands tied behind your back while someone screamed obscenities into your ear.

"*Uncle* Leander," Araminta said, sitting down at the counter. She eyed the spread I'd laid out, then picked up a cheese knife. "Honorifics, Lottie, are never wasted words."

"Yes, Aunt."

She arranged herself a plate of Brie and grapes and water crackers, then, to my surprise, passed it to me. "Eat," she said. "You're still underfed for your frame. Though, thank God, nothing like the last time I saw you."

I took the plate.

"Eat," she said again, and, obligingly, I put a thumb's worth of Brie in my mouth and chewed.

"Good girl," she said, then watched my throat until I

swallowed. "I could murder your father."

Before I could say anything to that—could I, in fact, say anything to that?—she had moved on. "Did you learn to do this from films?"

"Lay out a spread?" I asked. "I—"

"Films," she said, "or your housekeeper, or Leander. *Uncle* Leander. It's one of the three. Most likely Leander. Though I shouldn't count out your Jamie."

"Jamie doesn't know how to make a stir-fry," I told her, and then reeled at having sold him out so easily.

"He *doesn't*," she said, with delighted interest. I watched her file that away. "Fascinating. We should teach him. Eat, Charlotte."

I put a grape in my mouth. She squinted at me. I put in two more. "Also," I said, mouth full, "I don't know how to make a stir-fry."

"Of course you don't," she said. "You know how to slit a man's throat and how to get Lucien Moriarty extradited back to Britain, but you don't know how to make a stir-fry."

I nodded.

"I could kill your father," she said, "*kill* him," and at that, Watson rapped on the door.

In short order she had the three of us on the sofa, though Watson tucked himself behind me in case Araminta should want to bite him. I didn't blame him—I had a number of family members who were, in point of fact, vipers—but he shouldn't have worried. The two of them got on famously.

There aren't very many stories about my aunt. The one

that's told over and over in my family is perhaps the most dramatic—her uncovering Walter Moriarty's dastardly plot; his killing her cats in revenge—and it is also, perhaps, the only story about her they know. When Araminta quit her job at the Home Office to keep bees in Sherlock Holmes's little cottage, my family had assumed that she had quit them as well.

That she had quit the world entirely. Shriveled up like some old crone.

That night, I remembered that other people can't tell your story for you. And also that my aunt had a book club.

"I think you met my mother at a charity auction," Watson was saying, "a long time ago?"

"Oh, yes," Araminta said. "Grace is lovely. Very strong, very intelligent. I know you're worried about her after that Lucien business—"

Watson winced. It *was* a rather euphemistic way to say "a Moriarty married your mother."

"—but give her time, and she'll come out of it unscarred. I know you're worried that she blames you for it. She did warn you to never get involved with our family, didn't she?" Her eyes flitted between us. "It wasn't bad advice. But really, she doesn't blame you."

"I'm glad to hear that, but how—"

"She blames your father," Araminta said succinctly, and ate another grape.

Behind me, Watson coughed. "How exactly do you know that?" he asked, a bit strangled. "Did I say—or do—could you tell from my shoes, or—"

Her mouth twitched, and then she burst into a hearty laugh. "Oh, you poor boy. You've been running around with Lottie for far too long. I talk to your mother maybe once a month."

"Oh," Watson said, and I leaned back and squeezed his knee.

"Don't be disappointed. You don't actually want someone to read your whole history from your body. Can you imagine what I'd be able to tell about what you've done the past few days?"

Watson's eyes flickered to my bedroom door and back again.

"Dear God," she said, "*now* I know. An idiot would know. Never mind that. Have some more cheese." She pushed the cutting board toward him. "The Mimolette is very good. Lottie, did you get it at a cheesemonger?"

"Sainsbury's," I said, as behind me, Watson did his level best to disappear into the ground.

She huffed. "Well. It's very good Mimolette. Jamie. *Eat.*"

"Has Charlotte told you about our case?" Watson asked, in an admirable attempt to change the subject. He was piling up a plate. "It's *Hamlet. Hamlet*-adjacent, I guess I should say. It looks like there won't be a production after all."

"No," she said. "she hasn't. Though it's getting rather late, don't you think?"

"Late?" Watson paused. "It's half past seven—"

"But you haven't eaten," she said, heaving herself off the couch.

He and I glanced down at our heaping plates. "No," Watson ventured. "I suppose we haven't."

"You can tell me in the car," she said, gesturing us toward the door. "Your uncle does have a car, doesn't he, Lottie?"

He did, a little brown Fiat with a backseat sized for toddlers or mice, and it was there that I found myself squished in as we drove. We could have walked quite easily to most of Oxford, or taken a bus, and so in a way I wasn't surprised as she drove us out of the city and west, into the gathering night.

In the front, my aunt kept up a lively conversation with Watson, though perhaps it would be more accurate to call it an interrogation. I hoped he didn't take it personally. She took pleasure, it seemed, in asking you a question, then answering it herself. Did Watson have any siblings (*oh, you do, how could I have forgotten*) and how was Shelby doing this summer, would she come visit, did she keep in touch with Leander after he helped to free her from that horrible American school?

Watson began to respond, but Araminta shook her head, nimbly passing a Peugeot on the right. "Someone should have stepped in sooner."

"It was a mess of my own making," I reminded her quietly. "I had to sort it out."

Her fingers flexed on the steering wheel. "You," she said, "were a child, and 'sorting it out' nearly killed you both."

"Shelby's doing fine," Watson said after a moment. "Do you know the story? How Leander and my dad broke her out of that 'school' in Maine?"

He told it well. My Watson, the consummate storyteller. We had been on the run from both Lucien Moriarty and the police, and the two of us had holed up in a safehouse in New York City. We could do nothing for Shelby. Shelby, Jamie's little sister, who had always loved horses, who had a vivacious smile, who talked a mile a minute about her friends and her paintings and about L.A.D., her favorite boy band. She wanted nothing to do with Lucien Moriarty, in his guise as her mother's boyfriend, and Moriarty had used Shelby's resulting rebellion as a means to persuade Grace Watson to shuttle her to this "school" in Connecticut that was, of course, no such thing. What it was was the sort of wilderness rehabilitation/punishment facility with which I was intimately familiar. I had been threatened with many of them over the years. The difference?

Lucien Moriarty owned this one.

Araminta shook her head as if to clear it. "I never heard this story," she said quietly.

"There was nothing we could do," Watson continued. Though the police—and Lucien Moriarty—were desperately hunting us down, Watson had risked a message to his father. *Get Shelby out.* And he had gone to rescue her, Leander by his side. The drive from New York City was four hours; they had made it in two.

They'd argued the whole way about the plan. James Watson had wanted to go in with proverbial guns blazing (Shelby was his daughter; emotions tended to cloud one's judgment), while Leander, true to form, had argued for a more subtle approach. They would be state inspectors on an emergency call. They would be electricians, plumbers. They would call the local police and a judge friend of Leander's and get Shelby out the legal way.

None of it was enough for James Watson. *I want my daughter. And then, when we ride out of there, I want that place burning down behind me.*

You sound like a cowboy, Leander had scoffed, and it was then, as they'd crossed the state line, that they hit on a plan that appealed to the both of them.

"Horse thieves," Watson said, with some satisfaction. Araminta coughed in the driver's seat, but offered no commentary.

Leander had grown up taking riding lessons; James had insisted he'd worked as a trail guide in college. ("He had not," Watson said, "worked as a trail guide in college.") They'd stopped at a twenty-four-hour Walmart and changed from their formal wear into flannel shirts and Carhartts and hats to hide their faces. They bought bolt cutters, shovels, fertilizer, two long-handled lighters, and three twenty-five-packs of Saturn Missile Extremely Loud Fireworks.

They'd paid for it all in cash.

After parking the car in the woods, they'd approached the facility on foot. The "school" was protected by a twelve-foot-high fence crowned with barbed wire. Luckily, it wasn't electrified; less luckily, it was surrounded by cameras. They chose a spot close enough to the stables for their purposes.

Then James chose a spot a mile farther along, laid down both bags of fertilizer, and started a massive fire.

At the same time, Leander cut a hole in the fence big enough for a palomino, ducked through, and set off his pack of fireworks. They sang like missiles into the sky as he made his way to the stables. James Watson went for his daughter.

In short order, the school was surrounded by fire engines and police cars. Those horses that hadn't escaped through the fence were panicked, whinnying, galloping to the far corners of the enclosure, and as Leander watched from the woods, he saw something he hadn't counted on—students, at first a slow trickle of them, then a flood. Stealing out of their dorms and through the hole cut in the fence. Backpacks on their shoulders, escaping into the woods to try their luck anyplace else than the prison they'd been kept.

During the mass confusion, James Watson had broken into the infirmary—Shelby's last known whereabouts—and found her there alone, left handcuffed to a wooden desk chair. She'd been hacking away at it with a paperweight when her father found her. *They're coming back,* she'd said, through tears of rage, *he said he was coming right back, and they're putting me into the Isolation Pit—*

He didn't wait to find out what that was. The two of them hacked away at the wood until it gave, and then James Watson, his daughter, and the chair arm still handcuffed to her wrist disappeared into the forest, never to be seen again.

"Until they met Leander by his rented Saturn in the woods," Watson said wryly. "Though my dad likes to end the story before that."

"Leander—" My aunt gave me a look. "*Uncle* Leander

made some calls in the morning. The ones he wanted to in the beginning—the police, the judge, his lawyer. It took some time, and finesse, and a few massive fines for setting fires near a national park—among other things—but in the end, the facility shut down. I think what finally did it in was one of their board members getting arrested for attempted murder of a child."

"And that, kids, is why you don't let a Moriarty buy your school," Watson said.

"That's quite the story," Araminta said, turning off onto a gravel lane, our tires kicking up dust and rocks behind us.

"Well, it ends there. That was the last time James and Leander saw each other." Watson peered out the windshield. "Other than Holmes's hospital room, that is. My father is too busy fucking up his life. Is this—is this where we're going to dinner?"

Araminta had kept him talking for the full half hour it had taken us to arrive at our destination. We'd driven past a full-to-bursting parking lot into the circle drive of a manor house. In the waning light, I had the impression of flowers. Pots of them around the entrance, an arch over the entrance to the garden.

"It's lovely, isn't it?" she said, handing the keys to a silent valet. "I thought you two deserved a treat. Come, our table's on the terrace. You don't mind dining al fresco?"

Our table was bedecked in candles. The waiters brought duck eggs, carpaccio with capers and artichoke hearts, a risotto with salmon and beetroot, a sea bass the width of my arms wrapped in a delicate, fragrant leaf. We didn't talk much about the program; Araminta didn't press me on the classes I wasn't attending, and Watson was loath to discuss a story when he was in the middle of writing it. Instead, I told her more about our case—the mysterious entrance into the theater, the missing girl. The conversation between Theo and George Wilkes.

"It isn't Theo after all," Watson said, spearing an asparagus, and I agreed, and I didn't agree, but I didn't offer my opinion aloud. Not yet. Araminta had her head cocked, almost as though she was listening for something, and then she came back to herself all at once, calling the waiter over for more wine.

As we waited for the dessert cart, I saw that Watson's eyes had fallen half-shut, whether from the wine or the food or the long day, I couldn't tell, and he settled back in his chair to look out over the grounds. Couples were playing lawn games, sipping cocktails. Tail flagged high, a spaniel ran loose through the croquet wickets, and a girl gave chase, laughing, a leash in her hands.

The shadows began to lengthen across our table. Araminta talked about her bees, the new young queen. As the evening cooled, Watson took my hand between our chairs and let them slowly swing back and forth, a pendulum, and I was happy.

I was happy.

But it had been some time since we'd seen our waiter, and Araminta was toying with her wineglass. "Lottie," she said at length. "Would you pop into the bar and order me a decaf coffee? Here, take my card. Jamie, would you like anything?"

"No," he said with a yawn. "I'm fading out. But thank you so much for dinner, Araminta. Aunt Araminta . . . ?"

She grinned. "Cheeky monkey. You can call me aunt."

"Aunt. You didn't have to do all this. I think it's wasted on me."

"Experience is never wasted," Araminta said. "And you're welcome."

It took me a few moments to pick my way through the tables to the door back into the hotel, and as I reached out for the handle, I found myself turning back to our table. I didn't know why. Watson was telling a story with his hands.

Araminta was staring at me.

Go on, she mouthed.

Ignoring the disquieting prickle at the back of my neck, I let myself inside the hotel. There were a number of dining rooms I passed through, some with stained-glass windows, some with paneled ceilings, pink-veined marble floors. It was like something from an old movie, or one of Watson's favorite novels. *Brideshead Revisited,* everyone in evening wear, in pincurls and ten-thousand-dollar watches, everyone polished bright with white, white teeth. They were lovely, and they were threatening, and though I'd thought our dinner to be extravagant, there was clearly more extravagance to be had. I found myself holding my breath as I stepped through the final set of doors into the lobby.

At last. The bar. It was more crowded than I'd expected, perhaps because of the late hour, and it took me a moment to get my bearings. The bar was a looming thing, dramatically lit, and the bartender was rushing about in a crisp white shirt, a cloth tied into his apron strings. He had a polished cocktail shaker in his hands, and the girls sitting before him propped their chins on their fists and watched him work, giggling to each other.

I took a step forward, my aunt's card in my hand, and then I stopped.

I knew those hands.

I knew that waist, those shoulders. I knew the chin, with its proud upward tilt, and the gentle mouth that balanced it. I knew the Roman nose, the cheekbones, the sweep of the eyebrows. I knew that thick blond hair and how it fell over his forehead, and I knew his eyes, too, and before they could look at me I had ducked behind a column, gasping like a fool, telling myself I was wrong.

It wasn't hard to mistake one Moriarty for another. My brother Milo had done it on our lawn in Sussex when he had shot August Moriarty dead.

I had seen him do it.

Slowly, infinitesimally slowly, I leaned out from behind the column. I had to be sure. I had to know, beyond a shadow of a doubt, that I was right, that I had seen who I thought I'd seen, against all odds, against all logic, behind a bar in this manor house in Oxfordshire.

The shaker. The hands. The dazzling smile. I saw it in pieces, not as a whole, and I wouldn't stay any longer to look. I turned and ran back blindly through the dining rooms, one after another—tripping over tablecloths, dodging waiters, not caring about the scene I was making.

He hadn't seen me.

August Moriarty hadn't seen me at all.

nineteen

The moment we climbed back into the Fiat, I arranged my head against the window and shut my eyes, feigning sleep. I didn't trust myself to speak, to my aunt or to Watson or even to myself, in my own head.

Had one looked closely, the pulse point at my throat would have given me away. My heart was a hummingbird's.

We rode back in silence to the city. On our street, Araminta pulled up to the curb, and I pretended to rouse myself. "Watson," I said, "do you mind going up alone? I want to have a word with my aunt."

He had the decency not to look surprised. "Sure," he said, climbing out of the car. I followed, to move into the front, and he grabbed my wrist. "Are you okay?" he asked me quietly.

"No," I said, and shook my hand free, not caring, just then, for anyone else's feelings. He stepped back, wounded—why was he always so wounded? Was I such a monster, to always be hurting him this way?

I couldn't bear it.

I climbed back into the car and I slammed the door in his face.

"Lottie," Araminta said, not looking at me. "Was that necessary? He has nothing to do with this."

"You are not allowed to tell me what's *necessary*." I pointed to the road. "I suggest you get us out of here, if you're so concerned about Watson's feelings."

We left Jamie there on the street, hands at his sides, staring uselessly after us. I realized, too late, that I hadn't given him the keys. He'd be left there until we returned.

I turned my ringer off. I didn't care. I couldn't. I stared straight ahead with my arms wrapped around myself, and Araminta drove.

Fifteen minutes later, she found a small, well-lit petrol station on the outskirts of the city. She pulled into a parking space and turned the engine off, folded her hands in her lap.

"What do you want to know?" she asked.

"How," I said. "I want to know how."

She must have had her little speech prepared, because she started in right away. "I was traveling with a friend over the holidays. She'd wanted to see Blenheim Palace. I hadn't been away in some time. Months, really." Araminta studied the steering wheel. "We stayed far longer than we'd intended, far too late to make it back to London, where we planned to stay in Leander's flat. He didn't have the Oxford flat yet. It's how I can afford to travel—your uncle owns so much real estate, and you know that I . . . well. I make a modest living from my bees. Not enough to live like he does. Like your father does, or your uncle Julian. I chose my life, I'm happy with it, but I . . ."

She was babbling. I'd never heard her babble before.

"My friend, she . . . she looked up last-minute hotel rooms on some app on her phone, and that's how we ended up there. There was a deal. We checked in, she took a shower, and I went down for a nightcap at the bar.

"And he was there. I knew him from his photograph in the news stories, but he'd never met me. It was funny, he was this little axle on which our world turned, and we were strangers to each other. I almost left it alone. But the bar was empty, and in the end, I . . . couldn't help myself. I asked about his life. His story. He spun some tale about growing up in the Netherlands; he spoke with a slight accent. He'd been a teacher, he said. He told me his name was . . . Felix, I think."

I turned away.

I thought I was going to be sick.

"He didn't know who I was, Lottie. I was sure of that. I charged the drink up to our room—it was in my friend's name, he never saw mine. And then I went upstairs, and I called your brother."

"Milo," I snarled. Milo, who had shot August dead. No. Who *hadn't.* Who had lied, to everyone, who had fled the country rather than go to prison, who had stared at me in a safe house in New York like I was the angel of death come for him at last. I had hated him, how he had acted out his grief. The drunkenness. The unkempt hair. The hollow eyes.

I had scrubbed him from my life.

"Milo denied it. Denied it all. Told me I was delusional, a plague . . . some other choice descriptors. And then, just when I'd given it up and decided to believe him, he spat out, 'Don't tell my sister,' and he hung up the phone. I knew it then to be true."

"So you brought me there to see August," I said dully. "To be sure."

"I brought you there." She looked at me, her eyes two sunken pools. "So tell me. Is there any way that he can be alive?"

"I didn't check for a pulse," I whispered.

"When he was shot?"

Not trusting my voice, I nodded.

"Why not?" She asked it of me gently. "Why didn't you look for a pulse?"

It burst out of me, a torrent of words. "There was so much happening, and I was in such disbelief . . . my brother doesn't make mistakes like that. He's far too careful. You don't become the head of a *mercenary company* in your twenties unless you're a master of precision, and he shot him, he had a *scope* and I knew he could see August's face and he still shot him and said it was an accident, and I—" I gasped for air. "I couldn't believe it. I couldn't make it true.

"But I—" I shook my head. "I know why they did it that

way. Milo. August. I know why I wasn't told. I ruined his life already. Twice. Why would he trust me with it again?"

"I didn't bring you there to torment you, Lottie."

"Why, then?" I sounded so much like a child. "Why? I don't understand any of it."

"Lottie—"

"Can I ask you something? When you had me to your house, before I went to America . . . it felt like you wanted to tell me something. The day I dropped the hives. Did I imagine that?"

She twisted her hands. "I thought I might be able to offer you a home with me," she said. "You could work with the bees."

I stared at her. "I would have loved that," I said.

But she hadn't offered.

"But that day you visited . . . well, I was reminded that you were still so young. And so strange. How you just stood there, as those bees filled the air . . . mesmerized. It was unnerving. I didn't know what to do with a girl like you. And Lord knows that then, you weren't willing to hear any advice.

"But you've grown up so nicely. It feels like time, perhaps, for you to come under my wing. I took you out tonight because I wanted you to feel—free. You have so much ahead of you, and if August were really alive, I thought you could finally put the past to rest."

My kind, businesslike aunt, with her sensible face and her sensible shoes. Her sensible decisions. Her tucking herself away, safe and sound, while the rest of the world raged around her.

I came at her like a snake.

"I am fully done with other people telling me what to do with my history," I said. "My past *made me who I am.* There is no way to wipe it clean. *I* am the evidence. If you look at me and see track marks and too-skinny arms and hands that know how to hold a gun and a brain that is *sharper* and *faster* than yours, then that is not my problem. Do you hear me? I have regrets, and I have made mistakes, but I am who I am. I'm done pretending that I've wholly remade myself, that I'm going to . . . to hide myself away in some lecture hall for the next four years to make you all *comfortable.*" She was backed up against the door, now, her arms wrapped around herself, and I didn't care. "If you want to stop seeing it, you'll have to stop seeing me, and I am not going to *disappear.*"

It was what they'd done to Matilda Wilkes. It was what they'd done to me. Hide the problem away so you don't have to look at her. Put her on a train. Bin her somewhere. Shove her off to another country, shove her six feet underground, and wait for her to rot.

I was suddenly so very tired.

"I'm not going to hurt him. August. I'll leave him alone."

"Lottie," Araminta said. "I never thought you would—"

"He never saw me anyway." I turned from her then. "You can find yourself a hotel, I'm sure."

"Charlotte—"

Was that all she could say? My name?

"I just want to go home," I said, and it took me two tries to unbuckle my seat belt, but I did it. I did it with my own hands, and then I walked myself the five miles home.

Watson was waiting for me on the curb outside our flat. He turned his head when he saw me at the corner, and then looked straight ahead, his jaw clenched.

"I'm locked out," he said evenly, as I approached.

"I know."

"Can we not do this?" he asked. "The whole, me dragging an apology out of you?"

"Yes," I said. "I'm sorry, Jamie. I don't deserve you."

"You don't." He snuck a look at me. "How about an explanation, while you're at it?"

"I have one of those too," I said, offering him a hand up. "You're not going to like it."

"Holmes," he said, "are you okay? You seem a little . . . punchy."

"No," I said, and laughed. "No! What's that thing that Lena says? I am so not okay, Jamie. I am the opposite of okay. But don't worry—we'll go upstairs and sit down, and I'll tell you all about it. And very, very soon, you're not going to be okay too."

twenty

LATER, MUCH LATER, AFTER WE'D RAGED AROUND THE FLAT, after Watson had held a pillow so that I could punch it, after he'd cried in the bathroom where he thought I couldn't hear, we put on sweatpants and went down to the twenty-four-hour off-license and bought as much ice cream as we could carry. At the last minute, Watson threw in a thing of Tunnock's tea cakes so we could eat something on the walk home.

It was only five minutes, but we were in desperate need of chocolate.

"You don't want to see him, do you? August?" I asked, as we settled back into bed.

He considered it, his mouth full of marshmallow fluff. "Maybe eventually," he said, swallowing. "If he stays there.

He'd be stupid not to switch jobs every few months. He's already taking such a risk, working in England."

I stared at the pint of gelato I'd balanced on my stomach. It was beginning to melt. "Does this mean I need to forgive Milo?" I asked. "What are the rules?"

"There aren't any," Watson said, handing me a spoon. "I don't plan on forgiving my father."

I nestled in to look at him. "Can you unpack that a little more?"

"That," Watson said, "is therapy-speak."

"I've been in therapy," I reminded him.

He sighed. "I keep thinking about my brothers. Mal isn't even in kindergarten yet. Robbie was acting up before any of this started. And my dad is already doing the thing where he's escaped across an ocean. Back in London, waiting for someone to take him in so he can start the whole cycle all over again: marriage, kids, running away. I don't want to be a part of that."

"Is that fair?" I asked him.

"Does it have to be?" he asked me. "It's how I feel."

"You can call him," I said, watching his brows knit, his eyes shutter. "Talk through it all. At which point, you can forgive him, or you can tell him to go to hell."

"Pass."

"Or you could never call him again."

Watson snorted. "There. A workable plan. Anyway, I thought you were the one asking for advice on Milo."

"Fine. Enumerate my options, please."

"You can call him. At which point, you can forgive him, or

you can tell him to go to hell."

"You're funny," I told him. "Hilarious."

"Or you can never call him ever again. Or—"

"Precisely. Fuck him." I dug into my pint. It was mint chocolate chip, and it was a revelation.

"There are other options, Horatio," Watson laughed. "You don't have to make up your mind tonight. You can change it six ways til Tuesday."

"Tonight," I said, "I am going to fill myself with gelato until there is literally no room inside of me for feeling like shit."

"Cheers," Watson said, and extracted another tea cake from its packaging. "Do you want to talk about something else?"

"No," I said, and affected a smile. "Not really." And it was late, and soon enough Watson got up to shower, and when he climbed back into bed, he pulled me up against him and fell almost immediately asleep.

If anything could make me feel better, it would have been that.

And yet.

I slipped out of bed, taking up my phone from the nightstand, and crept through the flat in the dark. I checked the locks on the door and the windows, drew the curtains. I poured myself a glass of water. I was stalling, I knew. I didn't want to do it. It wouldn't do me any good.

And yet.

I locked myself in Leander's bedroom, at a far enough remove that I wouldn't wake Watson. It was spare, tidy, the lair of a man who was always on the move. The only extravagance was the bed, piled high with duvets and pillows, its mattress pillow-soft. I flung myself down onto it, buried my face in the quilt. *Someone in my family loves me,* I told myself, inhaling. *Someone in my family tells me the truth.*

I rolled onto my back, and I called my brother.

He picked up on the first ring.

"Lottie?" he said, thick with sleep. "What happened? What's wrong?"

I had it planned, an insouciant little snipe of a story—*guess who I saw tonight,* etc. What came out of my mouth was, "He's alive. You bastard. He's *alive.*"

"Oh," Milo said, and he sounded very, very awake. "I was wondering when I would get this call. Araminta?"

"Yes," I said. "Tell me how."

It was the same question I'd put to my aunt, but Milo, being Milo, answered it much more succinctly. "A blood capsule in the mouth. I fired into the hedgerow. He wanted to disappear, Lottie. It was the only way to make it work."

I breathed out through my mouth. "Jesus Christ, Milo."

"You didn't honestly think that I shot him with a sniper bullet traveling at *supersonic speed* and he survived?" He scoffed. "I thought our father taught you better than that."

"I was in shock," I said.

"You were." His voice gentled. "You didn't even check him for a pulse, Lottie."

"He'd even told me . . ." August on the plane, flying back to Britain. *I'll change my name. I'll disappear. They'll never find me.* "I still can't believe it. I can't believe you didn't tell me."

"Not then," he admitted. "You're in a fragile place, and last year . . . last year, you were a force of nature, and not one I could predict. This is still sooner than I'd like for you to know. I thought you could handle it eventually, when you—when things had calmed down."

I forced myself to keep breathing. *A force of nature. So strange. So unnerving, and so young.* "This is why you ran. Why you didn't want to go to prison."

"I don't kill without reason," Milo said tartly. "And I don't put my neck on the line for just anyone. I did it for you."

"For me," I said.

"I took August in for you. I gave him a job. A home. We became *friends*, Lottie, and we made a plan. And when you decided to run roughshod through Berlin, guns akimbo, acting like you suddenly knew best—*yes*, Lottie, you, the girl who'd stirred all this up to begin with—well, forgive me if I didn't think to bring you in on it." He sighed heavily. "Forgive me if I mourned the loss of both you and August in one fell swoop."

I shut my eyes. "Fine," I said, because it was always this—love and disapproval in the same breath—and I had to escape it.

He could tell I meant to hang up. Milo's instincts had always been razor-sharp. "Wait," he said. "Your case."

"What about it," I said. It was pointless to ask how he knew. My brother, the spymaster.

"Rupert Davies. He's living with your Watson." A shuffling sound, fingers on a keyboard. "Old family. Very old. Lots of history there."

"Get to the point."

"His grandfather was in Parliament. His father's brother was an MP as well. For years. He's only just retired. And . . . well, Lottie, on his staff—"

"No," I said, my brain speeding ahead. "Absolutely not."

"One of his staffers was a young Lucien Moriarty."

"That doesn't mean anything." I heaved myself up and off the bed and began to pace. "That family is everywhere. They have their fingers in everything."

"And once you're beholden to one, you are for life. At least that's the case for Lucien. Did you know that the Davies family owns a small plot of land outside of Oxford proper? What do you think is buried there?"

"It can't be. Rupert's the only one out of that whole wretched cabal who's a decent person," I said.

Milo sighed. "Can you honestly tell me it's a coincidence, that the only person in your program—your *whole* program, Lottie, I vetted them all—who has a connection to that family was assigned to live with your boyfriend?"

I stopped at the door, my hand on the handle. "I can't do this again," I whispered. "I can't have him in danger, Milo."

"Then walk away," Milo said. "August did."

At that, I hung up the phone.

It was three in the morning by the clock on my nightstand when I crept back in. I dressed as quietly as I could in the dark—Watson didn't stir—and picked up the bag I'd packed when Leander and I had first moved into this flat, the bag I thought I wouldn't ever need. In the kitchen, I looked over my uncle's plants, by the window, and picked up the one I had placed there that afternoon.

I sent three text messages, and then I was putting on my shoes at the door.

"Where are you going?"

Without looking up, I zipped my other boot. "New information," I said, straightening the cuffs of my jeans. "I need to act."

"I'll get my jacket," he said.

I looked up sharply. His hair was mussed, his feet were bare. "You're not going," I told him. He belonged back in bed. He belonged in a dorm room, in a typical summer, somewhere far, far away from me.

"I'm not."

"No," I said. "It's too dangerous."

"Holmes," he said patiently. "If it's too dangerous for me, it's too dangerous for you. Are we really going to play this game?"

I dragged my hands over my face. "The stakes just changed," I growled. "I might need to make some . . . decisions."

"Stupid ones?" he asked, creeping forward. "Tell me you're not going to go and make stupid decisions without me."

I laughed, despite myself, and I kept laughing despite the nervous hammer of my heart. "Watson. Go back to bed."

"No," he said, and caught me around my waist. "I heard you might be in some need of a partner."

twenty-one

We crept back to St. Genesius in the dark. It was late, far past curfew, and Watson had to hoist me over more than one fence before we made our way back to the quad. By the time we'd made it to his stairwell, I'd finished filling him in on everything I'd learned.

"Do you think that Theo was lying?" he whispered as we lingered outside the door. "About Matilda calling him?"

"My usual methods haven't been working," I said. It was something I hadn't wanted to admit even to myself. "I'm able to tell if someone's lying quickly, but . . ."

"But everyone here's an actor," Watson said, putting it together.

"Everyone. Even those that pretend they aren't. Rupert can

pretend all he'd like, but one doesn't swoop in and steal the role of Hamlet if you're talentless." I reached for the doorknob. "Or if you're working for a Moriarty."

Watson stopped my hand. "Are you sure you're okay?" he said.

I stared at him. "Watson. For all we know, Rupert is waiting at the top of those stairs with a cleaver."

"Right. Well," he said, looking again at the door. "After you."

THE TEXTS HAD DONE WHAT I'D INTENDED—THEY WERE all waiting in their kitchen when we walked in. Gathered around the table in their pajamas, like a scene from a sitcom. There was a bowl of popcorn in the middle that none of them were eating.

"It's three thirty in the morning," Anwen said, brushing off her hands. "I woke everyone up, like you told me to, but I hope you have a good reason for this."

Wordlessly, I unzipped my backpack. With gentle hands, Watson removed the tissue paper I'd tucked around the lithe, lovely potted plant, and handed it to me.

I placed it on the table.

An orchid. A yellow European *orphys*, to be specific. (Who knew you could buy them at the fancy grocery store?)

"Watson found this outside your door," I said, and waited for their reactions.

Anwen wrapped her robe around herself with shaking

hands. Theo shook his head, tightly, and reached out to touch one of its petals—then jerked his hand away. And Rupert? He looked as though he were about to cry.

I sat, and in the guise of tying my shoelace, I took a quick but comprehensive look at their feet.

Only one of them was wearing shoes.

Watson said, "Last summer, the orchids were only delivered after something had happened. An accident. What happened tonight?"

Theo shoved a lock of hair out of his eyes. He looked, suddenly, very tired. "Fuck all," he said. "Watched a film. Ordered in a pizza. Pepperoni. We had way too much." Beside him, Rupert nodded quickly, like a puppet. Anwen was staring at a point over my shoulder.

Watson was hovering behind me, his hands on my chair. "Oh, *amazing*," he said. "We went out to this posh restaurant for dinner with her aunt, and the food was all, like, mouse portions. Can I have some?" He walked over to the fridge and opened it, peering inside. "Oh. Is it somewhere else?"

"I mean, we *ate* too much," Rupert said. "I tossed out the box, it was huge."

"You didn't just wait for housekeeping tomorrow? That's nice of you," Watson said, and pulled out the chair next to me, sitting down at an angle.

"So you don't know why the orchid was out there?" I asked. "Watson and I took it straight down to the police station. They photographed it. Took samples. We talked to DI Sadiq for a long time, and they let us bring it back here."

Wholly untrue, quite implausible. But to Rupert and Anwen and Theo, I was Charlotte Holmes, renowned detective.

The rules didn't apply to me.

Rupert swallowed. "There wasn't an orchid left after Dr. Larkin's death," he said. "Not that we know of. Maybe it's from that?"

"But why would it be *here*?" Anwen asked with a slight quaver. "That doesn't make any sense. They'd send it to . . . her."

"She's *dead*," Theo said, turning on her. There it was, that revulsion. "What, are they going to plant one on her gravestone?"

"She has family." Anwen crossed her arms. "Friends. They could send one to them."

"Yes," he said slowly, like she was an idiot. "That's why it's ridiculous that one showed up here. Jesus Christ, we had nothing to do with this!"

The seams were beginning to show. It was the middle of the night. They were clearly lying about what they'd been doing. We'd interrupted a fight, or something worse.

"You act like you know *everything*, Theo," Anwen said, standing. She cinched her dressing gown: an extravagant blue silk shot through with gold thread. "You were never like this before!"

"Before *what*," he said, staring up at her. On the table, his hand seized into a fist.

"Before you started dating Matilda," she said, taking a half step back. Her words came out in short bursts. She was scared. It was clear that my and Watson's presence was the only reason she felt safe enough to speak. "Before you let her *change* you. You'd known her, what, two days? And suddenly you were calling her *lady* and letting her—letting her eat our food, and follow us around!"

"She was my *girlfriend*," Theo thundered. Beside him, Rupert shuddered and sank into himself.

"No," Anwen said tightly. "She was someone you could perform for. She acted like she had all this depth. Like she was some big, posh mystery. Well, I'm sorry—that was an *act*, Theo. She had secrets, but they weren't the ones you thought."

Tell me a secret, Matilda had said in the video, lolling across the lawn on a blanket. Drawling her words extravagantly, drawing every eye, and then laughing it off the moment before she became ridiculous. And Theo, just days ago in the auditorium, staring at me, haunted. *You've had this invitation to you. Like you want me to tell you all my secrets.* At the time, it had made me furious.

Now I thought I understood it.

"What's yours, Anwen?" I asked into the silence. Beside me, I heard Watson suck in a breath.

She remembered I was there, then, her head whipping to the aside. Her long, wavy hair was all in snarls and knots. "I don't owe it to anyone," she said. "But—"

"Tell Rupert," Theo said, shoving back and standing. "I don't care." He made for the stairs.

Like a child trying to tune out his parents' fighting, Rupert was staring fixedly at the orchid in the middle of the table. "Anwen grew up in care," he said. "In foster homes. Didn't you? You and your twin sister."

She had her arms wrapped around herself, the sleeves of her silk robe hiding her hands.

"You never stayed anyplace long. Bounced around Wales. Cardiff, mostly. Right? No. I know I'm right. You got top marks. Maybe you were determined to get yourself out. Maybe you were just naturally gifted, or it was some combination of both. But your sister got in trouble. Shoplifting, things like that. I've seen the records."

At the foot of the stairs, Theo ducked his head.

At the table, Rupert softly fingered one of the orchid petals. "You never mentioned her," he said. "Last summer. This summer. I kept waiting for you to mention her, but you didn't."

"She got pregnant," she whispered. "Had the baby." Theo took a step forward, searching her face.

Rupert nodded to himself. "Figured it was something like that."

"Why didn't you tell us any of this?" Theo asked.

She barked out a laugh. "Like you'd listen," she said. "I tried to tell you. So many times! But you never wanted to hear it. Next to Matilda, I was *boring* to you, and all the while I was dealing with *real* things, Theo, not just . . . fucking posh-people problems! Do you know last Boxing Day, when you called me losing your mind over that phone call—"

Rupert sat up straighter. This was news to him.

"—that was someone just fucking with you, Theo, someone who called you with a dummy number and pretended to be your dead ex-girlfriend, my sister and I were being thrown out of our foster home? The baby was too loud. The baby was too much. Those *assholes.* I ended up . . ."

"Calling me for help," Rupert said.

Anwen turned to him gratefully. "And you didn't ask me why. Just put us up in a hotel until I got ahold of my caseworker, and we got another placement." Her pale face hardened. "But you found out anyway."

"My father did," he said. "It was his money. He had someone look into it, when I asked."

Rupert Davies. The only boy at this program with a Moriarty connection. It would have been as easy as snapping his fingers to get that information.

"It isn't your fault." She reached out to touch his shoulder, but he shied away.

Theo groaned. "I'm sorry, Anwen," he said, and there was bitter irony in his voice. "I'm sorry you didn't think you could trust us. But what does this have to do with Matilda?"

"Everything," she murmured. "Everything."

And just like that, I had my solution.

There was a hammering at the stairwell door. "Police! Open up!"

The three of them looked wildly at each other. Rupert stood and backed up against the wall, and Theo shivered in his T-shirt, and only Anwen had the presence of mind to look at me.

I tried very hard not to smile.

The second text I'd sent had been received. DI Sadiq really did have impeccable timing.

"Someone should probably go answer that," Watson said, leaning back in his chair.

twenty-two

THE SNEERING PC USHERED US INTO THE INTERROGATION room. He was the one who'd told me I'd had an attitude; I didn't think his disdain was an act. "Come on, missy," he was saying.

Anwen stepped into the room like she was a princess visiting a pigsty. "How long will we have to wait?"

"We'll get to you," he said, and shut the door behind us.

Gingerly, she sat down next to me at the table. I was trying not to obviously catalog the room: where the camera was, where the smell was coming from. Something like rotting fruit.

"Did you know they were coming?" she demanded. "The police?"

The two of us had been read our rights, stuffed in separate

cars, and placed here, together, in a room. All as I'd requested. I hadn't seen Sadiq since we'd arrived, but I had the feeling she was on the other side of the "mirror" across from us, watching intently.

"No," I said. "I mean, Jamie and I were here earlier with the orchid we found. I was worried he was in danger."

She folded her hands. "Well. It seems like they suspect you now, too."

"I don't know why," I said.

Anwen shot me a sideways glance. "From what I've heard, you're supposed to be something of a psychopath," she said. "Maybe that's why."

All that arrogance plastered over her pain. Knowing that didn't make me like her any more. But it did make me understand.

We lapsed into silence. My chair had one leg far shorter than the others, and I rocked back and forth a few times experimentally. They'd really done everything they could to make this room as wretched as possible.

"Will you *stop that*," Anwen said, rewrapping her silk robe over her pajamas. "I can't believe they wouldn't let me change."

"You're wearing clothes," I pointed out.

"I'm wearing *slippers*."

I rolled my eyes. "What you're wearing," I said, "is something like two thousand dollars' worth of vintage Christian Dior. I imagine that's fancy enough for an interrogation."

Anwen paused. "You know clothes," she said, sweeping my outfit with her eyes. As usual, I was wearing all tailored black.

It wasn't remarkable, but every piece was expensive.

As I'd dressed for tonight, I'd made sure of that.

"I do," I said, straightening my shirt. "Is that surprising?"

"No. Yeah, maybe. Is that a Comme des Garçons jacket?"

"Yes," I said. "How long have you been collecting vintage?" I reached out to touch the sleeve of her robe. "This is what, mid-fifties? Mint, right?"

She nodded, and glancing at the two-way mirror—*Aha,* I thought, *she knows what that is*—she shimmied out of the robe and handed it to me. "It really isn't meant to be worn. I was sorting through my collection when . . . when I got your text, so I threw it on and came downstairs."

That wasn't exactly the timeline, but I'd get to that later. I gently held the robe up to the light. It really was a thing of beauty. All silk. Raw edged. "Something like this runs for, like, four hundred pounds on eBay."

"I know," Anwen said, with some pride. "It's part of my escape fund."

"Your escape fund?" I asked, casually checking the label inside the robe. *Christian Dior,* and underneath, in small handwritten letters, *Larissa.* I affected not to notice and began looking at the stitching.

"I have a fee waiver for Cambridge," she said. "And a bursary, money to help support me when I'm there. And the rest of it is coming from these clothes. I got them for, like, nothing."

I whistled. "You must have a good eye, to find all this thrifting."

She reached out for the robe, and put it back on carefully.

"I've been collecting since I was fourteen. It's where I've put all my pocket money, paying one pound for a piece in a bargain bin, five pounds for designer shoes stuffed in with a bunch of trainers. Sometimes charity shops don't know what they have. I wear it for a bit, and then I sell it online. I've made almost three thousand pounds."

I thought about the clothing in her wardrobe, the pieces that hadn't been marked with Larissa's name. They had been nice, certainly, but nothing near as expensive as the rest.

"It's a brilliant plan," I said, and it was.

Anwen was warming, visibly, to me. Praise did that. "And I set up Tamsin with a place of her own—my sister. She has a job, now, in a bakery. I think we're going to be okay."

"She's lucky to have you."

Anwen nodded, cleared her throat. "I'm sorry you had to see that scene in there," she said. "We've all . . . we've been a mess since Matilda's gone. Lots of fighting. It's been so awful."

"I'm sorry," I said. "I've seen that before, when I've worked other cases. It seems like it's been really hard on you. Knowing what you did about Matilda."

I said it as naturally as I could, as though I'd just been finishing a thought.

"It was so strange," Anwen said, the words slipping out quietly. She was exhausted. She'd just allowed herself to relax, a bit. "Being the only one who saw . . ."

". . . that she was pregnant."

Slowly, Anwen realized what she'd done. "How did you know that?" she hissed.

I put up my hands. "You know who I am," I said, and it was true. "I put it together when Rupert was talking about your twin sister. It made sense, having seen Tamsin's pregnancy up close, that you might recognize someone else's."

Anwen buried her face in her hands. "Oh my God," she said, muffled. "You can't tell anyone."

The irony of where we were—an interrogation room covered in cameras—had escaped her. "I won't," I said.

"I wake up early," she said, rubbing her eyes. "I always have, that's why I'm so knackered right now—I've been up since five. Sometimes I go down to that coffee shop, Blackmarket, to study. It's how I fit all my work in. Anyway, last summer, I'd be getting ready in the bathroom. And Matilda . . . she stayed over with Theo most nights. Three mornings in a row, at like, five thirty in the morning, she burst in there to throw up."

I nodded, listening. I hoped that Sadiq was taking copious notes.

"We were three weeks into the program, and all that crap with *Midsummer* had already happened, them canceling the show because of Matilda's feelings. Titania's an amazing role. Amazing costumes—she's a *fairy queen*." Anwen shook her head. "Larkin pretended she couldn't get the rights to the show. Please. It's not like we're idiots—it's Shakespeare! So they stuff everyone into a production of *Earnest*, and Theo . . . he knocks her up."

"It must have happened almost immediately," I said.

"I think it did," she said. "They'd hooked up the first or second night, but it wasn't until later that they started dating."

I took a deep breath. "Maybe she was using him," I said. "Maybe she knew she was pregnant immediately. Some girls do. And then she decided to trap him."

I hated everything I was saying. It was the worst part of this job: telling criminals what they wanted to hear.

"Yes," Anwen said, slamming her hand on the table. "Exactly! Everyone was so up her ass that they couldn't see it. But I knew that if he got any more attached to her, that he'd be roped in for life. And Theo's a genius. You saw him audition, right? Matilda was overrated, but Theo is just as good as everyone says."

"Matilda would have ruined his life," I said. "You had to intervene."

"It's not like it was hard." Some door inside her had been unlocked. From exhaustion, or from my sympathetic ear, or from both. "Rupert was working in the sound booth. He knew the theater techs well, had them teach him a few things. And you know *Rupert.* He'll do anything I ask." Anwen waved a hand. "He showed me how the lighting rig worked. Where they kept the props. Where the back entrance to the theater was, and where Larkin hid the spare key."

"You didn't hurt anyone."

"Well." Anwen laughed. "I didn't do in Dr. Larkin, this year. That one was bizarre. And really sad. No, I didn't hurt anyone except that cow, Harriet. She was so disgusting, couldn't shut up about her family's money. Nothing like Rupert, you know, who's so modest. I thought—two birds, one stone. I didn't do anything to her that doctors couldn't fix."

"People like that should know better." After all this was over, I was going to need a shower.

"But they didn't cancel the show." She stifled a giant yawn. "I couldn't understand it. Dr. Larkin just refused. I liked her a lot—we all liked her—but it was just ridiculous. And Theo and Matilda were *inseparable.* I was running out of time."

"So," I said, laying down my final card. "You called Matilda's father."

"George," she said. "Dear old George. He's a homophobic piece of shit, you know, but everyone has their uses. Matilda was always admiring herself in clothes from his costuming business. 'This was used in the Old Vic production of *The Crucible.* Isn't it witchy and amazing? I made him give it to me.' She was always acting like she had something on him."

"Did she?"

"I'm sure she did. Who cared? She was born on third base and acted like she'd earned a home run." Anwen snorted. "Theo said that once. Not about her, of course, but isn't it amazing?"

"Amazing," I echoed. "So you called him?"

"I did," she said, and yawned again, fit to split her face open. "I made him a deal. In exchange for information on his daughter, I wanted a payout. Not money. You can trace money. No, I wanted—"

"Clothes."

"Exactly. I already had the online shop. And he wouldn't give me anything from his shop directly, so he took things from Larissa's closet. Things he'd set aside to give to her. Not like she'd notice they were missing, she was all drugged up.

My plan was, I wouldn't sell them all at once, of course. I'd do it bits at a time. And in exchange, he'd drag Matilda home by her hair."

"But Anwen," I said, far more gently than I felt, as the girl settled herself down in her chair. "She didn't go home. She just disappeared."

"I know," she said, her eyes tipping shut. "Isn't that strange?"

I waited a long moment to see if she would slip into sleep. Her actions had been callow and desperate, and I wish I could say that no part of me understood them.

Except I had once been the girl who'd framed August Moriarty for a felony, and all because he didn't love me back. I was still that girl. Just tonight, I'd insisted that I was.

I stood, brushing myself off, and walked to the two-way mirror. "Is that enough?" I asked my reflection. "Is that enough, now?"

twenty-three

SADIQ USHERED ME OUT OF THE INTERROGATION ROOM. She looked exhausted, but then, we all were. Watson was still in with Theo and Rupert, she told me, but he hadn't gotten much out of them.

"Did you dust Rupert's hands for pollen?" I asked. "He was touching the decoy orchid I brought over, but there should be at least one other kind under his fingernails."

Sadiq dropped her glasses to the end of her nose. "Any particular reason?"

"You know . . ." I smiled. "Actually, don't. Don't dust him. Just have someone tail him the next few days. The Davies family owns a plot of land outside of town. They're farmers. I'll bet you anything that there's a greenhouse there, and that you'll find—"

"Orchids inside," Sadiq said. "Noted." She smiled at me. "Nice work, Charlotte. You live up to your reputation."

That usually wasn't a compliment. I found myself smiling back. "Thanks."

"You know," she said, leaning back against the wall, "I didn't think that Rupert boy was up to any of this."

"His friends brutally underestimated him," I said. "Counted on his good nature. I can't tell you if he helped Anwen because he's just that obliging, or because he's in love with her, or because, secretly, he wanted to have *some* of the power that everyone was denying him."

Watson padded up behind me. "Hi," he said, and tucked his arm around my waist. "Got her?"

"Got them both. Her and Rupert," I said.

Watson sighed. "Everyone except Matilda, then. Where *is* she? And who killed Dr. Larkin?"

The detective gave us a measured look. "Larkin," she said, "was injured by that falling light. Badly injured. She's currently under guard in the ICU."

She had hinted at this before, but I was still surprised. Watson shot me a look. "It's sort of cruel," he said tightly, "to let all those students think their teacher is dead."

Sadiq raised an eyebrow. "It's crueler to let a criminal go unpunished. She agreed to it, you know, as soon as she woke up after surgery. That we let everyone think she had died. Tear the bandage off. Throw everyone into a panic. Confuse the real culprit, make them paranoid."

"And?" Watson said. I could tell he was still angry; I didn't blame him. We'd had enough deception for one lifetime. "Does she know who did it?"

"There was a power surge in the college," she said. "The lights flickered. The lighting board was being raised and lowered without an operator, since that tech was in hospital. Dr. Quigley had been playing around with the settings."

"It was an accident," I said wonderingly. "I never would have guessed."

"It was," she said. "We just made hay while the sun was shining."

So to speak. "And Matilda?"

Sadiq smiled again, more toothily this time. "I have an appointment with George Wilkes in the morning, remember? Shall I call you after?"

"You've put quite a lot of trust in me," I told her, and reached out to shake her hand. "Thank you."

"Help is help," she said. "Go get some sleep, you two."

When DI Sadiq called, it was nearly noon, and we were both still asleep. I shook Watson's shoulder and put her on speaker, and the two of us dragged ourselves up to sit against the headboard.

George Wilkes was in custody, charged with a number of crimes. Conspiracy, fraud, kidnapping.

After learning that his daughter was pregnant, Wilkes had tried to drag her home from the program. But she'd refused to go. She was going to get an abortion, she told him; she had the appointment already. She would stay and perform her role and come home that fall to apply to conservatory programs, and there wasn't anything he could do about it.

Why?

Because Matilda had blackmail. The year before, she'd come home early from a rehearsal to find her father *in flagrante* (Watson's phrase, quite excellent) with another woman while her stepmother was out running errands. Her stepmother, nervous and gentle and rich; her money supported her father's costuming business, which had prestige but not a lot of cash flow.

"Convenient," Watson said, "that Anwen asked for payment in clothes."

Matilda threatened to tell her stepmother if her father so much as *suggested* he'd bring her home. She would have her torrid affair with the boy her father despised, and she would return to her childhood bedroom and go off to conservatory the next year. And he would pay.

George Wilkes wasn't one to be bossed around, especially by his daughter. He went to Oxford the night of her final dress rehearsal and plucked her directly off the street. The argument bystanders had heard was between the two of them. He and his wife bundled her into their car, and drove her home to London, where her grandmother was waiting.

She was put on a train and taken up to her grandmother's

house in Scotland, up in Caithness. Quite literally as far north as she could be sent. She'd been homeschooled. Had her baby. Was living there now, far away from her friends and the rest of her family, from her acting, from her life.

"She must have managed to get her hands on her old phone," Watson said, "to call Theo last Christmas. God. I can't imagine what kind of lock and key they had her under."

"We'll find out when we raid it," Sadiq said. "A team should be breaking down the door right about now."

"Was he . . ." This was a strange question for me, and I wasn't sure why I was asking. "Was he sorry?"

Sadiq sighed. "He was insistent that she was a bad girl. One who needed to be punished. And as her father, he was the one to do it."

"Got it." I found myself staring at nothing. "Thank you for calling. I'm still very tired. I think I need to go back to bed."

Watson touched my arm, and I turned to bury my face in his shirt.

"Thanks, Miss Holmes," Sadiq said. "We'll be in touch again soon."

LEANDER AND STEPHEN RETURNED THAT NIGHT, AFTER I called to tell him the news. He insisted on tending to me like I was a child—making steak and kidney pie, tucking blankets in around me on the couch. Stephen and Watson played Scrabble at the kitchen table, and the television droned, and I slept. I slept, it felt, for days. And when I wasn't sleeping, I was coming to some decisions.

And then, one morning, I woke to an empty flat. Watson was in his tutorial, discussing a new story of his. It was quite good. Elegant, and spare, and it had a peacock in it that appeared at opportune moments. With each new tale, he was getting better.

Leander and Stephen were down at the farmers' market, and the street was quiet. I dressed myself and went for a walk.

I knew, by then, what I wanted to do.

MEET ME AT THE BOATHOUSE, I'D WRITTEN HIM.

By the time I'd made it there, Watson had already paid and was hauling a stack of cushions over to the punt.

"Leander could have paid," I said, picking up the long metal pole and bracing it against my shoulder.

He grinned, tossing the cushions in one at a time. "I didn't want him to tease us about what we were doing."

It took some maneuvering to get the both of us in the boat—we pitched in our things, and he held the pole while he helped me in, and then I braced the pole and helped *him* in. The punt listed from side to side as the two of us got settled, him standing at the back, in the "huff," while I settled down cross-legged to watch him.

He stuck the pole into the shallow water and pushed us off into the River Cherwell. "Can you dig into my bag?" he asked.

"For what?"

That smile again. "For my straw hat," he said, and caught it one-handed when I chucked it at him.

"You're very confident for someone who hasn't ever been punting before," I said, as he lazily maneuvered us down the river. The Cherwell had a current, but it wasn't a strong one. Every now and then Watson dipped the pole back into the water to steer us back onto course.

"You do realize," he said, "that most punters are drunk."

I considered this. "Still." He cut a dashing figure, like some Venetian gondolier who'd given up the striped shirt for a blue oxford and boat shoes. The hat was a bit silly, but Watson wore it at the back of his head, like the hipster he was always pretending he wasn't. His thick hair curled up under the brim; his trousers were loosely cuffed. It was all endlessly charming.

"So you're saying," I clarified, "that you can punt only middling-well for a sober person."

"Do I need to make this thing do backflips?" Watson asked, and dug the pole into the muck. Our boat tilted crazily to the right. I made a high-pitched sound, then clapped a hand over my mouth.

"You *squealed*. Did you just squeal?"

"If you have to ask," I said, with some dignity, "then no, I did not."

He dug in the pole again, and we spun in a neat circle.

I bit my lip while he laughed at me. "Jamie, I swear to God I will pull this boat over—"

He lifted the pole again, threateningly. I lunged forward, and Watson leaned backward, and then began windmilling his free arm to keep his balance. I considered pushing him in, but the water smelled a bit like bad fish, and anyway, I liked his shirt too much to ruin it.

"You were going to let me drown," he protested, pushing us off again.

"Yes. In knee-deep water. It would take some skill, but I believe in you."

The water was quiet this evening, so close to sunset. A pair of ducks paddled alongside us, and on the bank, I watched a stealthy little fox work the underbrush. The water was dappled green from the trees that listed low along the water. Watson must have seen me studying their canopies; he pushed the boat on an angle, and we drifted through the long, slim arms of a willow tree. I traced it with a finger. It left a handful of leaves in the bottom of the boat.

"You have one in your hair," he said fondly, and I plucked it out and tucked it behind my ear. "Did you send a photo to your uncle?"

"No," I said, taking out my phone. "I should." The light had taken on that effervescent quality it did around sundown. Watson was smiling, one hand on his hat, the river out behind him.

Leander responded almost instantly. *Adorable! You two are breaking my heart,* he said, along with a row of (unbroken) heart emojis.

"I wonder how often they did this," Watson said. "Leander and my dad." They had been at Oxford at the same time, though they hadn't met until an alumni event after graduation. In their twenties, though, they'd returned quite a few times together to their old stomping grounds.

I settled in against the cushion. "I'm not sure. They talk about it enough."

We drifted in silence for a moment. Knowing Watson, he was painting the scene in his head. Leander trailing his hand in the water, James inexpertly steering, some sandwiches and a bottle of wine in a wicker basket. The two of them spinning out some merry argument the way we'd heard them do so many times before.

"How's your father?" I asked finally. "Have you responded to him at all?"

Watson stabbed the pole back into the water. "No. I don't understand him, sometimes. It's like he can maintain the illusion that he's a normal, healthy human for about ten years at a stretch. That's how long he was with my mom. How long he was with Abby. And then he . . . he burns it all down. Gleefully."

I was with him until that last adverb. "I don't know if he enjoys it."

"Some part of him has to," Watson said, making a face. "I keep—I keep waiting for him to show up at Leander's door, here in Oxford. It's the absolute last thing he should do, which means it's probably at the top of his list."

"I'm not defending him," I said, but he didn't seem to hear me, pushing us along down the river.

The evening was starting to cool. I took my sweater out of my bag and slipped it on.

Watson's eyes refocused on me. "I'm sorry," he said.

"Don't apologize," I told him, pulling my hair out from the

collar. “You have every right to be mad.”

With his father, and with me.

“You’re here now,” he said, and he dragged the pole against the riverbed to slow us. “You aren’t going anywhere.” The taut line of his shoulders. His eyes everywhere but on mine.

“Watson,” I said. “I have to tell you something.”

twenty-four

WATSON SHOOK HIS HEAD AS THOUGH TO CLEAR IT, AS though a fleet of sirens had gone screaming by.

"I'm going to bring us ashore," he said stiffly. "Can you grab that paddle out of the bow? Give me a hand."

Together, we maneuvered the punt toward the bank. Watson kicked off his shoes and stepped into the shallow water. We carried the boat ashore to rest in the soft bed of leaves under the willow grove.

He dropped down to sit on the till, hands folded. "Why is it," he said, "that when you have to tell me something, it's usually that we're about to die?"

"It isn't anything that terrible," I said, though I knew, in a way, that I was lying. "Why do you think it's always something terrible?"

He opened his mouth, then thought better of it.

"Most of my past behavior notwithstanding," I allowed.

"Spill," Watson said, and there was an edge to it. "We're paying for the punt by the hour."

"I've dropped out of my summer classes," I said quickly.

It wasn't what he'd been expecting, that much was clear. "Really?"

"Really."

"But that means you won't be able to enroll this fall."

"I know," I said.

"I thought you were taking chemistry," he said. "Really advanced-level chemistry. I thought that was what you'd wanted?"

It had been. And yet. "I can't . . . I can't see myself doing it."

He nodded. Watson, of everyone, would understand this: a boy who lived enough in his head that he rehearsed each moment before he lived it. "It makes sense," he said. "You've been all caught up in this case."

"Watson," I said, somewhat louder than I intended. "That's not the point. Do you understand? None of that is the point! I never . . ."

I'd run out of words. All I had was the sharp pulse in my throat.

"Hey," he said, standing. "What are you trying to tell me?"

A punt went by on the water—four blond children with ice lollies, their blond mother with an ice lolly, the father steering them onward, steering them home.

"I'll always take a case if it seems like someone needs me," I said. "But Jamie . . . I don't know if I can see myself doing this, either."

"So, not chemistry," he said, more lightly than I think he felt. "And not detective work."

"Not this kind of detective work. Not solving cases that the police could easily take on, and I'm not planning to join the force. I don't do well with institutions."

"That's an understatement."

I smiled. "I want to know how *I* can be of use."

"What, then?"

"Is it okay if I don't know?"

"Of course it is. You don't need my permission." He reached out to tuck a strand of hair behind my ear, and I leaned into the warmth of his hand. "Is there anything you *can* see, when you look into your future?"

Scotland, perhaps. The winding streets of Edinburgh's Old Town; it was the only British city that hadn't been bombed during the Second World War. I hadn't seen them since I was a child, and the child in me wanted too to disappear into the highlands, see cows wander across a field, their faces like kindly, bearded old men. I wanted to go even farther, to Sweden and Iceland and to Norway. Up to Tromso to see the Arctic Cathedral, to Reykjavik to see the night stretch long into the day. I was as pale as the snow and as wicked-looking. I thought that was a landscape in which I'd fit.

"I pick up languages quickly," I was saying, "and I notice

things, and I can get into places no one else can. There are other girls out there who need help they don't even think they can ask for. Girls like Matilda. I always felt so alone, you know, but now? I think I could be that person for them. Their . . . champion, I suppose. I want to find a way to put all that together."

He took off his hat, held it loosely by his side, waiting. He could hear it, I think. What was coming.

I laughed hollowly. "These past few months have been the happiest I've ever been."

I hadn't known why my aunt had taken me to that little gilded restaurant where August had been tending bar. The towel tied in his apron strings. His hair longer, now, falling around his temples. His smile quicker than I'd ever seen. I'd never see it again.

I'd thought it was a punishment, of sorts. That had been so much of my past few years: people coming out of the woodwork to punish me for being who I was. A girl who'd been fashioned as a weapon, then left to rust out in the rain.

But it hadn't been a punishment. She had offered me a kind of freedom.

And Watson was just looking at me.

"I love you," I said. "But I don't know if I can stay here, after all this is settled."

He nodded once, twice. Took a step off to the side. Pinched the bridge of his nose. "I'm sorry," he muttered, and turned from me, walking out of the grove and into the darkening night.

It was selfish to follow, but I did.

"Jamie," I said, crashing after him. "Jamie!" He sped up, but I lunged forward, close enough now to catch him by the elbow.

He stopped there, his back to me still. "You say the two things like they go together. That you love me, and that you have to go. Do you understand how—I have no idea what to *say* to that, Holmes."

"Come with me," I said. "I never said I didn't want you to come."

At that, he spun, so close to me that I could feel the heat of him through his shirt. "I don't have the money," he said. "I don't have the time. I need to go to college. That's what I'm doing this fall, Holmes. *College.* Not—not *Tromso.* Despite everything, I got into a good school, and I need to get a degree. And then maybe I'll make, like, a *wild* decision and go to grad school for fiction instead of immediately getting a job as . . . as a copywriter. Which I would be lucky to get! I can't just hare off after you while you go extravagantly find yourself. I think, actually, that would kind of defeat the purpose, don't you?"

He shut his eyes, hard, and I felt childish. I felt like a fool. I had rehearsed all this in my head so many times. What had I expected?

"I can't stay here," I said desperately. I had to make him understand. "I can't. I've changed. For the better, I think, but there's still this . . . shadow over me. No one trusts me. No one but you."

"I trust you," he said. "How long? How long before you

go—fuck, before you go wherever you're going to go, and—" He was crying now, and he wiped at his eyes with his knuckles. *"God."*

I couldn't help it. I reached out and pulled his arms apart and stepped between them. He stood still and resistant for a moment, and then he collapsed, his arms going around my waist, tucking me up close. I could hear the hard echo of his heart.

"I love you," he said quietly. "I've never in my life loved anything more."

And somehow, somehow, that had been the last thing I'd imagined him saying.

"I'll be back," I promised. "I won't be long. A year. Maybe two. And even if it isn't to stay—maybe you can take a long summer, and come away with me."

"You're asking me to wait for you," he said, pulling away. There was something broken in his eyes. "And you know I will. But I can't make you feel better about this. I can't. Not right now."

"Jamie—"

"Come on," he said, walking back to the boat. "I'll take us home."

Epilogue

Two years later

THE TRAINS FROM LONDON PADDINGTON STATION TO Oxford ran more than 150 times a day; the journey itself took about an hour. It cost seventeen quid to go there and back, twenty if you factored in the sausage roll I liked to buy in the station. I usually didn't have a seatmate, but if I did, more often than not they'd be someone who looked like me—a university student with a weekender bag and a textbook they weren't reading, off to visit a friend in another town.

She had a small little set of rooms in East Oxford, near Cowley Road, the sort of place with a half kitchen and radiators that hissed and a bedroom that didn't have a door. But the view from the sitting room window was magnificent—you could glimpse the dreaming spires of the university from her gray velvet sofa, and she sat there in the mornings, her silk blanket tossed over her shoulders, while she saw clients during her business hours. Fridays only, ten to two, and what she made in those sessions covered her rent, because she had to pay her own rent now. Her reputation had gotten round town to her satisfaction in the year since she'd been back. There wasn't ever a wait to speak with her, but she was never in want of work, either.

I'd rearranged my classes this term so I could sit in and assist where I could. It meant forgoing the Robert Louis Stevenson tutorial I wanted in favor of one on American poetry, but in the end I found I didn't mind. Mrs. Dunham would be proud of me, carrying John Berryman's *77 Dream Songs* around, reading even the ones I hadn't been assigned. The rhythms of them got into my head, and as I took the stairs two at a time to her door, I ran compulsively through my favorite bits. *I don't know how Henry pried / open for all the world to see survived.* A one-two tap, and then I'd call out, "Charlotte?"

There wasn't ever an answer, but I wanted to give her a moment, in case she was on the phone or wasn't dressed. Sometimes I thought if we lived in the same city I'd be more comfortable treating her flat as my own, but as it stood, I showed up with my duffel and my train ticket home, and when I got to her door, I knocked.

I was a visitor here.

Inside, I'd find her at her little stove, the electric kettle already going. She made herself breakfast now, two hard-boiled eggs and a green leafy something. Gone were the experiments that she'd made for me in Leander's kitchen; when she cooked for herself now, it was with the grim determination of a soldier tearing into rations. If the first of her clients arrived at her door during breakfast, she took her meal to her bedroom and let me entertain her visitor until she'd properly finished.

"Entertaining" maybe wasn't the best word for what I did for the shivering wrecks who showed up on those Friday mornings. Even when it wasn't raining, they gave you the feeling of having wandered in the dark and wet for days, waiting for ten o'clock on Friday morning to finally roll around. In the beginning it had been only girls our age, university students and bartenders and shopgirls, the occasional younger one snuck out of her morning classes. At first it galled me to think that there were boys out there who needed Holmes's skills, but who refused to trust themselves to a mere *girl*. She read that thought from something I did (my posture, a frown, all those signals I let myself project so that she could pretend to read my mind) and told me that, no, in fact, her name was passed like a secret between girls—you came to this flat if you needed a particular kind of assistance, if you needed your case to be heard. She would decide if she would help you, then if you had to pay, and when that was settled, you'd have your problem solved within the week.

One girl, still in her work polo, told us of the man who came to her bar every night for months who now was making cameos at her bedroom window. Her boss refused to do anything about it, told her if she called the police in, he'd lose his clientele—and she'd be fired. Another had an ex-boyfriend who was currently still teaching her chemistry lab; he gave her failing marks on problem sets she'd done correctly, but she didn't want to report him, she was afraid of retaliation. Another had the wrong kind of stepfather. That sort of awful, ugly thing.

Usually, after listening to the story, she'd come up with a solution on the spot. Something that didn't require much risk. The lab assistant had a superior, and our client had all of her old quizzes she could bring in as evidence, and after he was removed as her teacher he would be watched, carefully, and if something further needed to be done, all the client needed to do was come back. Sometimes she called her contact at the Thames Valley Police, a colleague of DI Sadiq's who was discreet, and who didn't mind, on his off-hours, following a man from a bar to a bartender's house and making some not-so-veiled threats. Sometimes she loaned out little cameras, taught her clients to record audio on their phones, gave a brief, explicit lesson in Blackmail 101. Once she listened in total silence and then asked a few simple questions about *how long* and *when did it start* and *how gone do you want him*, then said if she showed up the next day in their homeroom or their French club or at their front door dressed in a school uniform to treat her like a long-lost friend and then to let her do what she had come there to do.

The next week, it came out that her target had committed a number of crimes. This was vigilante justice, of course, and terrifying too, and I didn't ask too many questions about it. My opinion wasn't wanted, or necessary, and though I often wanted to know what happened to the girl after her life was turned right side up again, she never returned to the flat by Cowley Road. The clients had their marching orders, and they followed them.

So did I. She sleuthed on Saturdays, after I had gone back to London, and as much as I wanted to be there and help, a silent line had been drawn between the work I did in her living room and the work she did in the world.

Her clients' secrets never came out, not in any way I knew of, but the secret of who was helping them did. It had to. A secret grew in you like a pumpkin seed in the tales, the dark vine of it climbing inexorably up until it spilled out from your mouth in a fury of stem and leaf. It was girls at the door for the longest time, but the guys came eventually. Their problems were often more prosaic, though not always, and she had the same rules for everyone. If she could solve it from her sofa, she would. If the client was in danger, she'd take it; if it interested her, she'd take it; if neither of those things and they could pay and she was behind on her electric bill, she'd raise an eyebrow at me and I'd shrug at her and we'd toss a coin to decide.

The clients never liked when we did that.

The man today was that, a man, a few years younger than my dad and nervous in his business suit. I could tell he didn't like how young we were, though I could also tell he didn't know exactly how young that was. When my old wire-rim glasses had finally broken, I'd begun wearing a pair of tortoiseshell wayfarers. They'd been a cheap placeholder for contact lenses until I'd arrived at Cowley Road that week to find her looking at me with a warmth I'd almost forgotten. The glasses stayed. The warmth was gone the next Friday, replaced by the calm, kind regard I had grown used to, and I think the both of us were relieved. As for her, she had a few streaks of gray in her dark hair that would be surprising to anyone who didn't know our past. But then, no one knew the whole of our past except for the two of us.

No matter. The man was speaking, and it was my job to take notes.

"She was someone I'd known for a very long time," he was saying, eyes flitting back and forth between us. *Focus on her,* I thought at him, until finally he did, settling back into his armchair with studied ease. "Since we were children. I thought she loved me, but she's seeing someone else behind my back, and I need to find out who, and why."

"I need more than that," she said, rearranging the fringe of her blanket.

"What do you mean?"

Her tone was patient. "I need more information than that, or I can't take on your case."

"Like where she goes? Or what she does for a job? That's easy. She works mornings at the bakery on—"

"No." She waved her hand to cut him off. "I meant that I'd like to know the depth of your relationship with her. Why you're so desperate to keep her, or catch her out."

The man looked at me, attempting to find an ally. I shrugged.

"I haven't seen anything fit to write down," I said to her. "I'm sorry."

"Miss Doyle," the man said, pinking in the cheeks. "You're going to decide whether to take my case based on whether you like my *story*? I'm sorry, but I don't know if you have the sort of name recognition to allow you to do that sort of thing. I didn't even have to make an appointment to see you."

Charlotte Doyle leaned forward on her elbows, sizing the man up. It had only been her name since she'd returned from her travels; she'd taken it then as an added layer of anonymity, but she'd legally changed it when she'd returned. Her family name neatly scratched through.

Though, looking at her now, there wasn't any doubt whose descendant she was.

She steepled her fingers under her chin and said, "Other than the fact that you're a barrister down on his luck with a large dog he can't control and a number of friends from school that you see often and are hoping to impress today—male friends, I'd imagine, though of course I don't know that for certain, I'm not a magician—the only thing I can tell you is that, from the way you lingered on the sidewalk for a full twenty minutes before coming up, this case means far more to you than your attitude suggests."

He crossed his arms. "How can you possibly know that."

"I saw you from the window," she said impatiently.

"Not that," he said. "The other things."

"I saw you from the window," she said again.

He looked at me mutinously.

"If she tells you," I said, "you have to promise not to say it's absurdly simple."

"Do I really have to do this?" she muttered at me.

"You made your bed," I said. "Now deduce it."

She sighed and turned back to him. "You were up late last night working. That's the jacket you keep at your office—it isn't as pressed as everything else that you're wearing, and though it's similar to your pants, it's a half shade darker. You have a good eye; both the pants and jacket are a decent cut, but the material they're made from is cheap and thin. I can't tell if the shirt is one you keep at your office, but I rather imagine it is as well—from that, and the shininess of the jacket's elbows and the ink on the side of your dominant right hand, I can tell that you worked the night through and didn't get home to shower. This is a common enough occurrence for you that you've laid in spare clothes for it. The clothes are cheap, so you're not doing well, but your briefcase is beautiful, and it was a present on your law school graduation. Why else would your initials and credential be monogrammed on it? You'd never be so tasteless as to do so, but the bag is very fine, so you carry it. Another point toward your impecunity. As for your being a barrister—you really should know better than to have contracts sticking out of your bag in plain sight. And as for the *rest*, there's a lick mark from a large dog on the back of your jacket at about the height that a mastiff could reach—clearly you're not controlling it, if it's licking your suit—and at first I thought you were in such a rush because you needed to get home and feed it, or get back to the office, but no, it's Friday lunch, there's a pub three blocks from here, and I saw you there last month with a gaggle of bros who clearly weren't also lawyers. You don't have time to make new friends. Ergo, from uni."

The man looked uncomfortable, as everyone does when they're called poor. "That was actually quite—er—it wasn't difficult," he amended, seeing the look on my face.

"No," she said. "But I can't tell you anything about the girl. You can, however."

He looked down at his hands miserably. "I love her. We're not—we're not together now, exactly, but we were for a while, and I thought we would be again. But my work schedule is ridiculous, as you pointed out, and I think she got tired of waiting. She says she isn't seeing someone, but on the weekend, when I can actually get away, she's never around. I only want to know if she's telling me the truth."

"Have you asked her?" she asked.

"Yes. I think she's lying. I thought maybe you could find out for me, so I know whether to move on."

She did that thing where she opened her mouth, then went silent. I knew she was trying very hard not to snap at him.

"There's the kettle," I said, jumping up. The kettle was, of course, not whistling. "Tea?"

"You need to move on," she told him, and there was a burn in her words. "She doesn't trust you as a friend—how could she trust you as anything else? I can tell you that now, and save you the cost of me tailing her for two weeks straight. Fix your friendship because you want to be her friend, not because you're laying the groundwork for some future that only you see. Or leave her be."

The man looked miserable. "Thanks, Miss Lonelyhearts."

"Cream and sugar?" I called from the kitchenette, but he had already picked up his expensive bag and his cheap umbrella and banged his way out the door.

At least this time she didn't call out, *That'll be twenty pounds.*

The kettle whistled after a moment. I fixed myself a cup and got her a glass of water and we settled into the living room to watch, out the window, as our ex-client stomped over to his car.

"At least this time he didn't tell me I wasn't Sherlock Holmes," she said. "That always happens when you make me explain my methods. I'm getting tired of it."

"It's not that Miss Lonelyhearts is much better, Miss Doyle."

She rolled her eyes, as she always did when I used her new name. "The 'miss' is the problem. It masquerades as polite. It isn't; it's condescending."

"Was she actually dating someone else?" I asked.

"I don't know," she said. "All I can tell you is that he didn't care about her enough, not in the right way. I couldn't see traces of her anywhere on him. That doesn't mean anything, of course."

I set my mug on the coffee table and wondered privately if she could see herself anywhere on me.

She didn't look me in the eye. "We're all over each other," she said, and that was that.

Over the next few hours, we had a few more clients. I fetched tissues, asked questions, took notes. But they were problems she could solve from her sofa. She made about a hundred pounds, all told, and a promise to follow up on one case the next week, and then we had the afternoon, as always, in front of us.

Now that it was May and the weather was warmer, we'd taken to wandering the university grounds. It was easy to walk and watch the punters on the water, to buy each other books in the secondhand stores outside of campus. It was a game we had, where she'd pay for some wretched ancient history or a German language primer and slip it into my bag without my noticing. I left her Golden Age novels, puzzle stories, locked room mysteries on the table beside her bed. It wasn't something we talked about; it was just something we did.

I was a visitor here, and it made us better with each other. More careful. She was more careful with everyone, now, and though I couldn't see inside her head—I never could; I'd learned that by then—it seemed to me she treated herself with that same care. There had been a night or two, right when she'd returned, where day had turned to night and I'd stayed over in her bed, but I'd slipped away at dawn while she was still asleep.

Once, I had loved her so much it was like a needle through my heart. Maybe I still did. Somehow, though, it seemed beside the point.

Today, we prowled the city for iced coffee, her hand in the crook of my arm. I'd begun drinking it this past fall, and though I felt guilty dragging my aesthete of a friend in search of something she'd sworn off, she didn't seem to mind. She didn't touch any of it now, caffeine or nicotine or drugs or booze.

It was a decision she'd made, in Norway, during the months she was assisting in a chemistry lab. I'd only heard bits and pieces about that year—more often than not, when she'd arrived in a new city, she'd gotten swept up into some investigation. Paris. Kyoto. A long two months in the American West: Lena Gupta had ended up at college in Los Angeles, and the two of them rented a homestead in Joshua Tree. From her letters, I knew that she'd been conducting experiments in the desert and catching up on her scientific journals, while Lena did . . . whatever it was that Lena did. Buying designer clothing? Plotting a coup? Their sublease ended in August, and Lena stayed in California, and Charlotte moved on.

I went to my classes. I watched my father and mother reconcile, begin dating. They kept separate flats, but Shelby reported finding the two of them on the sofa at night, watching old movies and laughing over popcorn. I suppose my father was the only person who could understand what my mother had been through, with Lucien. It made a strange sort of sense, and so did the way I found myself home again some weekends, in my mother's old flat, sharing a bottle of wine with my parents while my father told stories about his and Leander's adventures and my mother laughed a real laugh.

Had I been twelve years old, it would have been everything I wanted. It was, and it wasn't. I spent spring break of my freshman year out in Connecticut, visiting Abby, watching her boys so she could have a few nights to herself. I couldn't atone for anyone's mistakes, but I had two hands, and I could help.

In Oxford, Leander and Stephen kept that lovely old flat, and they had my father and me over every now and then, for roast duck and board games. Stephen had a wicked sense of humor, and sometimes, laughing with them all around a candlelit table, I forgot that Charlotte wasn't just in the next room.

Her letters came every two weeks. Sometimes through the post, sometimes through email. She often didn't say where she was, but I could glean it from the postmark, and inside would be a few lines about what she'd been reading, an odd deduction she'd made about a stranger. If she missed me. She always said she missed me. I couldn't respond; by the time my return letter reached her, she'd often moved on.

Finally, in December, the night Lucien Moriarty was sentenced to twenty years in prison, she'd called me.

I'd been at a party and stepped out onto the balcony. *"Jamie,"* she'd said. She sounded as though she'd been crying. "Jamie. Would you mind it if . . . I came home?"

"Come home," I said, closing my eyes against the city. "Come home. Tomorrow. Come home *tomorrow,*" and she'd laughed wildly, and for a moment I thought it was going to be all as it had been.

The flat in Oxford had come around this January. Leander had to travel to China for a case, and though he'd given her the option of accompanying him, she'd taken a place of her own. I think deep down she wanted to be close to the university, even if she'd decided against getting a formal education. She'd made a life here. She had a chemistry tutor, and sometimes she'd mix her witch's brews in her kitchen. She'd joined a string quartet that was starting to do weddings, and sometimes she played her parts for me to see what I thought. In an attempt to "exorcise some demons," she'd said, she'd joined a bare-bones production of *The Merchant of Venice*. Sometimes we'd run her lines in a café overlooking the water. *The quality of mercy is not strained. It droppeth as the gentle rain from heaven . . .*

Today, I drank my coffee. She took off her jacket and slung it over an arm; the day was growing warmer. Soon I'd have to catch my train. I told myself I was dreading it because of the flat in London I was returning to—five other English undergraduates, us two to a room, a filthy kitchen and no one ever replacing the toilet roll except for me. I could be living at home, I supposed, but I wanted to give my parents' romance a little space to breathe.

"I was thinking about a publishing internship for the summer," I was saying as we picked our way back to Cowley Road. "Finals are next week, so I have to decide soon. And publishing's writing-adjacent, not writing-*writing*, but that's fine, right? I need some kind of job when I finish school. Though maybe I could just do more school."

"So the solution to school is school?"

I grinned. "I guess I like institutions."

"You don't. You have an authority problem and you know it."

"I do not."

"You can't even take a correction from me. How many of your teachers do you actually like?"

"King's College isn't Sherringford, H— Charlotte." It still felt odd in my mouth.

She pretended to ignore my slip. "So they're not trying to bug your room, then. Not a major improvement."

We rounded a corner onto a prettyish street not far from her flat. The houses were brick, and they had window boxes, and a few of the doors were painted bright red. "This isn't our usual way back," I said.

"We're looking at a place," she said, and pointed to a FOR LET sign near the end of the block. "I thought you could give me your opinion. My sublet is up at the end of the month."

We were the only showing. She'd booked it for two o'clock and, in her usual way, maneuvered us there so subtly and determinedly that we'd arrived exactly on time. The letting agent opened the door and left us to it.

It was quite a bit bigger than her current place, a second-floor flat with low ceilings but lots of light, and a proper kitchen that wasn't nice, exactly, but not terrible either, with a big old table that came with. The room she'd sleep in was just beyond, with a generous-sized bed, and there a door beside it that led to what I thought would be her study. It was a good size, with a closet and ceiling fan, which I thought would be good to blow away the fumes from her chemistry table. Though she'd have to get rid of the bed in there. Most flats in England came furnished; the only furniture I knew she had to her name was that ridiculous velvet sofa she'd taken from Leander, and so we wandered back to the living room and measured with our arms to see if it would fit. There wasn't an amazing view from the windows, but then, Holmes didn't seem to mind those things.

Charlotte. Charlotte didn't.

"I like it," I said, and I did. I was also ridiculously jealous of her having her own space. "Though the question is—"

"How can I afford it. I know."

"Is your brother helping?" She hadn't been taking money from Milo, though I knew he'd offered. His company had been doing quite well; they'd expanded their operations to South America. He had more power than before, though Milo Holmes was hardly someone to trust with it.

Still, he hadn't forgotten his sister. That was something. Despite her protests, sometimes he sent her groceries, or paid her water bill, and she huffed for a day or two about him meddling in her business and then texted him to say thank you.

"No," she said, frowning. "I think I'll have to get a flatmate."

"Oh."

She turned to face me. I was still getting used to the new sorts of clothes she wore—a forest-green sweater over a pair of black jeans, a long necklace with a pendant that looked like a tooth, the fawn-colored jacket slung over her arm. She looked like herself. She looked nothing like herself. The changes had been both gradual and incredibly sudden. In this light, her eyes weren't gray, but slate-blue.

"Are you going to advertise? For a flatmate?"

"The bookshop you like," she said. "The secondhand one, not the Waterstone's. They have a help wanted sign in the window. I went in and the owner asked about you, since we're always in there, and I—I told him you might be looking for a summer job."

"Am I?" I asked slowly.

"And then on Fridays, we can work together. It's not publishing, I know."

I looked around. There was a fireplace, an armchair; there was a wall of built-in bookcases. There was Charlotte, standing in front of me, biting her lip.

"I don't have to take it," she said, as I stood there, saying nothing. "I can find my own—"

"What happens after the summer?" I interrupted. "My classes start up again in September."

"I thought we'd decide then," she said.

"And then you might end up without a flatmate."

"I could move again."

I was stalling for time, I knew it. "That's a pain. Three months in, and—"

"You could commute. It's only an hour."

"Maybe—"

"I can't plan my whole future all at once. I'm done with that. I just thought—"

"Watson," she said, and I nearly bit my tongue. I hadn't

heard that name from her in forever. "Don't you want to try it? Don't you want to know?"

"I—I don't know if I trust it," I said. "You. I don't know if I trust you."

The two of us so long ago in Berlin, talking about getting a place, taking cases together. The two of us hand in hand, running through the night. After all the missteps, all the mutual destruction, we'd been strong together, steady and right and true—and it had been then, and only then, that she had wanted to be alone.

"Not like that," she said, her eyes searching mine. "Not like before."

"And not like it is now?"

"Watson—"

"Holmes," I said, then winced. "Sorry."

"You can call me that."

"It isn't your name anymore."

"You can call me that. *You* can," she said.

"Holmes," I said. "What is it that you want?"

She reached out and took my hand, her fingers twining with mine.

I stepped toward her. "We'll be taking cases? You'll have to double your rates. I don't come cheap."

"You're not that expensive. Anyway, we don't have to decide today. I know you need to catch your train home."

There was a reckless light in her eyes I'd thought I'd never see again.

“Is it that late already?” I asked her, smiling. “We should go.”

It was so bright there in the flat that I had to blink against it. We’d have to put in curtains. I didn’t tell her that, though, as we went down to the street. I was too busy counting the steps down to the door. *Sixteen, seventeen, eighteen.* Outside, she was waiting for me, her hands clasped together in the sun. I hadn’t had to say a word. She’d already known what I was thinking.

ACKNOWLEDGMENTS

THANK YOU SO MUCH TO KATHERINE TEGEN AND EVERY-one at Katherine Tegen Books, especially my amazing editor, Alex Arnold, Jamie and Charlotte's fairy godmother. This was a hard one, and I can't imagine getting through it without your insights and your support. You are an incredible reader, a rock, and a dear friend. Thank you, too, to Rosanne Romanello, Gina Rizzo, and everyone at Epic Reads. I am so lucky to have you all!

Lana Popovic: we've had such an amazing run. I adore you. Thank you, from the bottom of my heart, for taking a chance on me. Sandy Hodgman, Terra Chalberg, and everyone at Chalberg and Sussman: thanks so much for your time and efforts on behalf of Charlotte!

Thank you to Kit Williamson, my platonic other half, for all your work behind the scenes. To Emily Temple, my heart. To Becky Hazelton, Chloe Benjamin, Corey Van Landingham: endless, truest love to my girl gang. To Emily Henry, for every last-minute read that magically fixed my book. Let's get in that convertible and start driving. To Jeff Zentner, gentleman scholar, and one of my kindest, truest friends. To Evelyn Skye, Parker Peevyhouse, Mackenzi Lee, Angelo Surmelis, Jennifer Niven, Kerry Kletter: you make this community better and brighter, and I am so lucky to know you all. Mika Perrine, Joe Sacksteder, Lesley Tye, and Interlochen: thank you for your wonderful support.

Thank you to Sir Arthur Conan Doyle for letting me play in your world for a while. I'm never happier than when I'm there.

Love and thanks to my family, especially my parents. And to Chase—my husband and my home.

And thank you to my incredible, incredible readers. This last one, especially, is for you.

READ THEM ALL!

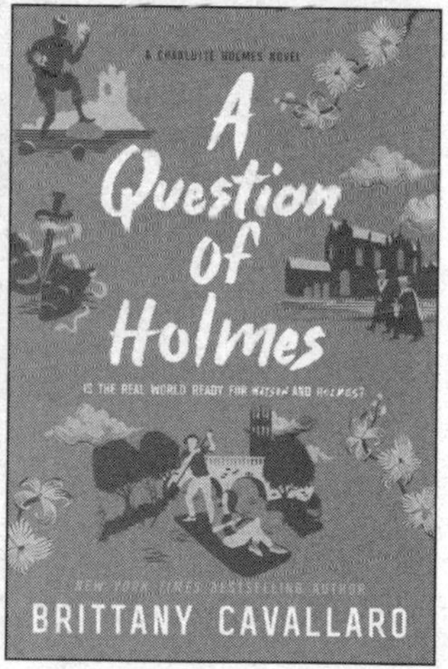

You've never seen Watson and Holmes like this before!

KATHERINE TEGEN BOOKS
An Imprint of HarperCollinsPublishers

www.epicreads.com